T0357137

A Spirited Blend

Books by Lauren Elliott

Beyond the Page Bookstore Mysteries

MURDER BY THE BOOK
PROLOGUE TO MURDER
MURDER IN THE FIRST EDITION
PROOF OF MURDER
A PAGE MARKED FOR MURDER
UNDER THE COVER OF MURDER
TO THE TOME OF MURDER
A MARGIN FOR MURDER
DEDICATION TO MURDER
A LIMITED EDITION MURDER

Crystals & CuriosiTEAS Mysteries

STEEPED IN SECRETS
MURDER IN A CUP
A SPIRITED BLEND

Published by Kensington Publishing Corp.

A Spirited Blend

Lauren Elliott

Kensington Publishing Corp.
kensingtonbooks.com

KENSINGTON BOOKS are published by

Kensington Publishing Corp.
900 Third Avenue
New York, NY 10022

All Kensington titles, imprints, and distributed lines are available at special quantity discounts for bulk purchases for sales promotion, premiums, fund-raising, educational, or institutional use. Special book excerpts or customized printings can also be created to fit specific needs. For details, write or phone the office of the Kensington Special Sales Manager: Attn. Special Sales Department, Kensington Publishing Corp., 900 Third Avenue, New York, NY 10022. Phone: 1-800-221-2647.

Library of Congress Card Catalogue Number: 2024949733

KENSINGTON and the KENSINGTON COZIES teapot logo Reg. US Pat. & TM Off.

ISBN: 978-1-4967-3522-5
First Kensington Hardcover Edition: April 2025

ISBN: 978-1-4967-3525-6 (ebook)

10 9 8 7 6 5 4 3 2 1

Printed in the United States of America

A Spirited Blend

Chapter 1

If the day had been a routine workday, like all the pre-ceding ones that Shayleigh Myers had enjoyed over the past two years, then this morning Shay would have climbed the spiral wrought-iron staircase to the second floor of her teahouse, Crystals & CuriosiTEAS. She would have paused at the top and closed her eyes as she passed her small alcove office to shut out the stacks of paperwork demanding her attention. If her universe hadn't felt lopsided, she would have stepped into her greenhouse and inhaled the heady, earthy scents of recently watered soil and the fragrances of blooming flowers and herbs growing in the raised planter boxes that filled her second-floor conservatory.

If things were normal, she would have sat on the bench beside the potting table, where for precisely thirty minutes, she would reflect on and give thanks for all in her life that had brought her to this moment in time. She would have her daily chat with the spirit of Bridget Early, her birth mother and the woman who, by her bequeathment, had led Shayleigh to this time and place. She was also the woman who had given Shayleigh the gift of second sight. Sadly, though—her heart ached with the reality of the situation—Bridget was the mother she would only ever come to know by trying to absorb everything she could about this incredible woman through the journals and letters Shay had unearthed while living in Bridget's cottage and running her tea shop.

However, the day was not normal, and the status quo of two years had left Shay feeling off-kilter. Her tranquility was threatened. Currently, she was huffing and puffing after ascending the spiral staircase, and her mind, much like the stairs she'd climbed, spiraled with whirling thoughts, and Shay was unable to settle comfortably into her usual routine. She exhaled and drew in a slow, deep breath in hopes that when she cleared her lungs, she would also expel the coiling, twisting energy eclipsing her morning meditation—but it was no use. The snaking energy had nestled into the base of her skull and curled in nicely, it seemed.

It wasn't a world-shaking energy, and she hadn't detected even a wobble in her universe. But if it was linked to what she suspected it was, it still held a great consequence, especially if she couldn't find the solution.

She glanced down at Spirit, her pure white German shepherd companion, who had followed her upstairs. "You've witnessed all my failures this week. What do you think the problem is?"

He let out a singsong groan and laid his large head on his front paws.

"I know. I'm just as stumped." Shay scanned the greenhouse and studied the various raised planters.

One planter housed common cooking herbs: thyme, rosemary, sage, oregano, basil, parsley, chives, dill, and fennel. Other planters blossomed with herbs she regularly used in tea blends, like mint, lemon balm, chamomile, lemon verbena, rosehip, and lavender. The remaining tables of exotic plants were beautiful to look at, but useless until she could learn all the benefits and the uses their blends could bring to her customers.

The amulet nestled in a leather pouch she'd inherited

from her mother, Bridget, warmed against her chest. She jumped to her feet and headed to one of the tables bursting with exotic plants. "That's where the answer is! Thank you, Bridget." She clasped her hand over the pouch. "I should have known you'd point me in the right direction sooner or later."

"Shay? Who are you talking to up here?" Her sister, Jen, called from the top of the staircase.

"Um . . . just Spirit?"

"Oh, I didn't see him. Hi, boy. I got our coffee. Do you want it now, or should I put it on the potting table?"

Shay's shoulders slumped. Another tradition she wanted to enjoy that her chaotic thoughts wanted to destroy. For the past two years, Jen had brought coffee from Cuppa-Jo, the coffee shop across the street, and they would sit and talk, enjoying the naughtiness of their ground coffee bean indulgence before they began a day of tea service. Since inheriting the tea shop, Shay had always felt like an imposter because, up until having to promote tea drinking, she had been a die-hard coffee drinker. Truth be known, the only tea she had ever indulged in was a common brand from her grocery store when she had a cold.

A small smile tugged at her lips as she gazed at the plants before her. The old Shay didn't exist anymore—well, that was, until after her daily morning ritual was completed.

Change can be difficult and painful. Ask the caterpillar, and then ask her again if it was worth it when she becomes a butterfly.

Shay closed her eyes and sighed as the words of Liam Madigan, her neighbor and the owner of Madigan's Pub, next door to the tea shop, floated through her mind. If she'd learned nothing over the past two years, she'd at least learned that. The difficulties, the pain, the changes, and the current doubts coiling at the base of her skull were a testament that she hadn't reached butterfly status and still had much to learn.

"You didn't answer, so here." Jen handed Shay a take-out cup of coffee.

Shay blinked at her sister and gave an apologetic smile. "Sorry, I'm struggling with something this morning."

"Why, what happened?"

"I'm at a loss about what to do with the tea we planned to serve at the Halloween carnival."

"That's it?" Jen eyed her uncertainly. "I thought we'd settled that weeks ago when we decided to put food-grade dry ice in that huge cauldron you found. Have you changed your mind about doing that?" Jen's pale blue eyes glimmered with concern, and she swept a lock of her golden-blond hair off her face and tucked it under the top of her single long braid.

"No, creating the steam effect isn't the problem. It's coming up with a tea recipe that will continue to bubble after it's poured into glasses. We don't want to put dry ice into the cups because if anyone inadvertently touched their mouth to it or swallowed the chip of dried ice, that would be disastrous. Besides, the Health Department would never approve that."

"Can you blame them?"

"No, I can't, but in all my research, I haven't been able to find anything nontoxic that will sustain the bubbling affect."

"You're overthinking it." Jen sipped her coffee. "Remember, it's a family-fun weekend, with lots of kids and prizes and games. No one is going to critique us on whether our witch's cauldron brew actually bubbles in the glass."

Shay could almost feel her sister's eye roll, and she looked at the plant table again with an even more resolved eye. "I know, but this needs to be realistic. You know as well as I do that Madam Malvina is going to have a display for her tea shop that will knock the socks off everyone in town. She's still the shiny, bright new toy in Bray Harbor and has already managed to steal away a lot of our business as it is." Shay studied the table intently and shook her head. "No, this year our display has to be like something off a movie set."

"The cookies Tassi and I have been baking will help with that. She found some great decorating tips with gelatin eyeballs and gummy worms—"

"I know, and they look fantastic. It's just that I know Madam Malvina will use this community event as another opportunity to one-up us. She already stole the Little White Glove Society ladies away with her offer of one free pot of tea per table for a year, and that's really hurt our bottom line."

"Maybe we finally need to start doing our own baking," said Jen. "Tassi's really got a hidden talent there. That way, we will be serving something different than Madam Melvina, and it might draw the ladies back because, as it is, we're both getting all our goodie orders from the Muffin Top Bakery, and it doesn't make us stand out from her shop."

"I know, and when we first started the teahouse, that's what I planned to do, but the cost of refitting the kitchen so we can bake in it is way beyond our reach now, especially since we've been losing customers to *her*." Shay sipped her now lukewarm coffee, crinkled her nose, and set the cup on the table. "As it stands now, some weeks I can barely make payroll, let alone keep the lights on."

She looked past the table of exotic plants and focused on one particular table in the corner. "No, this must be the best display we've ever had. We have to show the people of Bray Harbor that Crystals & CuriosiTEAS isn't going out of business yet."

"What's that old saying you like?"

"When things fall apart, better things fall into place."

"Yes, that one." Jen gave Shay's shoulder a reassuring squeeze.

"I don't see how that applies to our current situation."

"You're thinking Madam Malvina is going to put us out of business, but what if something else is meant to happen? Come on, you're the one who gets those *inky* feelings. They must be telling you that everything we've done here, all the work we've put in, and everything you've learned from Bridget's journals and from Gran Madigan can't have been for nothing."

"You're right. I'm not going to roll over and play dead. Madam Malvina took advantage of our relationship."

"She did. She kept tabs on you to see how far you were coming along, and when you got to the point of equaling her knowledge, she moved in and declared war."

"She did, didn't she?"

"She sure did. So what are we going to do about it?"

"Beat her at her own game. She doesn't have any staff other than her son, Orion, and he's only part-time now because of college. Plus, she told me she can't cook or bake for the life of her, and you and Tassi are my secret weapon, so . . ." Armed with a renewed sense of hope, Shay felt the heaviness that had descended over her begin to lift. "We are going to have the best display at the carnival, and we are going to win first place. Madam Melvina's going down!"

"Darn right she is. One bubbling cauldron at a time." Jen applauded. "Remember that, and stop overthinking the whole carnival and try to have some fun with it. Speaking of fun . . ." She pulled her cell phone out of her apron pocket and checked the time. "I'd better get down there and open the doors."

"Not much urgency there. Since the summer tourist season ended, I think we've averaged four customers a day before noon."

"I know, but with this new attitude, things are bound to pick up. After all, it's you who is always telling me we manifest our futures." Jen gave a cocky grin and headed down the stairs.

Shay retrieved the harvesting basket tray and clippers from the potting table and walked to the planter that had caused her amulet to warm earlier. Her skin tingled as she approached the exotic plant with bright yellow flowers and needle-like leaves that resembled small brooms.

"That's it, rooibos!" She shook her head at her own forgetfulness, but it was easy to overlook these plants and this particular plant table, as it was far removed from any of the overhead sprinklers because the plants needed dry soil to thrive. "The rooibos will be perfect, with its seasonal reddish color when it's brewed. I can just add sparkling water and Jell-O powder to create the effect I'm looking for."

"Shay? Are ye up here?"

Normally, the singsong lilt of Liam Madigan's Irish brogue was all it took to make her pulse race, but not today. She knew exactly why he was here, and she was in no mood to give him his monthly pep talk. She had a battle to plan and a war to win.

Chapter 2

Shay sat silently on the bench by the potting table, her fingers instinctively stroking the fine hairs behind Spirit's ears. Her head unconsciously bobbed from side to side as Liam's lilting voice cast its enchanting spell over her. However, if he were to give her a test and ask her to recite back to him everything he'd been saying, she knew she'd fail miserably. The thing was, she didn't care what the words were that tumbled out of his mouth. She'd heard the same old who-should-I-date-now question over and over for the past year, and the conversation was getting really old. Nope, she wasn't in the mood.

She defiantly met his expectant gaze and realized he was waiting for an answer to something.

"Well, what do ye think?" He held his hands out, palms up, as if expecting her to plop an answer into his awaiting grasp.

"About . . . ?"

"About me asking Maggie Somers to the Monster Mash dance on Sunday night?"

"Maggie Somers to the Halloween dance?"

"Yeah, ye know, the lass from the bookshop up on Fifth Avenue."

"I know where it is, and I know Maggie quite well."

"Good, then ye know if we'd be a good match, right?" His electric-blue eyes lit up with flickers of hope.

"I think . . ."

He leaned closer and steadied his expectant gaze on hers.

"I think she's as good a match as Lillie Andrews, Adeline Price, Gwen Helton, and Beverly Lewis were. Oh"—she snapped her fingers—"and let's not forget Teresa Boyer from Teresa's Treasures or our dear sweet friend, Zoey Laine, Spirit's veterinarian, who shockingly did manage to last longer than a month or two."

"It wasn't my fault Zoey ended it. It was the situation of her and Gran living under the same roof." He shrugged. "As for the others, I may have had a hand in it not working out, which is why I'm asking ye what do ye think about Maggie and me? Do ye think I should ask her? Is it worth a shot? Do ye think she'd be interested?"

Shay narrowed her eyes at him. "Did you just hear what I said?"

"Aye, I'm not daft, ye know."

"Then I want you to really think about what I said."

"I have, and all the women you mentioned have something in common, right?"

"Yes . . . and?"

"They own their shops." He impishly grinned at her. "I can't help it if I'm attracted to successful businesswomen."

"And you didn't see any other pattern in that long list?"

"Aye," he nodded slowly, and his eyes lit up. "I see what yer saying. I suppose I could start looking at some of the workers downtown, not just shop owners. There's even a couple of nurses and a new doctor at the hospital that have caught me eye. Yer right. I should be expanding my dating pool."

"That's what you've taken away from what I said?"

He sat back on the bench and studied her while he

stroked his chin. "Aye, but now that I think about it, maybe ye aren't very good after all about giving me advice in the affairs of the heart since none of those women turned out to be the right one."

"Sooo," she said, coaxing him on, "what does that mean?"

"It means I should be talking to someone else who's a more experienced seer than you are." He snapped his fingers. "Madam Malvina. She's the ticket."

Shay shot to her feet. Her body shook as she glared down at him, and she clenched her fists at her sides to keep from slapping him.

"Aye, and here's me thinking ye, being a seer and all. Ye could steer me in the right direction, but so far, all ye've done is make a complete mess out of me personal life, and my reputation in town is suffering for it."

"Me? *Your life?* Why, you shallow . . . toad! I . . . I can't even . . . Get out of here and don't come back. Do you hear me? Out!" She pointed to the staircase. "Now!"

"Ye want me to leave?"

"Yes, and I want you to take your own advice and go ask someone else, someone who cares. Because, Liam, I don't care who you date or do anything else with. Not then, not now, not ever, not anymore. Do you hear me?"

"Aye." He rose to his full six-foot-three-inch height and looked down at her. "I think ye must be having a bad day, so I'll come back later."

"No, don't bother ever coming back here again!" she said, her body vibrating with fury.

"Certainly, ye don't mean that?" His eyes narrowed, and concern flickered within their electric-blue depths. "Ye're me best mate. Ye always know just what to say when things in my love life don't turn out. Move on, you say, and I think ye did after yer ex, so I can too." His hand lay gently on her arm. "I don't know what I'd do without you in me life."

"And there lies the problem," she whispered and pulled away from him as though his touch had burned her.

"Say what?"

"Nothing." She rubbed her arm. "Just go, please."

He nodded his head slowly and eyed her skeptically, his questioning gaze not wavering until he'd descended past the top of the stairwell.

"Madam Malvina!" she hissed through a jaw locked by the rage coursing through her. She gasped in a series of breaths, trying to release her pent-up anger, and reminded herself she had done the right thing, that sometimes when things fall apart, better things fall into place.

It was time she refocused her energy on someone other than Liam Madigan. The hoped-for romantic evolution of their relationship clearly wasn't ever going to happen. It was time to face the truth. He didn't fancy her in a romantic way, and it was time she accepted that fact. The past year's door of revolving women proved it.

She took another deep breath. It was time to stop believing the energy between her and Liam was anything other than a close bond of friendship. A sharp pain twinged her heart, and she rubbed her fingers over the spot. If the universe didn't want them together, then . . . Shay's shoulders slumped. Could this really be what the universe planned for them? Some seer she turned out to be. How could she have been so wrong about them? And Gran? She kept encouraging Shay, telling her their lifelong bonding was fated because she and Liam were both royalty of the fairy's High Seelie Court.

After discovering she was even a tad bit attracted to Liam two years ago when she arrived back in Bray Harbor, she had hoped that she could actually move on from her cheating, thieving ex-husband, Brad, who had ruined her career and her reputation back in Santa Fe, New Mexico. Her attraction to Liam then signaled that the heart she thought broken beyond repair from Brad's betrayal was indeed not destroyed and could, and wanted to, love again.

The problem was she wasn't sure she could move on easily from a man who she once thought too perfect. Even though Liam's electric-blue eyes, framed by raven-black hair, and his muscular build stirred her to her very core, Liam Madigan wasn't the perfect man she'd thought—or hoped. The past two years had proven he wasn't for her. Obviously, she wasn't that shallow, and it wasn't just his good looks that called to her. There was something intrinsic about him that pulled her to him. If only she could . . . she shook herself from her fantasy. No, he wasn't even close to perfect, but in her time of crisis last year, he had proven to be a loyal friend of substance.

Clearly, he wasn't the man she thought him to be. She had to get him out of her head and her foolish heart, and take it as a lesson learned. Fables and myths belonged in storybooks. They made for great reading, but not so much in real life. It was time to put the dream of her and Liam to rest. If she could survive leaving Brad, she could survive the loss of Liam. Forcing herself to believe the lie that she didn't need Liam Madigan, no matter how much he said he needed her, she finished harvesting the parts of the rooibos.

"Gran!" Her chest tightened as she set her basket on the potting table. Her decision today to move on now meant Shay had the monumental task of breaking the news to her that they both needed to move on from Gran's foreseen romantic future for Shay and Liam. How could Shay explain to someone like Gran that her usually unfailing second sight was faulty when it came to matters of the heart? Maybe she and Gran had missed the chapter in the seers' handbook that says, "You can see for others, but never yourself or never for matters of the heart when family are involved."

"Shay, can you come downstairs? There's someone here who wants to see you," Jen called up the staircase.

Spirit cocked his head, and his tail thumped against the brick floor.

"Two to one that's you-know-who."

Spirit let out a high-pitched yip that sounded uncannily like Gran.

"I know. It's scary how she does that, isn't it? Let's go see if we're right." Shay trotted down the stairs and into the tea shop's back room and nodded her gratitude at Jen. "Gran, what a surprise." She winked at Spirit, who ignored her and trotted over to Gran. "Is everything okay?" she asked, straining to keep her tone innocent.

"Trust what ye feel, not what ye hear, lass. There, I've said me piece, and I'll be off now." Gran walked toward the door.

"No!"

Gran halted, her hand on the doorknob.

"It's just not what I've heard, Gran. It's what I have had a ringside seat to for the past two years."

Jen looked blankly from Shay to Gran and then back at Shay. "Is this some kind of secret code you guys are speaking in?"

Shay knew exactly what Jen meant. Sometimes Shay and Gran were so connected that Shay herself often wondered if she and Gran could read each other's minds. "Not a secret code. I just happen to know what she's talking about, because the timing of Liam leaving and her arriving isn't a coincidence."

Shay crossed her arms over her chest and thrust out one hip, feigning nonchalance. "So, what did he tell you when he went back to the pub? No, don't tell me. Let's see if I can guess." Despite Gran's faded blue eyes gazing intently at her, Shay forced a detached tone to her next words. "He told you I was having a bad day and told him to leave and never come back. He plans on waiting a few hours until I settle down, and he'll come back and ask me again if he should take Maggie Somers to the dance Halloween night, right?"

"Would ye like a nice cuppa tea?" Gran's white hair, pulled high on her head like a dollop of whipped cream, jiggled as she marched over to the sink. She plonked the teapot on the counter and tossed in two spoonsful of dried chamomile leaves from a tin on the counter. Shay watched her in silence, knowing what Gran had planned and trying to think of a way out of a tea-leaf session.

Before Shay could think of a reasonable excuse, Gran gestured to a chair. "Sit, dear. Gran will make ye a nice brew, and I can do a reading, and then ye'll see that—"

"Sorry, Gran, not this time. This isn't me being in a bad mood. This is me being fed up waiting for him. I knew it would take time. The first year, he was waiting for me to get over my horrible marriage, and I did. Since then, I've given him so many hints that I'm truly starting to think he's as dumb as a box of rocks or absolutely clueless. And in that case, I don't want him." She swallowed the bitter taste on her tongue. "Face it, he still acts like we're kin." Her eyes widened. "Unless we really are and—"

Gran emphatically shook her head.

Relief flooded through Shay's veins. "Good. Look, I know he's your grandson, and you love him to the moon and back, but he's—"

Gran waved off Shay's words. "He's a lost soul right now, lass, and it's our job to put things right."

"No, it's not. Not my job anyway. If you feel you need to take your grown grandson by the hand and lead him in the right direction, that's up to you. But in my life, I've learned that unless a man is actually a baby, there is no woman who can change him, no matter how hard she tries. It's something he willingly has to do himself." Shay took the teapot out of Gran's hand and set it on the table.

"But, lass, it's in the leaves and me dreams and—"

Shay took Gran's hand gently in hers. "Yes, they were in mine too, but if they're not in his, it's not going to happen. Let's face it, Gran, we got it wrong this time."

"No!" Her messy bun jiggled with her brisk head shake. "I can't accept that. It's written. It always has been, don't ye see?" Her eyes filled with tears. "The fairy queen decreed it."

"That may be true, but don't you see, my feelings haven't changed. I've just run out of patience, and I don't—can't— wait anymore. It's too painful, and, quite frankly, I'm exhausted. I need to move forward so I can focus on what's really important and not run Bridget's legacy into the ground."

"Don't give up yet, lass."

"I have to. It's been too hard to stand on the sidelines and watch him get all twisted up about women I know he's not a match for. Every time he crashes and burns, I end up helping him pick up the pieces just so he can move on to the next one."

"Dat's what I'm saying, lass. He's a lost soul. He's struggling with something." She placed her hand over her heart. "Something in here, and it's our job to help him see what that is so he can move on too, in the right direction, the one the fairy queen decreed all them years ago."

Shay recalled Zoey Laine claiming Gran suffered from dementia because Gran would ramble on about it not being good for fairies to mix with others not of their kind whenever Gran argued that Zoey and Liam wouldn't last. That was the year before, and, of course, Gran had been right about the inevitable end of the couple's relationship. The jury on the mixture of mortals and fairies was still out, though.

Shay knew the old Irish legends were important to Gran. In her yearlong experiences and conversations with Gran since she arrived from County Clare, nothing except this kind of talk ever made Shay wonder about Gran's state of mind. However, the pain and sadness that radiated from Gran's eyes made Shay see there was only one of two things she could do. She could either send Gran packing and inform Liam his grandmother really did need medical intervention or allow her to do the reading and see how it all played out.

"You could always ask the leaves about you-know-who," Jen, always the peacemaker, offered.

Shay looked at her blankly, having no idea who exactly she was talking about.

"You know the person we were talking about this morning. The one who seems to have weaponized her association with you against you."

Shay nodded her understanding. Yes, being angry and overreacting was not going to solve anything anyway. Taking a deep breath, Shay refocused her anger at the person at the center of it all, and it wasn't Liam for being an idiot or Gran for being . . . well, Gran, but Madam Malvina. The woman's true colors were showing from under Madam Malvina's fake cloak of friendship, and Shay realized that her jumbled feelings and erratic energy weren't anger. She was hurt. Madam Malvina had broken her trust and her sense of goodness.

Ashamed of how she'd taken out her misplaced emotions, Shay sank into the chair Gran had indicated earlier. She had no reason to take out her frustrations on Liam for being a fool when it came to love and on Gran for believing all was good. She was just frustrated with herself for allowing the situation to continue and for not moving on it sooner, so she at least could have put an end to the conversations. If she was honest with herself, it was actually her inability to expose her own feelings that led to this point.

However, that still didn't let Liam off the hook. She would find a way of dealing with him and his wayward spirit later. After dealing with Gran's impending tea-leaf reading, of course.

Chapter 3

After drinking her tea, Shay began the tea-leaf reading ceremony by swirling and turning the cup in her left hand in three full rotations from left to right. With her left hand, she placed a serviette on top of the saucer, turned it over and set it over the cup, and slowly inverted the cup, leaving it upside down for a minute, allowing any leftover liquid to drain onto the napkin. At Gran's nod, Shay rotated the cup three more times with her left hand, turned it back upright, and positioned the handle so it pointed south.

After completing the procedure, Shay pushed the cup toward Gran and sat back, waiting for the same story she'd heard a year ago, that Liam and she were fated to be together because they were both royalty in the High Seelie Court or some such thing in the fairy realm.

Gran peered at the variety of tea-leaf shapes and clusters on the bottom and sides of the cup. Her craggy face lit up, and her broad smile made her appear twenty years younger. Shay tried to peek into the cup to see what Gran saw that had amused her so much, but the woman waved her hand and blocked Shay's view. She got up, washed the cup, and, without a word, tottered out of the back room.

"What?" Shay called. "You have nothing to say today?"

Gran's schoolgirl-like giggle mingled with the overhead bells jingling out her departure.

Jen poked her head into the back room. "What did she say about the reading?"

"Nothing, absolutely nothing, which translates into the same thing she's been saying since the first time she did a reading for me," Shay said, clearing off the table.

"Then she's still convinced you and Liam are going to be married and have half a dozen babies and all live together happily in your little cottage, right?"

"Pretty much." Shay shook out the dishcloth over the sink. "Some days I really do wonder if she's losing her grip on reality."

"Gran? Nah, she's eccentric, but she's still as smart as a whip, and there's always something behind her seeming moments of madness."

"I know, and I'm not being fair to her. It's only this is the one thing that hasn't shown to be true with time, and it makes me wonder. Just because you want something to be true doesn't make it so. Maybe it's time she leaves it alone, and we all focus on what's really important."

"Which is?"

"Me coming up with something that will take first place in the Halloween booth decorating contest and put Crystals & CuriosiTEAS back on the Bray Harbor proverbial map."

"How are you going to accomplish that?"

"I have no idea." Shay shook her head as she rinsed out the teapot and set it on the drying rack. "I'm blocked right now because I feel so, so . . ."

"Hurt?"

"Yes, I'm hurt and angry, all at the same time. Does that make sense?"

Jen nodded.

"I thought Madam Malvina finally thought of me as an

equal and we had started to become friends, but I see now that she was only using me, and then wham bam . . ." Shay drew in a deep breath. *Inhale and draw in your power, exhale and release your anger, and focus on who and what you are.* "It must be quiet enough this morning, or you wouldn't be hanging out in the back with me. Do you mind if I go out for a while?" Shay removed her apron. "I'll be back soon, but there's something I need to do so I can unblock this energy and move forward."

Within less than five minutes, Shay reached Madam Malvina's shop on the boardwalk, where, two businesses down, she skulked behind a large sandwich-board sign that read COLD BEER AND ICE CREAM, focused on the doorway of Celestial Treasures and Teas, and was hit by a renewed burst of anger. "I should have known what she was up to when she moved here and opened her new shop one street over from mine," said Shay, under her breath, trying to refocus on what she thought she was going to accomplish by stalking her target. "All's fair in love and war, though, right?" But when she gripped the side of the sandwich board and peered around it, she immediately questioned her actions.

After all, her impulsiveness hadn't served her well so far, and, between her and Gran, she questioned which one of them was losing touch with reality. The Little White Glove Society would soon be arriving for their usual morning tea and scones, and they were the last people she wanted as witnesses to a confrontation between her and Madam Malvina.

She used the edge of the sandwich board to help her out of her squatting position and, as inconspicuously as possible, retrieved her vintage red bike from the bike rack and readied to power-walk it away from Madam Malvina's tea shop as fast as she could on the busy boardwalk.

"Shay! Yoo-hoo, Shay!" a shrill voice called out from behind her.

Shay winced at Cora Sutton's very distinct nasal tone. As the mayor's wife and the chairperson of the Little White Glove Society, Cora was a hard woman to miss, and her voice was unmistakable.

Shay plastered a smile on her face. "Cora? How nice to see you," Shay lied. "I didn't know you were back in town." She gave a finger wave but firmly stood her ground by the sidewalk sign, forcing Cora to come to her.

The last thing she wanted was for the other ladies in the group to peer out of her competitor's tea-shop window and see Shay speaking to their leader. It wouldn't take long for rumors to spread that Shay was begging for them to return to Crystals & CuriosiTEAS. Even though that was exactly what she wanted do, she wouldn't give them the satisfaction of witnessing her desperation.

Cora huffed and quickly walked the fifty or so steps toward Shay. "I had no idea when I returned that our little group wasn't holding our meetings at Crystals & CuriosiTEAS any longer. I was just floored by the news." She studied Shay's face with open curiosity, no doubt looking for a reaction she could report back to the ladies who had chosen to be taken in by the promise of a free pot of tea.

Shay wasn't going to give her the satisfaction and masked her face, much as her adoptive mother had done when little Shay questioned her on the existence of Santa Claus.

"Well, that's neither here nor there, is it?" Cora gave a slight shoulder shrug, but kept her eyes glued on Shay's face. "Say, I did want to talk to you about some very interesting information I stumbled on when I was in San Francisco."

"I heard your mother took ill, and she passed away. I'm so sorry for you and your family."

"Thank you. It has been a difficult few months, but . . ." Cora glanced over her shoulder and lowered her voice. "It's precisely my family I need to talk to you about."

Shay hadn't seen Cora since the summer's Founders Festival, when Cora had made the public announcement that she'd discovered she was a direct descendant of John O'Toole, a fisherman from Howth, Ireland, and founder of Bray Harbor in 1854. Shay hadn't had time to discuss the discovery because Cora had left soon after to care for her ill mother.

Cora scanned the boardwalk again, leaned in to Shay, and whispered. "Not here. I'll drop by your shop later." She turned and rushed off toward Madam Malvina's, paused at the door, tossed her head of brown, short curls high, plastered a smile on her face, and entered the rustic, brick-red, seaside clapboard building.

The meeting Cora wanted to have with Shay piqued her interest. Ever since Cora made the big announcement at the Founders Day festival and said this was a fact that been kept from her previously, Shay had been dying to talk to her about it, since it sounded similar to her story. Cora's need to share something about it with Shay, out of the earshot of others, intrigued her even more.

Not risking the southern path that led her past the large picture window of Celestial Treasures and Teas, Shay meandered north, away from the direction of her own shop a street over on High Street, and pushed her bike along the boardwalk, all the way down to Swirls Ice Cream Shop. After an ice cream cone and a chat with the shop's business owner and her neighbor, Pearl Hammond, Shay headed back to work.

As the familiar overhead bells jangled out her arrival, Shay stopped short at the sight of Cora. "Cora? I thought—"

"I know." Cora waved for Shay to join her at the back

corner table. "As soon as I finished my hellos to the ladies, I made an excuse to leave." Her eyes lit up with a mischievous glimmer. "I'm just busting at the seams to tell you what I discovered about my family."

Shay glanced around the empty tearoom to the back counter, where her sister was filling a tea tin with dried herbs. "Okay. Jen, if you don't mind, I'll just be in the back with Cora. Call me if you need me." She motioned to the back room and allowed Cora to go ahead.

"Did you want me to need you?" whispered Jen as Shay passed by her.

Shay discreetly shook her head and then went in and closed the door behind her. "Would you like a cup of tea while we talk?" she asked, plugging in the electric kettle.

"That would be lovely. I didn't even stay long enough to enjoy one at . . . well, that other tea shop." Cora sat at the round table and laced her fingers together in front of her.

Cora's nail tapping grated on Shay's nerves, and she concentrated on placing four stalks of lemongrass and four sprigs of mint leaves into a teapot. Lemongrass and mint tea was supposed to pep up a person, even on the most trying days, and from the day she'd had already, Shay needed all the help she could get. What in the world could have Cora so excited to share her news with Shay that she abandoned the very group Cora had founded over two years ago? And on her first day back after being gone for months, no less?

Shay sighed and shook her head. The day was getting weirder and weirder, and her energy was still blocked. If she wasn't so dang mad at Gran for not sharing what she saw in the leaves, she could go ask her for another tea-leaf reading that didn't focus on Liam. If she could stand facing that backstabbing Madam Malvina, she'd go ask her what the planets were doing. There had to be something mysteriously esoteric or, at the least, planetary about all the craziness. Saturn or Jupiter or one of them must be in retrograde, right?

Shay poured the boiled water over the herbs and set the teapot on the table. "There, this should be ready in about ten minutes." She placed two cups on the table and took a chair beside Cora. "Now, what is it you discovered that has you grinning like a Cheshire cat?"

"Well," she leaned closer to Shay, "after I uncovered the fact that I was a direct descendant of John O'Toole, I was most curious about my Irish ancestors. My parents never talked about any of that. So, in the evenings after I finally got Mother settled, I started to research more of my family genealogy, and you aren't going to believe what I found out." She looked expectantly at Shay.

Shay shrugged and motioned for Cora to continue her tale.

"I have a family link to Killanena, County Clare! That's where your Irish kin are from too, if I'm not mistaken."

"You have kin from the same village that my ancestors are from?" Shay's stomach lurched as she heard Cora's words, and she blocked out whatever else she was droning on about.

"Yes." Cora squealed with glee. "Wouldn't it be something if you and I were related?"

Chapter 4

Shay opened her mouth, but on second thought, she quickly snapped it shut. Ever since discovering the people she thought were her birth parents had actually adopted her, she'd lost part of her identity. She wasn't of the same Scandinavian lineage as her adoptive family, but was, in fact, Irish. She'd longed to connect with any Irish blood relatives she might have, but—she uneasily squirmed in her chair—however strong the need to make family connections, she wasn't certain the mayor's social-climbing wife, whose career aspirations for her husband exceeded even his own, was what she had in mind.

Cora's voice droned on and on in the background as Shay fixated on the fact that they might be related and all that could mean going forward. She inwardly cringed. *As the saying goes, you can't pick your family like you can friends*, so . . . if it was true, she'd have to make the best of it, wouldn't she?

". . . Biddy Early—" Cora's nasal voice broke through Shay's thoughts.

"I'm sorry, did you just say the name Biddy Early?"

"Yes," replied Cora. "It seems I'm related to her, which means you and I are related. How exciting. Bridget Early was your mother, right? And she came from the same county as the 'wise woman of Clare.' " A smug expression crossed Cora's face. "That's what they called the real-life witch, Biddy Early, you know."

"Yes . . . I think I recall reading something about her in one of the books I have out front, but—" Shaken by Cora's words, Shay got up and refilled the teapot with more hot water from the kettle. "However," she added, fighting to keep her voice steadier than her knees were behaving, "I'm fairly certain Early is a common name in Killanena, County Clare, and I have no knowledge that Bridget was related to anyone claiming to be a witch, of all things."

If Cora had researched Biddy to the extent that she knew what locals called her back in the day, what else had she discovered? Dread reared up inside Shay as an edgy sensation settled into her chest. The last thing Shay needed was for Cora to discover she was a blood relative.

This declaration also meant that, in her research about Biddy Early, Cora would probably have also read the stories around Biddy's little blue bottle and guessed it was the supposed secret of the Early women's powers. The last thing Shay needed was for Cora to make a fuss about finding it to keep it within the family.

The amulet pouch Shay wore around her neck grew warm against her skin, and a whispered voice brushed her cheek. *Don't let Cora learn the truth, no matter what.*

"Coincidence is all," said Shay, with a short laugh, as she placed the refreshed teapot back on the table and retook her seat, not missing the skeptical look in Cora's eyes.

"I just think," said Cora, "it would be wonderful if we were actually related. What a small world it truly is, right?"

"It's not that small, and it would be quite a long shot. How many millions of people live in Ireland?" Shay laughed, fighting to keep the nervous tension quivering inside her from reaching her voice.

With trembling hand, Shay started to refill Cora's cup. Tea sloshed over the lip and onto the saucer, and she immediately set the teapot down. Still, she needed to keep Cora here long enough to discover exactly what she knew about Biddy and her blue bottle. Filled with renewed determination, Shay took a breath and refilled the cup, meeting Cora's gaze. "Tell me what you discovered that makes you think we might be related?"

"It seems I have a great, great"—she flapped her hand wildly in the air and softly giggled—"a whatever aunt. She was married to one of Biddy Early's great, great, great, whatever nephews. That side of my family's last name isn't Early, so my connection to them is through marriage, it seems, which means we must somehow be related. It makes sense, doesn't it?"

No, it really didn't, and Cora seemed to be grasping at something she wanted to be true rather than what really was. She eased out the breath that had been pressing on her chest. "Like I said, Early is a common name and—"

"But that's not the best part and the part that tells me I must be an Early like you. Did you know—you must know because I know you've researched her too, that Biddy Early had a magical blue bottle. It was reported that she could see the future with it." Cora rested her forearms on the table, leaned in toward Shay, and dropped her voice. "It apparently vanished when she died, and no one has seen it since."

Shay choked on a gasp, seized her cup, and took a tentative sip, stealing some precious time to come up with a game plan.

Cora's voice broke through her spiraling thoughts. "I found it to be a fascinating fairy tale and nothing more."

Shay eased out a constricted breath. If Cora didn't put much stock in the tale, then everything was—

"That is, until after my mother passed"—Cora crossed

herself—"and I was cleaning out her house and found something that made me wonder if the fairy tale might actually be true, and if I was a direct descendent of Biddy." Cora's eyes gleamed, and she pulled a folded lace handkerchief out of her purse.

Shay struggled to fill her lungs. She didn't know what the wrapped item was, but she didn't like the tingling at the back of her neck nor the burning of the amulet against her chest.

"I came across this in her jewelry box," Cora said, carefully unfolding the lacy package, "and it made me realize that my own connection to the Early family was closer than I'd originally thought. It seems that what I had put down to superstition and fairy tale might actually be true." She smiled as she revealed a small blue bottle, removed the cork, and dropped a dark-blue gemstone into the palm of her hand.

Shay's frazzled nerve endings ceased firing, leaving her mind blank, her breath stuck in the back of her throat, and her heart missed a beat.

"I thought that since you are a trained gemologist, you could identify what kind of stone this is?" Cora tilted her head and studied Shay. "Are you okay? You look pale."

Shay waved away Cora's concern. She sat up straight and timidly smiled. "Sure, I can look at it for you." With her system gradually rebooted from her initial shock, Shay made a show of examining the blue gem closely.

She knew, of course, that it was nothing more than a piece of common, blue, polished beach glass and not the priceless rare blue diamond the real bottle contained. Her mind raced while she played up the show of examining the bottle's contents to bide time while she thought through the consequences of Cora's discovery.

If Cora thought she had the real bottle, she would never suspect that Shay had the genuine magical one. But that meant that, if Cora left believing her bottle was real, it also made her a target. The trick was going to be convincing Cora her bottle wasn't real without her suspecting that Shay possessed the real one. As long as Cora never learned that that part of the Biddy story was, in fact, true, everything would be fine.

"Do you think," Cora's voice wobbled on the verge of hysterics, "this bottle and stone might be the mysterious blue bottle that Biddy Early was known to have but that disappeared after she died? Since I now know about my Irish roots, I'm guessing my mother's family must have brought it over from Ireland with them, which was why everyone thought it had disappeared. But it didn't. It just left Ireland with the family and has been safely stashed away in San Francisco for all these years."

Shay picked up the bottle, studied it closely, and reexamined the piece of polished glass. The relief she'd felt earlier about Cora thinking she had the genuine article faded. Shay had no doubt that Cora would tell everyone she knew—which was all of Bray Harbor—about the mysterious blue bottle she had found and its supposed magical qualities.

It wouldn't be long then for Doyle, the Irish crook and murderer Shay suspected might be her biological father, to find out, and Cora would have made herself his target. After all, he had sworn to stop at nothing to get his hands on the Early magic, and by the time he discovered Cora's bottle wasn't the real thing, it would be too late for the woman.

I'm sorry to tell you." Shay forced an edge of authority in her voice to sound convincing for Cora's own good, "but this isn't old enough to have been Biddy Early's. If what is recorded about her is even half the truth, then it's not from the same time as she lived. To be honest, I'd say it's maybe a 1930s or '40s mass-produced replica of what people said the blue bottle looked like and was sold in souvenir shops."

"That can't be," cried Cora in disbelief.

"I'm sorry, but the stone isn't a magical gem. It's a piece of beach glass, and the bottle has seams, meaning it was machine produced, not handblown, like bottles in Biddy Early's time would have been. It is old, though," Shay quickly added when hope disappeared from Cora's eyes. "It would be a collector's item, I think, since, to my knowledge, they don't make anything like this these days." Shay softened her tone to alleviate Cora's crushed hope of a fairy tale come true. "But as far as I can tell, it's not old enough to have belonged to the 'wise woman of Clare.'"

Cora whimpered, and her bottom lip trembled.

"However, since it is of some value, because it's an antique and a collector's item, it might be best to keep it under your hat. Especially since there are so many tales and rumors surrounding the actual mysterious blue bottle and the magic it possesses, it might be best if you don't tell anyone that you have this and instead put it away for safe-keeping."

Cora looked curiously at her.

"Think of it as a memento of your Irish family and something precious to your mother, who kept it all these years because it meant something to her. Perhaps it was a gift from someone special in her life at the time or she picked it up on a vacation she took to Ireland before you were born?"

"But," Cora eyed Shay skeptically, "if it's not priceless and not the real thing, why can't I tell anyone about it? I'm quite certain the society ladies would love to hear the stories around the real one and to have a replica to show them—"

Shay's mind flashed to Doyle. "I just think it's—"

"You know," said Cora collecting the bottle and blue

glass piece and wrapping them back up in the handkerchief, "it has been a few years since you worked as a gemologist, and you don't have any of your testing equipment.
I think I'll take this to someone else, because I have a hard
time believing that this isn't the real thing, especially after
all the research I've done into my family tree and about
Biddy Early."

"As I said, Cora, I believe it to be a collectible, but—"

"There, you just said you believe it to be. Well, my
mother never went to Ireland, and so it had to have been
gifted to her by her mother and brought over by my ancestors. Like I told you, I found proof I am related to Biddy
Early, so this"—she waved the folded hankie in Shay's
face—"might very well be the real thing." She harrumphed
and stalked toward the door. "If it is, and it does hold
magic," she said as she pulled the door open, "just think
how I'll be able to use it to help boost my husband's political career." With that, she banged the door closed behind her.

"Wait, Cora," Shay cried, flinging the back-room door
open. Doyle would undoubtably make Cora his next target. He knew the bottle was in Bray Harbor and might assume his spies had never found it because Shay didn't have
it after all. Cora did. "Let's do a reading and see if it can
give you a clear path forward."

Cora stopped, her hand on the front door's handle, turned,
and fixed her gaze on Shay. A smile ticked up the corners of
her lips. "You know what? I think you're jealous."

"Jealous?" Shay headed across the empty tearoom, not
missing the confusion on Jen's face as she passed the sales
desk.

"Yes, jealous, because I have the Early magic even though
I don't have the name, and you have the name but not the
magical bottle." She held her head high and nodded. "Yes,
I think a reading is exactly what's needed since I can see it

as something I should be performing in my future, as I'm related to a real-life witch and all." She crushed her purse tightly to her chest and marched toward Shay. "Shall we?" Triumph rang in her voice, and she gestured toward the back room.

Shay nodded in agreement. "You go ahead. I'll just make sure Jen can handle things out here while we do the reading."

When Cora shimmied past her, Shay let out a shaky breath and double-checked to make sure the amulet pouch she wore around her neck containing the real blue bottle was safely tucked out of sight.

Chapter 5

Shay sat alone in the back room and stared down into Cora's cup. No matter how many times she examined them, the odd leaf formations still looked like a large raven sitting off to the side, a butterfly, and a fairy ring spread out across the bottom of the cup. Did they really point to an ominous outcome to a situation that her feelings of impending doom now suggested? She just wasn't sure.

She pushed the cup and saucer away, comforted by the thought that she'd followed Gran's advice and kept all her readings positive and had told Cora all was well. She was comfortable telling Cora they were, in fact, good omens, in spite of an ill-omen-induced tension that snaked up Shay's spine when she peered at the images.

There was no harm in telling Cora that the fairy rings are where fairies dance and play and that the image of it meant positive changes. She saw no need to tell her that, if humans interrupted their fun, it could be deadly for the people involved. As for the black butterfly, in some cultures, it was an omen of death, while in others, it was a sign of positive change. Besides, the color could be read as black because of the heavy clumping of the leaves. It was the ambiguity of the images in her cup that helped Shay placate herself, comforting her in the thought that these were all actually good omens, right?

After all, Shay had read some positive interpretations of those images. The raven, for example, was often described as a bird to be revered for its intelligence and memory, and not, as some articles said, a trickster or one to be feared as a sign of bad things to come. Bridget had also echoed the positive interpretations in her journals. So it must be true.

However, if it was, why had a sense of something ominous appearing in the leaves begun to send shooting pains up the back of Shay's head? So much so that, when Cora left, Shay became unnerved and couldn't help but repeat her warnings not to tell anyone about the blue bottle and to promise again to keep it hidden.

Shay had reemphasized the importance of Cora not even carrying it around in her purse because it could easily be snatched. Instead, she had advised Cora to wear it in the small leather pouch Shay gave her from the shop and had tied it around Cora's neck, giving her instructions to keep it tucked discretely under her blouse.

Much to Shay's surprise, Cora had appeared to listen to her and didn't even comment about Shay coming across as dictatorial, something Cora would have normally pointed out. Shay hoped that meant she now either considered Shay kin by way of her research or that Cora had recognized the urgency in Shay's voice. Either way, it didn't matter right now. What mattered was that, even if the woman might not agree with or believe the reason Shay had given her with her far-reaching explanation about the blue bottle being an antique and a valuable collectible, she still headed her warning.

After Cora left, Shay would have loved to have breathed a sigh of relief, knowing she had done everything she could to keep the woman safe. However, as she studied the images again in the bottom of the cup she had pushed away, she was struck by an even more overwhelming premonition of impending tragedy. Why? Was there something Shay had missed when she'd warned Cora, right from the beginning, that, if she wasn't going to lock the blue bottle away in her husband's safe, it was important for her not to tell anyone she had it—that she had to keep it hidden? Shay replayed her words of warning over and over in her mind.

Then, once satisfied she had said all she could without telling Cora it was Shay who actually had the real bottle and gemstone, there was nothing left for her to do but cross her fingers and hope Cora would heed her words. Because if the prickly, stabbing sensations dancing along her spine and the unease swirling in her gut were any indication of what might lie ahead, even her innocently sharing the news with the other Little White Glove Society ladies—well, a move like that would only bring about a catastrophic event in Cora's life.

Shay needed Gran. She quickly covered the cup with a kitchen towel so as not to disturb the contents, cradled it in her hands, holding it close to her body, called out to Jen that she'd be back soon, and dashed next door to Madigan's Pub.

Shay blinked repeatedly, willing her eyes to adjust to the dim bar interior, and turned to her left in the direction of the bar, hoping to catch a shadowy image of Liam or Carmen, his usual day-shift bartender. Her vision finally adjusted, she made her way over to the woman with silver spiked hair and a weathered complexion. "Hi, Carmen. I'm looking for Gran. Is she upstairs in the office?"

"Hi, hun. She's not here right now. She left a while ago and said she had some shopping to do."

"Oh . . . okay . . . um . . . how long ago did she leave?"

"Maybe half to three quarters of an hour ago."

"Is Liam upstairs?"

Even though she really didn't want to see him, let alone speak to him, she knew if she left the cup with him, he'd make sure Gran read it, and she could get back to Gran about her thoughts later. She really didn't like leaving Jen on her own in the shop, and Tassi wasn't due to come in until four, after her college classes were finished for the day.

"No, sorry, luv. He's gone out too. Said something about going to see Maggie or something, I think."

"He went to Stacks Fifth Avenue?"

Carmen looked questioningly at her.

"The bookshop on Fifth Avenue?"

"Yeah, I guess, if that's where Maggie works. I can take a message if you like?"

"No, that's fine. I'll come back later." Shay turned to leave, but stopped when Gran bounded through the front door, paused as her eyes adjusted to the change in light, and grinned at Shay. "Just the lass I want to see. Can ye come up to the wee office and we can sit a spell?" Her words came off more like a command than a question, leaving Shay no option but to comply.

"I have so much news fer ye." Gran giggled mischievously, as she often did when something stirred her fancy, and they walked across the main floor of the pub to the double-wide staircase at the back of the room that led up to the office and the rooftop patio.

Once they were settled in the office, Gran behind the walnut desk and Shay in a chair across from her, Gran smiled broadly at her. "I've been over to that Madam Malvina's shop." She hesitated, studying Shay's face, as though she were waiting for a reaction. Getting none, she shifted in her chair and leaned forward. "She isn't what or who she pretends to be, ya know," Gran whispered, and her face lit up with smug satisfaction. "She's a fake, she is. I'd bet me life on it."

Shay cocked an eyebrow. Madam Malvina knew far more than she did about plants and herbs used for teas and was rather an expert on what went with what, which ones to avoid blending, and which ones were poisonous. "What makes you think that?"

"I know she knows her teas and herbs and such alright." Gran nodded knowingly as though she had read Shay's thoughts. "But she has no powers, only what she's read in books."

"That can be said about most people who run tea shops and do tea-leaf readings, can't it?" Shay swallowed the lump at the back of her throat, recalling the imposter syndrome she often experienced. "I can even say that about me."

"No, yer a seer and have other special powers ye've not yet mastered. That woman, I tell ye, has none. She has made a living off guessing, she has." Gran eyed the kitchen towel Shay had clutched in her hands, and the wrinkled etchings around her eyes deepened. "What da ye have there, lass, dat yer holding like the Holy Grail itself."

Shay gazed down at the towel-covered cup and saucer in her hands. She'd forgotten all about it in her curiosity as to why Gran was suddenly convinced Madam Malvina was a fake. "It can wait. Go on, tell me why you think the woman is a fraud?"

"All in good time, me dear." Gran laced her fingers together in a prayer pose and sat back in her chair. "She isn't the only thing fake I saw in that wee shop today, though."

"What do you mean?"

"When I left, she was doing a reading for that Cora Sutton—ye know, the mayor's wife?"

"Wait, what?" Shay set the teacup and saucer on the desk. "She was doing a tea-leaf reading for Cora?"

"Aye, she was that, and from what I heard, that Madam Malvina had no idea what she was talking about."

"Are you sure it was Cora Sutton? About five-foot-six, short, dark curly hair, talks with a nasal tone, and speaks like she's sucking on a lemon. Sounds hoity-toity or something."

"Aye, that be her." The etchings at the corners of Gran's eyes deepened. "But that's not what I need to tell ye. Cora had a pouch with a wee blue bottle inside it and was telling Madam Malvina how the gemstone inside was the key to the Early magic and that she was an Early and needed Madam Malvina to teach her how to use it."

"Oh no." All the blood rushed from Shay's head to her feet. She went on to tell Gran what Cora had told her and shown her earlier. "I told her to keep it hidden. I didn't want to scare her, but if word gets back to Doyle—"

"Clearly being in the spotlight is more important to the woman, and ye did the right thing by warning her. If she didn't listen and something happens, ye did yer best. Rest easy, lass, ye've done all ye can."

"I can hope I have because of this too." Shay removed the towel from the cup and saucer. "Just over an hour ago, I did a reading for Cora—"

"You also did a reading for Cora today?"

"I did, and to be honest, the leaf patterns were rather disturbing, and I wanted you to tell me if what I saw is actually there."

Gran cupped her wrinkled and age-spotted hands around the cup and studied the patterns. "Ye see this here raven on the side of the cup?"

Shay nodded.

" 'Tis a message to the reader, not the seeker, saying listen, watch, and learn. So be like the raven lass. Miss nothing and remember all, because dis black butterfly . . ." She pointed to the impression in the bottom of the cup. "It can be a symbol of death, meaning rebirth or re-creation. More importantly, 'tis the 'death' of anything misfortunate. Aye, they say 'tis de freedom of the mind, body, and de spirit. Ye see, lass, in Irish folklore, black butterflies are associated with the spirits of passed loved ones and often appear at funerals. 'Tis a good sign. It means da person in question is moving on to the spirit world."

Lightheaded, Shay sat back, not aware she'd been holding her breath while she waited for Gran's interpretations.

"Breathe, child," Gran said, without even looking at Shay. "Yer soul can't speak to you if ye don't breathe." She shook her head and squinted at the other pattern in the bottom of the cup. "Now this!" she cried excitedly, "dis fairy ring represents a powerful spiritual portal." Her bushy white brows knit together. "But I'm not sure how this connects to the mayor's wife." Her eyes widened before they narrowed as she looked at Shay. "Ye did tell her not to ever enter the center of a fairy ring, didn't ye, as that could bring misfortune and death, given the black butterfly image too?"

Chapter 6

The next week passed quickly, and nothing had come of the tea leaves, Madam Malvina, Cora, or the dreaded Doyle. Shay's nerves were in shambles, and she busied herself in organizing her herbs and spices in hopes that, in doing so, her mind would follow suit and organize her scattered thoughts in neat piles, so she could begin to sort through them. Thirty minutes in, and while the shelves looked tidy, her thoughts were still a jumbled mess. Add on Cora's breach of promise and going to Madam Malvina, of all people, and Gran's ominous warning about entering fairy rings, and Shay contemplated just going home and hiding under the covers. But she had work to do and last-minute touches to do on the spiderweb and cauldron display in one of her shop's bay windows.

The doorbells jingled, and Mayor Cliff Sutton silently stood in the entrance of the tea shop. Shay glanced at her watch. Nine a.m. It was the same time that he had shown up over the past few days, scanned the tea shop, and left before Shay or Jen could ask him if he needed help with anything.

"Good morning, Mayor Sutton." Shay moved quickly and headed off his escape out the door. "What can I do for you this morning?"

He wiped his brow and studied the toes of his brown, wing-tipped shoes. "I . . . uh . . . am looking for my wife. Have you seen her?"

Despite the sliver of worry niggling at the base of her skull, Shay forced a smiled. "I haven't seen her for a while." She studied his worried expression. "Is everything okay?"

"As you know, Cora's the chairperson of the Bray Harbor Halloween committee, and every day this week, she's left the house just before seven for her morning walk and then gone to the tea shop for a scone before her committee meeting at eleven." He cleared his throat. "I don't usually check up on her whereabouts, and I'm rather embarrassed, but it's just that . . ." He looked from Shay down to the wide planked, wooden floorboards, and a blush worked its way from under his shirt collar to his cheekbones. "According to some of the committee members I'm friends with, she hasn't been attending any meetings this week."

"Really?"

"That's what I was told, and the other members are concerned because she is one of only two on the committee who has signing authority, and there is still so much left to pay for and do before the carnival kicks off in a few days."

Shay opened her mouth to offer words of consolation, but snapped it shut when he fixed his anxious gaze on hers.

"Shay, I'm really worried. I have no idea what's going on." He raked his hand through his thick, salt-and-peppered dark hair. "When she does come home, she's not herself. She's snappy and seems disoriented and confused about everything. That's why I come in here every morning in hopes she will be where she said, and I can stop worrying about the alternative." He sucked in a breath and then exhaled it. "You know her well. After everything that happened last year, do you think"—he swallowed hard—"do you think she could be having an affair?"

"An affair?" Shay didn't want to add fuel to the fire and offer up her own fears that Doyle might somehow be behind Cora's strange behavior. However, it had been nearly a week since Cora showed Shay her fake bottle and had her leaves read, and Shay hadn't seen Cora since. "Not Cora. She loves you and wants nothing but the best for you." Unable to confide in the mayor about what she knew about Cora, Shay blurted out the first thing that came to mind. "Maybe she's planning a surprise for you? Any special dates coming up?"

The mayor smiled. "Our wedding anniversary is two weeks from now. Yeah, you're probably right." He patted her hand. "Thank you. I'll let you get back to work." He walked out the door, looking far better and less anxious.

"What did he say?" asked Jen, sliding up beside Shay. "I hope he explained why he's been acting so weird this week?"

A large group came through the door, sending the overhead bell dancing in a frenzy. "I'll tell you later."

"Love your window display," called a stout, gray-haired woman as she tottered over to a table, where she was joined by others in her group, filling up the entire tearoom.

Through the next few hours of tea and lunch service, Shay learned they were a seniors travel group from Seattle, Washington, and were on a bus tour down the Californian coast to San Diego. They'd heard about the upcoming Halloween carnival in Bray Harbor and begged their driver to stop so they could check it out. They loved everything about the picture-perfect village so much that they decided to stay for a few days to take in the first night of the carnival.

Shay worked with extra perkiness in her stride. This

was news she needed. If she could make them fall in love with her shop, they'd be bringing back their much-needed business.

The entire group had smiles on their faces and nothing but good things to say to Shay and Jen as they filed out. "We'll be back" were their final words as the door closed behind them.

The music of those little words drowned out the frantic ringing of the overhead doorbell, and Shay's heart burst with pride when she glanced over at Jen bussing the tables.

Tassi would be in soon, and invigorated by the successful service, Shay nearly skipped to the back room to begin working on the tea blend for the carnival. She grinned at Jen, who rolled her eyes at Shay's newfound spirited attitude, and they sat at the table and discussed what remained on the checklist to be ready for the kick-off at six p.m. on Friday evening. While Shay readied a teapot for their afternoon tea, Jen created a timetable for remaining tasks and assigned a role to either herself, Shay, or Tassi.

"Done." Jen joined Shay at the sink. "So, are you ever going to tell me what Cliff Sutton had to say about his weird flyby visits this week?"

"Right. With everything going on, I forgot. It was an odd conversation, that's for sure." Shay dried her hands and sat back down, giving her sister an abbreviated version of their conversation. "I'm telling you, I wasn't sure what to say when he said his wife was lying to him about coming here for tea and scones."

"Do you think she's—"

"She was going for tea, but not here," said Tassi from the doorway.

"Sheesh, you'll scare the bejeezus out of us." Jen half-gasped, half-laughed and patted her chest.

"That's odd," added Shay. "Spirit never yapped a hello at you when you came in."

"He's not out there."

"He must have left when that big group did," said Shay, then turned to Tassi. "But what was that you were you saying about Cora?"

"It's just that every morning this week, on my way to school, I've seen Cora heading into Madam Malvina's shop."

"You did know the Little White Glove Society has made that their new meeting place, didn't you?" asked Jen, taking a chair beside Shay's.

"Yeah, and that's what's strange about it. This is hours before the society meets and before her tea shop is open. I leave for school at seven. So you tell me what she'd be doing in there at that time of the morning?"

"You see her going into the shop just past seven in the morning?" asked Shay.

"Yup, I thought it weird the first day I saw her going in, so every day since I've been hanging back so I could try and figure out what was going on."

"And?"

"And nothing. Cora knocks. Malvina opens. Cora goes inside. When I walk past the shop, the CLOSED sign is hanging on the door, and those fairy lights she has all around the window are off."

A jolt surged through Shay, and the amulet seared her skin. "Oh no, Cora. What have you done?" she whispered.

Tassi gave her a curious glance. Shay waved her off, grabbed the harvesting basket, and, without explanation, headed up to the greenhouse to sort through her thoughts.

A queasy sensation rolled through her gut. Whatever Cora and Madam Malvina were up to had something to do with the fake Early amulet. She tried to put her thoughts into compartmentalized boxes so she could focus and not accidentally kill the rooibos bush while she cut off the sprigs of leaves she needed for her tea experiments. It didn't work. Images of a black butterfly and the fairy ring she'd seen in Cora's teacup kept flashing through her mind like warning beacons.

"Stop it, Shay!" she chastised herself under her breath. "You heard what Gran said. These can be positive signs too, right?"

Cora was an adult and capable of making her own decisions, and Shay had warned her against telling anyone about her amulet, hadn't she? Shay snipped wildly at the needle-like, broom-shaped leaves and dropped them into her basket. "I know the amulet she has isn't the real thing, but . . ." She snipped another leaf. "So, unless someone else is familiar with the Irish tale, they wouldn't know about it or the magic that the blue bottle is reported to possess, right?" She trimmed at another branch on the bush, and then paused . . .

"Until it's too late for Cora, that is . . . Oh no. What have you done, Cora? Why Madam Malvina, of all people?" She dropped freshly cut rooibos leaves into her basket and tried to calculate whether it would be enough for the next experiment she wanted to try for the carnival. But it was no use. A black butterfly flitted around and touched down on every thought and every image that whirled through her mind.

Chapter 7

Shay glared at the recipe card in front of her on the back-room counter of Crystals and CuriosiTEAS. One more fizzy beverage to try before she gave up completely. It seemed that experiment after experiment had failed her, and this was the last chance she was giving herself to come up with a brew that would knock the socks off anything her main rival for customers could produce.

However, her recent recipe failures over the past few days were most likely due to the haunting images of black butterflies and fairy circles that refused to give up space in her brain. Even though she'd had Tassi keep a watchful eye on Cora, who appeared unaffected and happily clueless about the danger she was putting herself in, Shay couldn't shake a sense of impending doom.

Perhaps Shay had been wrong, and it was all a good omen, as Gran suggested.

Shay shook her head. Either way, she had to buckle down and focus on clearing her mind of Cora. She couldn't spend any more energy worrying about the what-ifs when she had a competition to win and customers to gain back. If she couldn't win her clientele back, the doors of Crystals & CuriosiTEAS would close forever, and her birth mother's legacy would be gone along with it.

Think positive. Manifest your own destiny!

She attached the recipe card for Halloween Fizzy Witch's Blood Tea she'd been glaring at to a clip hanging over the cupboard doorknob. She'd discovered the kitchen hack months ago, and as she was more disaster than master in the kitchen, the clip solution had saved her from many a mess and kept her recipe cards from harm's way and readable instead of smudged with ingredient splatter.

Jen needed help finishing their booth for the Halloween carnival, and she was running out of time. The recipe for Halloween Fizzy Witch's Blood Tea that hopefully would have everyone at the carnival stampeding their booth for refills had to work. Shay was out of options and read the instructions out loud:

Halloween Fizzy Witch's Blood Tea

Ingredients
- 2 cups of water
- 2 teaspoons of coarsely ground rooibos tea leaves
- 4 or 5 blood oranges
- ½ cup of frozen cherries (about 20)
- ¼ teaspoon of cinnamon powder
- 1 to 1½ cup chilled ginger ale or sparkling water
- 1 tablespoon orange Jell-O powder
- 1 tablespoon cherry Jell-O powder
- ½–1 cup of ice
- Sugar to taste
- Small white marshmallows (optional)

Instructions
Boil the water and steep the rooibos tea for 10–15 minutes. Strain leaves and discard.

Transfer steeped tea into a blender, allowing tea to cool. Squeeze the juice from the oranges into the tea brew.

Add the cherries and the cinnamon.

Blend until there are no cherry bits left, and then chill the mixture in the refrigerator.

When it's chilled, pour the mixture into a jug or carafe, and add 1 cup of the ginger ale or sparkling water, the Jell-O powders, and the ice. Stir well, and serve. Add sugar and/or more ginger ale until the taste and a high of level of nose-tickling sparkling bubbles in the fizzy witch's brew is achieved. If desired, the individual glass servings can be topped with the mini marshmallows.

Makes 2 to 4 servings, depending on glass size.

"Sounds easy enough." Shay screwed her face up in thought and tried recalculating the ingredient amounts to make a cauldron-size brew and sighed. Math was never her strong suit. She'd worry about the math later. She needed to focus on seeing if the witch's potion actually did what she wanted it to do: bubble in the customers' glasses and not just the cauldron.

She set about eagerly crushing, boiling, squeezing, and mixing. After adding the mini marshmallows, she peered into the glass jug. It had a frothy appearance to it and popped and fizzed as it was supposed to. The trick would be keeping it fizzy all night.

She snapped her fingers. "Why didn't I hold some back and make it one cup at a time? It would be easy to add the ginger ale and a sprinkle of Jell-O powder to each cup when serving it." She watched the effervescent bubbles popping and fizzing, and she sighed. "Of all the times to not have foresight." She took stock of the unused ingredients and winced. "Maybe, just maybe—"

"Talking to yourself again?" Tassi pushed in the empty serving cart and placed it beside the last stack of supplies to take over to the carnival site. "It smells good in here."

"Yes. I needed good advice, and no one else was around." Shay winked and grinned. "Wanna taste?" She held out a fresh spoon.

"Have you tried it yet?" Tassi took the proffered spoon and peeked into the pot. "Yuck! It looks like gooey blood."

"Good, that means it will be a hit with the kids," said Shay with a laugh. "Now, go on, tell me what you think. Will it outdo anything Madam Malvina will be serving?"

Tassi tasted the brew, closed her eyes, and made a contented purring sound. "This is so good. We should put this on the regular menu."

"Yeah, only if we want the reputation of being 'that witch's' store again, so no, I don't think so."

"It seems to be working for Madam Malvina," said Tassi. "She's not afraid to embrace her witchy powers, and you have more seer instincts than she'll ever have, so why not? Flaunt it if you got it."

"Because with her, it's a gimmick, and I don't think it's right for a true seer—if I am one, like Gran thinks—to put themselves out there like that just to make a dollar."

"Something is going to have to make us those dollars soon. Since I've been watching Cora, I've noticed there's a lot of foot traffic entering Madam Malvina's tea shop lately, and most of it appears to be from people we used to see in here."

"I know," Shay said, dropping her tasting spoon on the counter. "I keep hoping it's a fad and people will get tired of her gimmicks and yearn for the authentic teahouse experience we're offering. I just hope we can wait it out until then."

The air in the room grew heavy as the earlier celebratory mood about the successful brew dissolved. Shay immediately regretted her negative attitude and drew in a deep cleansing breath. *Refocus.* "Since you've been keeping an eye on Cora, have you managed to sneak a peek behind the screen Madam Malvina has set up in front of her booth before the big reveal at six?"

Tassi shook her head.

"Well, let's see if we can get one before the event starts, but we'd better hurry or mother Jen will ground both of us tonight for being late."

Thirty minutes later, Shay and Tassi carted the last of their supplies to their booth. They weren't the only ones struggling to hit the deadline, and business owners and booth exhibitors buzzed around the event grounds like time-crunched worker bees. Shay had attempted to use the chaotic environment to get a peek at what lay behind the curtain surrounding Madam Malvina's display, but with no luck.

Six o'clock arrived, and a town crier dressed in zombie garb and makeup made the rounds, calling everyone to the bonfire pit in the center green for the opening speech and ribbon-cutting ceremony by Mayor Sutton and his wife, Cora.

"You two go ahead." Shay shooed Jen and Tassi from behind the booth. "I'll hang back and finish arranging the counter so we can easily access the tea brew, Jell-O, and ginger ale without tripping over each other."

"Are you sure? I can do it, if you want to go and see what some of the other booths look like before we start." Jen adjusted the witch's black hat that sat on top of her long, fake, black braid.

Shay glanced at the stall kitty-corner to hers, which had a white sheet hanging around it. "No, there's only one other booth I'm curious about." Shay managed to smile at Madam Malvina's son, Orion, who, based on his stance in front of the curtain, was there to guard against prying eyes and nosy neighbors. Sneaking a peek was going to be impossible.

Tassi and Jen hurried off and Shay refocused her attention from Madam Malvina's tent by arranging the Halloween black cat adorned paper cups she'd purchase in the hope of not spoiling the bubbling brew illusion. She then organized the Jell-O powder and ginger ale on an easy to reach shelf just below the main counter, and straightened the CRYSTALS & CURIOSITEAS sign overhead. Once she had placed the finishing touches on the hay bales, jack-o'-lanterns, battery-powered candles, and witches' brooms that flanked the sides of the booth, she finally stood back and smiled in approval. With bats on strings flying overhead and the giant cauldron flanked by the gooey assortment of spine-chilling Halloween treats Jen and Tassi had created, she hoped she was making a *spooktacular* statement.

"Top that, Madam Malvina," she muttered and took her place behind the counter to await the first of many hoped-for trick-or-treaters who would stop by her booth that weekend.

"That was odd." Jen joined Shay behind the counter and tied on a black apron.

"You're back early," said Shay. "I take it the mayor wasn't as long-winded as he usually is?"

"He really didn't say much except for 'welcome.' " Jen's eyes filled with worry.

"That is odd. If anyone loves an audience, it's him."

"Not tonight. He couldn't get out of there fast enough."

"That probably didn't sit well with Cora. Any excuse to have her husband as the center of attention—"

"She wasn't there."

"But she's loves being in his limelight."

Jen shrugged.

Tassi joined them and whispered, "Something weird is

going on. Cora Sutton appears to have gone missing." She lightly elbowed Shay in the side and jerked her head toward the mayor, who was marching over to their booth.

"Shay, there you are," Mayor Sutton said breathlessly. "When I didn't see you at the opening ceremonies, I wondered if you were with my wife. Is she with you?" His eyes filled with hope as he leaned over and scanned behind the counter.

"No, sorry. I haven't seen her," Shay said.

"Any chance you could look in that crystal ball of yours or perform one of your hocus-pocus rituals to see where she is?" He laughed nervously.

"Sorry." Not sure if she should laugh or not since his eyes were filled with such sincerity and concern. "I really don't do that sort of thing."

"I know you don't. I'm just feeling a bit panicked, I guess, but I'm sure she's okay. It's just . . . well, you know the way she's been acting all week." He shook his head as though to clear it and gave her a faint smile. "She must just be running late." He glanced down the aisle of booths toward Madam Malvina's stall. "I'll just keep looking then. It's just so unlike her to miss an opening ceremony," he muttered and lumbered off.

"See," said Tassi, "weird, right?"

"Yes, a bit." Shay pushed the uneasiness in her gut aside, pasted a smile on her face, and served the two little fairy princesses waiting patiently for their cups of witch's brew.

Opening night flew by with a never-ending lineup at their stall. The parade of carnival attendees' colorful and original costumes intrigued Shay, Jen, and Tassi more with each passing hour, and they took a vote, deciding that each one of them could take half an hour to make the rounds and check out the festival's food and events.

When Shay's break arrived, she particularly enjoyed seeing the children's face paintings as they emerged from the craft tent and laughed until her sides ached watching the three-legged mummy races and pumpkin-toss events. She even tried her hand at bobbing for apples. Although she didn't win, she did get her teeth around a few of the bobbing crispy treats in the bucket, which she gladly took away as her participation prize. She hadn't taken a dinner break, and even though the smells from the food court beckoned to her, she knew she'd better get back. She tossed her last apple core into a garbage bin, turned around, and smacked directly into the chest of a towering Dracula.

Two firm hands grabbed her shoulders, steadying her.

"I'm sorry," she said, pushing her witch's hat up off her forehead and shoving stringy strands of snarled wet hair from her recent apple-bobbing adventure out of her eyes. She looked up, gasped, and danced a step backward. "Brad! What are you doing here?"

Her ex-husband, the man who cheated on her and stole everything she had in the world, including her reputation, was standing in front of her at the Bray Harbor Halloween carnival.

Fire and ice warred in her veins, and she thought she'd be sick. She blinked to clear her vision, but there was no mistaking his face. The same face she'd naively thought of once as looking a lot like her one-time screen crush, Ben Affleck, now resembled exactly what he really was. His costume couldn't have been more perfect. Dracula, the original life-sucking monster. No, there was no error in identity, especially with the Bride of Frankenstein, with her ruby-red lips, raven-black wig, and body-hugging bridal gown, otherwise known as Angela Powers, standing beside him.

Seeing them again, the one-time love of her life and her then best friend and assistant, who had become Brad's mistress, here, in her hometown, sent a renewed, piercing stab into her chest. It just couldn't be happening, could it? It must be a nightmare she was having. But the pain that reared its head afresh in Shay's heart, especially when Angela smiled at her like a Cheshire cat, was too real. No, this was not a nightmare.

She shook off his grip on her upper arms. "What are you doing here?"

"I was wondering if I would see you here tonight." He wrapped a stringy tendril of her dark-red hair around his finger, held it out, and snickered. "Although, I must admit, I really didn't expect to find you in such a, shall we say, realistic old crone costume."

"What are you doing here?" she repeated and pushed his hand away.

He leaned toward her. "Making the deal of a lifetime, my love," he whispered hoarsely.

"What do you mean?"

"We're looking at property in the area." He stood up straight and fixed his piercing, dark-brown eyes on her. "I can see why you came back here." He gestured to the lanky, dark-haired woman behind him, dressed as a monster bride. "Angela . . ." He paused, his eyes glimmering under the lights and leaned into Shay closely. "My new wife," he said with a grin, "has fallen in love with Bray Harbor, and we've decided to buy a winery just outside of town that went up for sale—right, dear?"

Shay pulled back to avoid more of his rancid breath crossing her face, and her eyes darted toward the Bride of Frankenstein, who flashed her a self-satisfied grin.

She grabbed at the amulet scorching her skin, and hurried away from the horrid, monstrous couple, holding the burning pouch away from her chest.

Chapter 8

With her head spinning and her nerves razor-edged swords stabbing at every part of her body, Shay stumbled back to her booth.

"What's wrong?" asked Jen. "You look like—"

"Brad is moving to Bray Harbor!" Shay gasped, unable to regulate her breathing. "He, he's . . . Oh, Jen, how can this be happening?"

"He's what? Moving here?"

Tears dripped down Shay's cheeks. "He and Angela are buying a winery." Shay sobbed. "I need Gran. She'll know what I should do."

"Why Gran?" asked Jen, with a hint of confusion in her voice. "What does she have to do with Brad?"

As much as Shay loved her sister, Jen hadn't seen her through Brad's infidelity and theft of her accounts, business, and reputation. Time and distance had separated her from Jen, and Shay hadn't bothered her with the details at the time. In hindsight, she probably should have, but they had drifted apart during her sixteen-year absence from Bray Harbor and only reestablished their relationship when Shay landed on Jen and Dean's doorstep one late-August night two years ago. And even in their renewed connection, the secret of the blue bottle still lay between them.

"Nothing, but lately Gran's been the glue holding me together, and I—"

"I don't know if I should be offended or not." Jen tilted her witch's hat back so she could make eye contact with Shay.

Shay took her sister's hands in hers. "No, don't be offended. It's just that . . ." *Think, Shay, think. Why do you need Gran now and not your sister?* "It's only that she can do a reading and tell me if I have anything to worry about." This was a nightmare. The last thing she wanted to do on top of everything was hurt her sister's feelings. "Honest, I just really need her skills right now."

"I get it. She's the perfect mother figure in your life. Well, you know, ever since you found out you were adopted and who your real mother was and, well, Gran being from the same area as her and all—I guess sometimes we all need that bit of mothering, right?"

"Right." Shay threw her arms around Jen's neck and hugged her. "I'm so glad you understand."

"I do, but I haven't seen Gran all evening. I thought she might stop by, but Tassi never said anything about seeing her before she went on her tour of the carnival. Since you didn't see her when you were off, maybe she's off with Cora?" Jen filled two glasses of brew and passed them to the waiting furry lamb and Little Bo Peep.

"Do you think?" Shay passed cups to a family of four zombies.

"Yeah, they must have gone off together because Dean stopped by after talking to Madam Malvina and said they still can't find Cora. So my guess is, if they are both missing, they must be together, right?"

"Probably," Shay said, deep in thought as she doctored four cups of witch's brew she'd ladled out of the cauldron.

Yes, Mother Jen made sense, as usual. It would be just like Gran to take Cora aside and warn her about telling anyone about the bottle she had. That, of course, would lead in to tales of the fairies, and Gran really could go on when she talked about the old ways back in Ireland. But that didn't help Shay with the Brad situation. Her universe wobbled unsteadily under her feet, and she needed Gran's wisdom and foresight.

Shay glanced down the row to see if she could spot the familiar white hair bobbing through the crowd, dragging Cora along with her. No such luck, and even more un-lucky was the line of people waiting to have their fortunes told at a certain tea-shop owner's tent. Although, for all Shay's foresight had done for her, she was no better or more genuine than Madam Malvina.

In truth, it seemed that, despite what Shay had thought and said about Madam Malvina's powers or lack thereof, Shay was no more of a fortune teller than she was. Some seer, right?

When the resident zombie town crier announced it was time for the evening bonfire, the timing couldn't have been more perfect. The cauldron was empty, and Shay was out of ingredients to refill it for the umpteenth time that night. Besides, her feet were killing her.

As nice as a community bonfire would have been to end the first evening of the carnival, Shay wanted to go home. The odds of her running into Brad and his monster bride were too good, and she'd already spent the majority of the evening looking over her shoulder.

As tired as she was, Shay was grateful to Jen for loaning out her black Explorer for the weekend. With Dean on duty and driving his police cruiser, Jen was only too happy to confiscate his Ford pickup, leaving Shay the use of her SUV. Not that Shay would do anything with her time by getting home sooner, but it would afford her the opportunity to wallow in this latest misery Brad and Angela had inflicted on her life and drown her sorrows with a much-needed cup of soothing tea on her porch with her faithful companion, Spirit.

Shay navigated the streets of Bray Harbor and swiped angrily at the hot tears pouring down her cheeks. Brad the vampire and Angela, his monster bride even without the costume, were moving here. How could this be happening? She struggled to describe how it made her feel, but she had no words; there was only a cold numbness settling through her.

When she pulled into the parking space at the rear of her cottage, the SUV's headlights reflected off two dark, shadowy figures on her back step. One was clearly Spirit, who had never made an appearance at the carnival, but it wasn't until Shay drew closer that she could make out the second figure. "Tassi? What are you doing here?"

"I hope you don't mind," she said, petting the top of the hulking white shepherd's head. "I walked around the fair for a while, then I ran into this fellow." She gestured to Spirit. "He was acting strange, like he wanted me to follow him, so I did, and he led me here."

"Really?" said Shay, taking a seat on the back steps beside them.

"Yeah, but since we've been here, I haven't seen anything that should have set him off. It's been quiet. I think everyone is still at the carnival grounds, but—"

Spirit jumped off the step, yipped, paced around the backyard, and barked at the trees behind the cottage.

"See, every once in while he does that. Do you know what it means?"

"No, I don't, except sometimes he hears critters in the forest and reacts to that. I'm sure everything is just fine." Shay had no sooner said those words than the amulet heated and scorched her skin. "Yikes." She winced and lifted it off her chest.

"Are you okay?"

"Yeah, it's just a twinge from sitting on this step, I guess." She stood and shook herself.

"Maybe it is a critter," said Tassi, eying Spirit. "Or maybe he's hearing the search party Mayor Sutton organized to find Cora."

"They've organized a search party?" asked Shay.

"Yeah, didn't you hear?"

"No, I hadn't. She still hasn't shown up?"

Tassi shook her head. "At least she hadn't when I left to follow Spirit."

"I wonder . . ." Shay peered at the dark, wooded hill behind her cottage.

"Do you think it's what's got him on edge?"

"I don't know, but I do know we'd better call your aunt and let her know where you are. Maybe she can pick you up when she leaves the carnival. The bonfire just started, so she might be a while, though."

"If you don't mind . . ." Tassi lowered her gaze. "Could I stay here? I'll sleep on the sofa."

"I guess it makes sense since we have to go back to the carnival in the morning."

"That's what I was thinking too." Tassi's eyes lit up, and she jerked her chin at Spirit. "I just think he wants me here for some reason."

A cool breeze tickled the back of Shay's neck, and she shivered, despite the warming amulet. "He did bring you here, didn't he?" She uneasily glanced back up the hill. "Wait." She squinted into the blackness. "Do you see that?" Shay pointed. "Right at the top, where that clearing would be, there was a light . . . there it is again. See it?"

"Yeah, I wonder if that's the search party."

"Why would they be up there?"

"Maybe someone in the cottages saw Cora heading in that direction."

Shay scanned the upper five cottages, all of which had no lights on and showed no signs of life. Even Liam's, directly across the lane from hers, was dark and empty. "Then where is everyone? This alley should be filled with cars and police cruisers. Call your aunt and tell her we're going to join the search party and you're going to stay here tonight. Okay?" Shay opened her front door. "I'll grab warm jackets and flashlights, and we can go up and see what's going on."

"Do you think it's them?"

"I'm not sure, but someone is up there, and whoever it is has Spirit on edge. Maybe it's Cora, and we can let her know that she's been reported missing. At the least, we can call her husband and tell him we found her."

Several minutes later, Shay closed the door behind her, handed Tassi a flashlight, and stuffed two water bottles, a small first-aid kit, and some granola bars into a small backpack.

At Tassi's raised eyebrow, Shay smiled sheepishly. "Always be prepared. Besides, I didn't eat at the carnival and figured a snack on the go wouldn't hurt. Let's get going." She switched on her flashlight and led the way to the path that would take them the top of the meadow outcrop behind her house.

"Wouldn't it be faster if we climbed the rocks from the beach up?"

"Too dangerous. The tide's in, and the surf's splashed the rocks probably halfway up, making them too slippery and hard to navigate, especially in the dark."

"Good point," said Tassi, struggling to keep pace with Shay and Spirit as they started the ascent. "You know, you two have an advantage over me here. You walk these paths almost every day, and this way is a first for me."

"Just stay close and point your flashlight toward the ground, because there are a few protruding roots up here you'll want to watch out for."

When they reached the top, Spirit stopped and stared into the darkness. His perked ears, erect tail, cocked head, and front foreleg doubled up as if ready for the next cautious step to forecast a danger Shay couldn't see. "Until we know who is up here, let's not broadcast our whereabouts," Shay whispered and clicked off her flashlight, then gestured for Tassi to do the same.

"I can't hear anything, but then again, dogs can hear things we can't," Tassi murmured and cocked her head. "No, nothing, but something must have gotten his attention."

"I can't see any sign of the light we saw earlier, and there's no noise that could be the search party up here."

"That's so weird. Why would someone be up here at this time of night?"

"I don't know." The amulet on Shay's chest grew warmer, urging her forward. "But let's at least go to the clearing that's over by the clifftop. That's where the light looked like it was coming from. "Come on." Shay dropped her voice and took a step forward. "Maybe it's Cora and she knows there's a search party looking for her and she's embarrassed and afraid to go back."

Spirit barked and snapped and bolted into the dark. Shay and Tassi flipped their flashlights back on and cautiously followed though the last of the woods and thick underbrush before stumbling into the windswept open meadow that stretched out toward the cliff's rocky edge.

A lantern, casting a faint yellow glow, sat on the ground in the center of the small clearing. Shay squinted and could barely make out what appeared to be human body lying beside it. A chill quivered across her shoulders, and she wheezed in a gulp of air and tiptoed closer. The prone figure lay in the middle of a ring of mushrooms and stones. The amulet's burning heat sent Shay's already ragged nerves into full-blown panic. Something about this scene looked familiar, but she couldn't place it.

Shay directed the beam from her flashlight onto the figure's face. Air rushed into her lungs and stuck. Only a muffled gasp escaped. She'd seen this scene in Cora's teacup reading.

"Who is it?" asked Tassi, tentatively approaching her. "Ahhh!" She jumped back. "Is . . . is that Cora?"

"Yes." Shay's knees shook as she crouched down and placed two fingers on Cora's carotid artery. "She's still warm, but she's . . . dead."

Chapter 9

Shay attempted to find a comfortable spot on the boulder that Dean, her brother-in-law the sheriff, had instructed her to sit on in case he had any more questions. She'd never been more jealous of Tassi and Spirit, who lay sleeping on a patch of soft grass. Although Spirit appeared to be in a deep sleep, his ears twitched with every movement and sound on the bluff top. He was fulfilling his guardian role to perfection, and Shay was sure Tassi was safe and warm next to the giant white dog. If only she could have stopped her mind from racing, she could have caught a few hours of shuteye too. She needed all her strength and sense to clear her head and put Cora's death into a clearer perspective.

She shook off the morning dew that had seeped through the blanket someone had given her at some point during the night. She'd lost track of how long she and Tassi had been at the scene, but it had to have been hours, and as the sun crested the eastern ridge of the hilltop, she shielded her eyes.

With the sun's light, Shay could see Cora's body from her perch a little easier, and she maneuvered her body every so often when the crime-scene technicians, still taking samples and snapping pictures, got in her line of sight.

The position of Cora's body struck her as odd. She obviously hadn't fallen as a result of being pushed or tripping over a rock or a tree root. It appeared that she had lain down and gone to sleep with her hands clasped peacefully over her chest, clutching a bundle of clover.

The position of the body wasn't the only thing that struck Shay as odd. Cora, a woman who normally dressed immaculately, now was barefoot and wearing a long, flowing skirt more reminiscent of a flower-power sixties hippy than a fashion-conscious, politically driven mayor's wife.

Shay shivered. The last thing she wanted to do was remember the initial discovery of Cora's body, but she needed to go over every detail to make sense of the woman's death. When she'd first crouched over the body, she'd seen the bulge of something tucked inside the clover bundle. Not wanting to disturb the crime scene, she'd only checked for a pulse and then backed away.

At the recollection and the realization that the whole scene, minus the dress and no shoes, was exactly what she had seen in Cora's last teacup reading.

Except . . .

Shay shot to her feet and stood on tiptoes to try and see past her old friend, Dr. Adam Ward, the area coroner, who was crouched beside the body. There was one important element missing, and Shay struggled to see what Adam and his assistant, Jacob, were doing.

"Did you see this, Jacob?" Adam rolled the body partially onto its side.

"What is it?" Adam asked.

"It looks like a crushed black butterfly."

Shay's heart flip-flopped in her chest, and her breaths became short and erratic.

"Those aren't common in these parts, are they?" asked Jacob.

"Not that I'm aware of." Adam examined the specimen he held clasped in his tweezers. "How very odd." He shook his head and dropped the specimen into an evidence bag. As he removed the bundle of clover from Cora's clasped hands, out dropped the leather pouch Shay had given Cora.

Shay gasped. *Oh dear.* Her gut told her she was going to have some explaining to do.

"Sheriff," called Adam. "Can you come here? I think you're going to want to see this."

Dean crouched down beside Adam, shared a few words Shay couldn't hear, marched over to her, and dangled the evidence bag in front of her face. "Is this one of yours from your shop?"

"Yes, but I can explain."

"Please do."

Shay patted the boulder, and after Dean sat next to her, she relayed her previous meetings with Cora, and how Cora had been convinced she was in possession of the Early family magical blue bottle.

"But that's not possible, because you have the real one, right?" Dean whispered and checked over his shoulder. He and Liam and Gran were the only people aware of what was hidden inside the blue bottle Shay wore under her shirt.

"Yes. And I told Cora to tell no one she had a blue bottle, but the moment she left my shop, she had to tell everyone about it, even Madam Malvina, of all people."

"Why am I not surprised?" Dean shook his head. "She probably thought it would elevate her standing in the community."

"Of course, without telling her I knew for certain hers was a fake, I did a reading for her, and . . ." Shay braced herself and told him about the reading and how she had seen all the elements of the crime scene in the tea leaves. "I didn't know what they meant at the time, so I asked Gran. You can ask her if you need to corroborate my story."

He waved away her suggestion and turned to walk back to the scene.

"Is the bottle inside the pouch?" she asked breathlessly when she completed her rapid soliloquy of events.

"No. It's empty." He puffed out a deep breath. "Which probably means someone was convinced she did have the Early bottle and the priceless blue diamond inside it."

"It seems so."

"Who besides me, Liam, and Gran know you have the real bottle and diamond?"

"No one."

His brown eyes clouded with doubt.

"Seriously," she said, "Jen knows I have an amulet left to me by Bridget, and Tassi knows I have Bridget's pouch and blue bottle, but I don't think she knows there's a rare blue diamond inside." She dropped her gaze in thought. "Oh, and Conor knows because of everything that happened last year with the whole Doyle thing, which, of course, means Doyle also knows."

"It appears someone else besides them now knows what's inside that blue bottle, and they have proven they are willing to kill for it."

"It could be Doyle, I suppose, and he sent someone here to retrieve it. Somehow, he always knows the goings-on in Bray Harbor. But if not him"—she shrugged her shoulders—"then it could be anyone who knows about the powers the bottle is supposed to possess. That information's all over the internet."

"You're right." He stared at her and then shook his head. "It means anyone she told or anyone who overheard a conversation she had could have killed her to get their hands on the bottle."

"Yes, given the way she's been telling the story to anyone who would listen and showing it off like a trophy."

"Okay." Dean let out what sounded like a frustrated sigh. "Thanks for that observation."

"Sorry." She leapt to her feet, meeting his slightly perplexed gaze. "I didn't mean to tell you—"

"No." He waved his hand. "It's just that you're right, and if the autopsy shows that it was murder, our suspect pool is everyone in town, and with the carnival this weekend, that means—"

"Thousands of suspects," said Shay. "Oh no." The gravity of the situation finally hit her. "Does that mean you're going to have to tell people they can't leave town? How would you ever enforce that?"

"I don't know. Let's just hope it was natural causes and we don't have to call in the national guard to help keep the peace once I lock down the town, especially when the murder involves the mayor's wife, of all people." He started walking away again.

Shay cleared her throat and latched onto his arm. "I was wondering if . . . um . . . because I'm—"

"You want to get a closer look, don't you?"

"Well, no . . . yes . . . it's not that. I think I could help, and I can't do that if I don't have all the details. Just this once. I promise. You won't even know I'm here."

Dean grumbled and walked over to Adam, but didn't stop Shay when she followed him and stood a few yards off. "Adam, any idea yet what the cause of death is?"

"I can't say for certain." Adam peered up at Dean, shielded his eyes from the bright morning sunlight, and flicked a gaze at Shay. When Dean ignored his quirked eyebrow, he continued, "But given the fact that my initial assessment hasn't turned up any evidence of trauma, your guess is as good as mine. She looks like she lay down and went to sleep and just didn't wake up."

"Can that happen?"

"Of course. It could be due to a stroke, a blood clot, a heart attack, or any number of things that could have caused her to pass away like this. Not sure there's a medical explanation of why she's laid out like this, though."

"Does this make sense to you?" asked Dean. "It doesn't to me. Cora was a level-headed woman, not someone given to flights of fancy and . . . whatever this is." He looked quizzically at Adam. "Do you know anything about her medical history? Was she suffering from some disease physically or a mental disorder that could have caused her to do . . . well, this?"

"I wasn't her family doctor, so I have no idea."

"I don't know if it's the season or the fact that I have two kids, who have talked about nothing but their costumes for days now, but could the old-fashioned hippie dress she's wearing be a costume? I don't think I ever saw Cora wear anything like that. Perhaps she's laid out in some sort of a ritualistic Halloween thingy that went wrong?"

Adam gazed down at the body. "It could be, I suppose. What's also weird is she has no shoes on, but there are no marks or scratches on the bottom of her feet to indicate she came up here barefoot. So I don't know."

"Are there any shoe prints in the dirt or grass around the body?"

"Not that we've seen," said Adam, "which is odd because there are no footprints at all. Not even hers. It's like she just appeared here."

"And all the crime team folks are wearing shoe coverings to exclude theirs. That means that someone cleaned up after themselves, and if you can't find any signs of a struggle . . . she was probably dead before she was posed." Dean puffed out his cheeks and exhaled a harsh breath.

"That's most likely, unless she jumped from the rocky outcrop over there to this grass around the mushroom and rock circle, then lay down right in the center without leaving any evidence of having walked into it. A jump like that and the jolt she would have had when landing would have been enough to kill her."

"Really? Do you think—"

"No, I was being facetious. It's been a long night. An impact like that certainly wouldn't have led to her being laid out as ritualistically as this, and I would have found signs of trauma, especially on the soles of her feet."

Dean watched as Jordan, the coroner's assistant, readied Cora's body to be encased in the black coroner's bag. "It's the ritualistic pose that gives me some concern too. Have you ever seen anything like this before?"

"Only in folklore books," said Adam, removing his blue rubber gloves.

Dean glanced curiously at him.

"I think they're called fairy rings. This does have the hallmarks of a ritualistic killing, so if it's got something to do with all the woo-woo stuff, Shay's probably the best one to ask about that." Adam jerked his head in Shay's direction. "But back to your original question. My best guess at this point, based on the condition of the tissue around her lips, her flushed skin and dilated pupils, is that she was poisoned. I need to complete the autopsy before I can say for sure."

"Okay," said Dean. "I'll check with the FBI to see if this"—he gestured to the scene at his feet—"matches anything in their database."

Dean gestured for Shay to follow him and, after gently waking up Tassi, ushered them and Spirit away from the clearing. Tassi followed Spirit back into the wooded area, and before Shay could follow them, Dean halted her with a touch to her arm. "Don't make me regret letting you listen in on Adam's and my discussion. If something bad happens because of that, Jen will put me in the doghouse with no option of parole. Ever."

"Your secret is safe with me." Shay hid a yawn. "I plan on doing nothing except going home and cleaning up before heading off to the carnival . . . again." Giving Dean a small goodbye wave, she headed back into the trees and toward home.

Poisoned? That word looped in her head as she showered and dressed for another day at the carnival—the last thing she wanted to do. Tassi had been the smart one. After they got back early this morning, she had curled up on the sofa, with Spirit on the floor next to her. Shay brushed her hair and swooped it up into a messy bun. Sadly, Shay hadn't been able to turn off her mind concerning the events of the night, much less catch anything resembling a nap.

Between the poison and the ritualistic pose, Shay's gut swirled. She needed to talk to Gran, especially since she had told Shay earlier in the week that Cora had come by the pub to see her, asking about spells to see into the future. At the time, neither had been concerned. Gran had given her a stern warning about messing around with spells, and Shay had figured Cora wanted to see her husband's political future. Cora had dropped more than a few hints over the past two years about being California's future first lady.

Surely, if Gran had foreseen this event in Cora's life, there would have been more indication of foreboding, right? Dean was right when he'd said Cora was a levelheaded woman. No one could have seen this coming.

Then why do I feel so guilty?

Shay glanced at the time, grabbed a sweater from the back of a reading chair, stuffed her arms into the sleeves, dashed across the lane, and pounded on the side door of Liam's cottage.

"*A chara?*" Liam cried when he opened the door. "It's not even eight yet. What brings ye by at this time of the morning?"

"I know, I'm sorry, but I really need to speak to Gran."

"What is it, lass?" The door opened wider, and Gran poked her head around the frame. "What's got ye all in a dither dis morning?" She seized Shay's hand in her craggy, cool one. "I can tell by the look in yer eye and the heaviness of the air that something is wrong."

"Yes, something is wrong." Tears that came out of nowhere filled Shay's eyes. She must have been more tired than she thought or perhaps Gran's soothing touch had given Shay the comfort she needed after finding Cora's body and spending a damp fall evening on a hilltop surrounded by police. She glanced at the table, where tea and toast for two was laid out. "Sorry to disturb your breakfast, but . . ."

"Don't worry about that." Liam's usual sparkling blue eyes darkened with concern. "Take a seat, and tell us what's happened." Liam flashed a look of unease at Gran, whose eyes, filled with concern, focused on Shay.

"Someone's died," Gran said matter-of-factly, allowing Shay's hand to slip from hers while they took their seats.

"Yes." Shay laced her fingers together on her lap and told them what she and Tassi had found on the bluff top.

Liam hopped to his feet.

"Sit," said Shay. "There's nothing for you to do up there." She rolled her eyes when he slumped back into his chair and growled out something that sounded oddly like "Ye can't tell me what to do" and turned her attention to

Gran. "Can you tell me more about the meeting you had with Cora when she asked you about spells to see into the future?"

"It wasn't much. She came into the pub a day or so after she'd had her reading with you, I guess, and told me about her family coming from County Clare and all. She said she wanted to find out if there were any old Irish spells or potions that would help her see the future. She was most curious about her relatives back there and wanted to know if she was ever going to meet them."

"That's what she said? I'd figured she'd want to know if her husband was going to be governor of California."

Gran shook her head, her white cloud of hair quivering. "Aye, she was too casual about it all for me liking, mind ye. I knew she wasn't being honest, but I didn't feel any vibrations from her that might have told me she would . . . end up like ye found her."

"I never got that feeling from her either, except I did warn her not to tell anyone about the bottle, which she seemed to ignore."

"Aye, and I warned her against messing with spells. She said if she was, in fact, Biddy Early's relative, she would have to learn them sometime. I told her Biddy was a healer, not a conjurer, and that spells weren't where her magic came from. I told her it came from de fairies."

"I did find her in a fairy ring, so someone told her about a ritual or a spell . . ." Shay's mind drifted to the clover Cora had clasped in her hands.

"I knew if she was related to Biddy Early, it wasn't closely, and her bottle wasn't real. So I offered her a protection stone instead. She wasn't happy when she left, but . . ." Gran shook her head and stared down at her cold toast. "I never thought . . ."

"Neither did I."

"What was it ye found on her person?" Gran whispered.

Shay described the way Cora had been laid out and the items she had clutched in her hands and added in the crushed black butterfly discovered underneath the body. "Don't you see?" she said excitedly. "It was exactly what I had read in her leaves."

"Was there any sign of a small amethyst stone?" Gran asked, her voice edged with hope.

"Not that I know of. Why?"

Gran shook her head and tsked. "It sounds like she ignored me warning too and was performing a conjuring ritual." She sat back, her eyes focused on Shay. "I sense that someone else was guiding her and that someone knew about Cora's fascination with Irish folklore and magic and used it against her to get their hands on what they thought was the Early magical bottle. They killed her by very real-world means, trying to make it look like some other-worldly death experience."

"It is Samhain this week, and the veil is thinning," Liam murmured and locked gazes with Shay.

Fingers of cold air snaked across Shay's shoulders, and she gave an involuntary shiver. "Why didn't I think of that? If Cora was looking for a spiritual connection with her family, especially her Irish family, Samhain is the perfect choice. What better time than the Gaelic holiday that marks the end of the harvest season and the beginnings of the coming winter." She glanced sheepishly at Gran and then Liam. "I guess, with getting ready for the carnival, I've had our modern holiday of Halloween on the brain for the past few weeks and forgot completely about the connection it has to the old-world Samhain celebrations and the thinning of the veil between life and death."

Chapter 10

The last thing Shay wanted to do today was fill cups of witch's brew and hand out eyeball cookies to all the trick-or-treaters at the carnival. She stamped her foot in frustration as she tried to adjust her uncooperative, wide-brimmed, peaked black hat, certain her sleep-deprived, sallow skin tone had turned an envious shade of green over her jealousy of Jen, who last week had won the coin toss to stay back and work the shop while Shay and Tassi played witch again. At the time, it had sounded like fun to spend another full day at the carnival, and she'd felt like she'd won the lottery. But with the discovery of a fresh body burned into her mind's eye, she now felt like she'd won an unwanted white elephant gift.

All the way from her cottage to the park, she had hoped that, with the discovery of Cora's body, Dean would close down the carnival, but since there was still no known cause of death, he had argued it wasn't fair to the town's people, who had prepared for the event, and all the tourists, who had turned out in droves, anticipating a fun-filled weekend. She knew he had made the right call, but dang it, why did it have to have been her and Tassi who made the discovery?

Deflated after last night, Shay glared at Madam Malvina's booth. If Gran was right and Cora had found help from someone else as she sought to learn conjuring spells, Madam Malvina was the best candidate to have taught her. The problem was that she hadn't seen the woman since Madam Malvina had unveiled her fortune teller's tent the night before. Shay had only spotted Orion, who stood in front of the tent, carnie-calling passersbys. The morning lineup outside Madam Malvina's fortune-telling booth was five deep and showed no signs of letting up as the Saturday foot-traffic stream only grew heavier with each passing minute.

"Tassi, there's something I have to do before it gets too busy today. Can you manage on your own for a while?"

"Um, sure," said Tassi, handing a little mermaid a glass of witch's brew and the chocolate spider cookie she had pointed to on the tray under her mother's watchful and approving eye.

Shay smiled at the girl and her mom and checked out the lineup in front of Madam Malvina's tent. It seemed Shay's witch's station was a hit with the under sixteens, and the fortune teller's tent was where all the adults were gravitating to. Had Madam Malvina won yet another round in this battle for tea-shop customers?

Shay hoped not and wiggled out from behind the booth, sidestepped Spirit where he lay snoozing behind the straw bales, and made her way through the throngs of carnival-goers. She crossed her fingers that the kids would convince their parents that Shay had the best treats and that they should take them there after a shopping trip. Jen had told her that kids and animals were the best judges of character, and it seemed that, between her main customers today and Spirit, Shay had the approval of both and Madam Malvina had neither. She hoped those kids' parents would check out her shop based on their children's recommendations of the goodies they received this weekend. She needed to ask Tassi if she wanted the job as chief baker.

As kids giggled when the sparkling bubbles hit the tip of their noses, Shay had another idea. She was going to ask her niece and nephew what kids wanted in an outing with their parents. She could hold more kid-friendly events. The parents would have to bring the kids, and it would boost her sales in more than one way, especially if the parents liked what they saw and came back. Shay filed the plan away and smiled down at Orion, who was seated at a small table in front of the tent, taking the names of waiting customers.

"Hi, Shay," he said. Despite his eyeliner-rimmed eyes, which usually shone with detached coolness, his face betrayed unease, and he seemed more flustered than normal. "I don't need your name. When the lady in there now comes out, you can just head in."

"I don't want to jump the line," Shay said, glancing uneasily at the woman whose turn would have been next and who was glaring at the lengthy list of names.

"Nay, it's okay," he said, looking pointedly at the indignant woman. "Madam Malvina needs a break, and I know you are her friend." He stressed the word and glanced at the woman, who was now tapping her foot and drumming her fingers on her forearms. "You're not here for a reading, but to give her a break, right, Shay?"

A collective sigh came from the people in line who were within earshot of the conversation.

When a woman dressed in a troll costume came out, Orion gave Shay a nudge. She took a deep breath and tried to organize her thoughts, parted the tent flaps, and entered a room draped in an array of deep, rich, jewel-toned fabrics of emerald green, garnet red, amethyst purple, citrine yellow, and sapphire blue. Shay was taken aback by the strong smell of overly sweet incense that hung in the air, which quickly settled at the back of her throat. While she recovered from a reflexive coughing spell, she scanned the small canvas tent and spotted Madam Malvina seated on the far side of the round table in the center of the room. She was dressed in her usual flowing black garb and had enhanced her fortune teller's costume with the addition of a black velvet turban, adorned with a jeweled, pewter-colored snake with red crystal eyes that dangled down her forehead.

"Come in," she said and dramatically waved her hand toward the chair across the table from her. The jangle of the silver bangles circling her slender arm filled the room. "I've been waiting for you."

Shay knew better than to take the bait and reply, "You have?" That would give Madam Malvina the upper hand, and Shay had vowed that this woman, who had traded their friendship for a few dollars, wasn't going to best her again.

"I imagine you have, since word has gotten out about Cora," said Shay, taking her seat.

"I'm sorry, but I don't follow. What does Cora have to do with me knowing you would come and seek my services?" She laced her creamy white fingers together on the table, made paler by her flowing black sleeves; her meticulously manicured, blood-red fingernails looked like bloodied claws. "I haven't seen Cora this weekend at all," Madam Malvina said. "How is our dear old friend?" Her questioning smile came off a touch too syrupy for Shay's liking.

"Surely, you have heard about last night?"

"Last night?"

"You haven't heard about her death?" Shay studied every nuance of Madam Malvina's expression in hopes that she would flinch or gasp or that her pupils would dilate or constrict, proving she was already aware of the death. But she was either oblivious to Cora's death or was very, very good at hiding her tells. "So you didn't know?"

"No . . . I can't believe it. Dead? Cora? How?"

"That's what I want to ask you about."

"Me?" Her bangles clacked and clanged with her erratic hand movements. "Why would I know anything about her death? I didn't even know she was dead until you told me."

"I'm not saying you do. I'm just saying there were a few irregularities discovered around"—as it wasn't clear if Cora was murdered or not, Shay changed course—"the death scene, and I wondered if Cora had come to see you this past week about learning how to perform . . . ah . . . spells."

"Spells?"

"Yes, spells about foretelling the future."

"The woman was very troubled about something, and I was trying to help her get to the bottom of her uneasiness, but we didn't discuss any spells, I assure you. I do believe, even in this day and age, that the actual practice of witchcraft can land one in jail or, at the least, cause one to lose their license."

"Then you'll be happy to know we don't have that bylaw here in Bray Harbor."

"You know this for certain?"

"Yes," Shay said and dropped her gaze, recalling how Tassi's father had wanted her to be arrested for fortune telling without a licence and dropped his case when he found out Bray Harbor didn't demand a license for it. "But that's neither here nor there." Shay met Madam Malvina's unwavering gaze. "She sought you out because she was troubled about something, but never confided in you what made her uneasy?"

Madam Malvina shifted uneasily in her chair and glanced toward the door, as if looking for Orion to help get her out of the conversation. "I believe that information is confidential."

Shay smiled. "I don't think confidentiality holds true for people like us, and I'm pretty sure when the sheriff comes around asking you the same questions, he's going to feel the same way."

"The sheriff? Oh alright!" she snapped and drummed her nails on the richly textured, blue-toned tablecloth. "She showed me what she'd found at her mother's house in San Francisco."

"And . . ." Shay said, making circling motions with her forefinger, urging Madam Malvina to continue.

"And I told her about an old Irish ritual that would call the fairies to her, and they'd confirm if her blue bottle was, in fact, Biddy's."

"You gave her a spell to use?"

"I never thought she really would." Madam Malvina scowled.

"What did you think she was going to do with it? Ignore it and carry on as usual?"

"No, but—"

"Did you at least perform it with her so she followed it to the letter? Everything I've read says it only takes a few misplaced or incorrect words or steps and the spell takes on an entirely different life—or death, in Cora's case." Shay rose to her feet and glared at the woman in black. "You, of all people, should know better, but then this just shows me you're a bigger fraud than I ever thought. Tell me"—Shay leaned across the table, her breaths coming fast and hard—"where were you last night between ten and one?"

"I don't have to answer to you," snapped Madam Malvina, rising to her feet and matching Shay's glare.

"No, you don't, but I'm pretty sure that after I tell the sheriff you shared an unproven spell with Cora about fairies to find out if her blue bottle was real, and that Cora was discovered dead inside a fairy ring, and that the same bottle, which she had on her, is missing, he will have a lot of questions for you." Shay marched out of the tent and was gawked at by a silent, wide-eyed audience who clearly had overheard every word.

Chapter 11

It was all Shay could do to finish out her Saturday shift at the carnival. It hadn't taken long for word to spread about the explosive encounter she'd had with Madam Malvina, and Shay had become a sideshow attraction. Everyone apparently wanted to get a look at the woman who'd stood up to the scary fortune teller and called her a fraud.

The lineups at Madam Malvina's booth had all but disappeared, and Shay's stall was five deep at any given moment. A sliver of guilt worked its way into Shay's conscience. None of what was happening was what Shay had wanted. She wanted—no, needed—her customer base to return to her, but not at the expense of someone else's business or reputation. And she certainly did not want to feel responsible. If the person brought it upon themselves by their actions, that was one thing, but she was not comfortable with being the catalyst.

The whole thing gave her a queasy stomach, especially when she saw Orion looking down the walkway forlornly at Tassi and Tassi blowing a kiss in return. There was always collateral damage when war was declared, and Orion and Tassi would pay, it seemed.

Hours dragged by, and Shay wanted nothing more than

to go home and hide under her covers for hours. Her cheeks hurt from forced smiling at cute children oblivious to the drama-infused adult issues surrounding them. Her feet hurt from standing in her uncomfortable, pointy witch shoes. And her heart hurt over Cora and Madam Malvina and Tassi and Orion and—

"Ah, Shay, you're just the person I wanted to see." Brad's voice cut through her thoughts.

Shay glared at him, hoping the loathing surely expressed in her eyes would make him disappear.

She had no such luck. Instead of disappearing, he leered over the table with a saccharine-sweet smile plastered to his lips. "Angela and I just signed the papers for the purchase of the winery. It's official, we're moving to Bray Harbor . . . and soon. I believe our realtor, Julia Fisher, is a *good* friend of yours, is she not?" he asked nonchalantly then frowned and casually inspected his hand flicking an invisible—to Shay's eyes—speck of dirty from his palm.

Shay gaped at him struggling to comprehend his words. They seemed to catch in her mind exactly as if she had just heard the sound of a snake hissing at her feet.

"Why so glum?" he asked in a mock-sympathetic tone. "I thought you'd be happy because we threw your realtor friend a bone by giving her our business, and it was a good thing we did too. Because . . ." Brad leaned closer, dropping his voice, "here's the best news yet. It seems she owns most of the cottages in a complex down on the beach. Crystal Beach Cottages or something like that and has one that's vacant now that the holiday season is over." He locked his sardonic gaze on Shay. "It's my understanding that you're familiar with them? She told us you live in one right on the beach, lucky you."

The hollow smile behind the rest of his words was a disturbing contrast to his overly friendly demeanor as his voice droned on and on. Shay heard nothing of what was said after that. She could only watch his lips form words. Then air she tried so desperately to inhale exploded in a violent gasp.

"Who knows," he said, "perhaps after we're settled I'll have to take a look to see if she has anything I could buy for investment purposes, or"—a cruel grin twisted his lips—"maybe she'll offer up your beach front cottage." Before Shay could gather her thoughts and tell him Julia didn't own her cottage—she did—he walked away and disappeared into the crowd.

Fourteen hours later, and after a heated phone call with her so-called friend Julia Fisher, who was clearly more interested in making her commission off the sale of the winery than she was about any friendships, Shay paced behind the sales counter at her tea shop.

She was in no mood for Halloween, bubbling witch's brew, scary cookies, or lookie-loos passing by her booth to get a glimpse of the infamous woman who dared argue with Madam Malvina. If she had to pretend to be happy for one more minute, she would go postal. Add on Brad's announcement from the day before and Shay wasn't sure she could tolerate any more people, events, or noise. Her stomach felt as if she'd been punched, and her head ached. There was no way she'd survive the Monster Mash dance later on that night, either. The odds of her seeing Liam dancing with Maggie Somers were too high, and she wasn't sure her already broken heart could take another hit, especially as it was his chest she wanted to curl into and his arms she needed to find comfort in.

Unwanted tears filled her eyes, and she tried swiping them away before Jen noticed, but she wasn't quick enough.

Jen wrapped an arm around Shay's shoulders. "Why don't you and Tassi stay here at the shop, and Maddie can help me for the rest of the day. She'll be ecstatic about being at the 'coolest' booth in the whole carnival, and I'm sure she'll want to brag about it to her friends. She begged me this morning to help, and I told her no, thinking that would just be adding one more cook to an already full kitchen."

Tassi sighed, and Shay didn't miss the forlorn puppy-dog eyes. Shay had no right to tear Tassi away from Orion, and Tassi assumed the role of a haggard old crone to a T and seemed to love playing to the crowd.

Still, Shay couldn't face it anymore. She needed time—time to heal and time to think about how she would pro-cess Brad and Angela invading her territory. Above all, she needed time to recover from finding Cora lying dead in a fairy ring. What-ifs plagued her mind, and it was all too much. But Tassi didn't need to suffer the consequences of Shay's shattered soul.

"No!" Shay wrapped her arms around her chest. "I'm making an executive decision. Jen and Maddie and you, Tassi, will all work the carnival booth today. I'm going to close the tea shop and go home and go to bed. I'll tear the booth down tomorrow morning before I come into the shop. That way you can all go to the dance tonight and not worry about disassembling anything later on. Sound good?" She looked from one dazed face to the next.

"You're going to close the shop on a Sunday?" said Jen. "With all these tourists in town that—"

"Yes, I need a break and some sleep, and we're getting far more mileage out of our booth at the carnival than we are in the shop this weekend—if we can go by yesterday's sales receipts, that is. So it's settled? The carnival for you three, and home and bed for me. Maybe when I get up, the world won't still be spinning out of control because Brad will have fallen off the edge, never to be seen again."

"You can only hope," muttered Jen.

*   *   *

The following morning, armed with a claw hammer and her brother-in-law's tool kit, which she found in the back of Jen's Expedition, Shay made her way through the deserted carnival grounds. The sea breezes had picked up, bringing with them a damp chill, and Shay pulled her cardigan sweater tighter at the throat. The weather was about to change for the worst, and her bones ached. Even though the skies were clear, the briny sea air clung to her lips as the wind swirled leaves around her feet. There was no crunch of dead leaves beneath her shoes, and her brown boots were already darkened with the saturated leaves. While she wasn't a meteorologist, Shay forecasted days of rain ahead. As much as she loved her little cottage right on the beach, when rain settled in, it could be an awfully dreary place. The last thing she needed.

When she passed Madam Malvina's still fully assembled tent, a chill raced across her shoulders, and she pulled her dampened sweater even tighter. All the other booths were disassembled and packed up or in some state of teardown. Even hers. Jen and Tassi had not taken her advice to leave everything for her to remove. They had taken away all the props and decorations, leaving only the shell of the booth for her to tear down, and she could easily achieve that with a few thwacks of the hammer.

As much as she tried to ignore Madam Malvina's tent, curiosity got the better of her, and Shay inched her way toward the entrance, closed her eyes, and hesitantly lifted the tent flap. Finding one dead body already over the weekend had played with her head and emotions, and she wasn't certain she could handle two. She took a deep breath and opened her eyes. All was as it had appeared on Saturday. The Moroccan-style fabric covering the walls and the table in the center of the room were untouched.

"Shay? Is that you I just saw go into Madam Malvina's tent?" Dean called.

Shay winced, lifted the flap, and peered into his hardened brown eyes. "Yes, I was just worried when I saw that nothing had been done to start taking it down, and I was afraid—"

"It might be a carnival tent, but it's still trespassing. So may I suggest you come out of there now," said Dean.

"Yes, of course." She shimmied through the opening. "But don't you find it odd that neither she nor Orion have started to take all this down?"

"They have until noon, and it's not yet eight, so no, I don't find it odd." He waved his hand at the carnival grounds littered with other tents and booths. "As you can see, some of the others are just arriving now." He crossed his arms over his chest and pinned her with a look of doubt. "Now, why don't you tell me the real reason you were in there."

"I was . . . Oh, I suppose you've already heard about the altercation she and I had on Saturday." When Dean's gaze didn't waver, Shay knew honesty was the best policy. Dean was no idiot, and he'd already done more than he normally did by allowing her close access to his conversation with Adam at the crime scene. She relayed what had happened and what the ultimate fallout had been with the town's people. "You see I never intended to hurt her reputation or cause her business any misfortune. It just all kind of came out because I guess when I found out she had been using me and we weren't really friends, I was hurt. I know it's childish, but it hurts to find out you were used."

Dean dropped his arms to his side. "How well do you know Madam Malvina?" he asked, his sheriff's glare softening.

"To be honest, I don't know much about her when I think about it. I know she and Orion's father are no longer together, but I have no idea what the story behind that is. I know she knew Bridget, but I've come to sense they weren't friends. I think she used Bridget like she did me. She does know a lot about teas, plants, and poisons. She really did help me a lot in the beginning with those—"

"What about belladonna? Would she know about that?"

"I imagine she would." Shay eyed him curiously. "That seems pretty specific. Are you saying Cora had ingested belladonna before she died?"

"The autopsy report come back and showed a couple of nondeadly elements found in her system, probably from some teas she'd ingested, but then there were two that caught my attention." His eyes narrowed. "It showed very low levels of an opioid, such as one used in long-term pain management." He looked at her questioningly.

"I know she mentioned a few times in passing, before she went to her mother's, that she was having back issues. Maybe they got worse there?"

"That must be it then. However, the coroner also found lethal levels of a poisonous alkaloid commonly found in belladonna."

"Also known as deadly nightshade," said Shay thoughtfully.

"That's what Adam said. He also told me it's a perennial plant with reddish, bell-shaped flowers that has glossy-coated black berries on it. Do you know much about it?"

"I'm familiar with it, but would never use it in my shop."

"Never? Adam said it's commonly used."

"Not by me. I don't even grow it. There's none in my greenhouse, but I have read about it." Shay shook her head. "Where in the world would Cora have gotten some of that?"

"I suspect it was ordered online. Adam said it can be found easily enough on the web and goes by other names, like devil's berries, naughty man's cherries, death cherries, beautiful death, and devil's herb."

"But who would do that? Certainly not Cora, as she didn't know anything about herbs and poisons or plants other than what grew in her flower beds."

"Could she have grown some there?"

"I suppose. Anyone could, really. Why?"

"Would someone have told her about it? Are there any redeeming features about it?"

"Yes, but there's such a fine line between how much is safe to ingest and how much is deadly that anyone who knows about it wouldn't recommend it for any treatments that I know of."

"Unless the person who told Cora about it wanted her dead," said Dean.

"Yeah," said Shay, meeting his troubled gaze. "It has been around for centuries, and throughout history, it's been known as the plant of choice for assassins."

Chapter 12

"Did you know that belladonna means *beautiful woman* in Italian?" asked Shay as she set the last bag of freshly packed sage in the barrel by the front counter.

"But it's poison, so why give it a nice name like that?" Jen dropped her cleaning rag and placed a bottle of dried herbs and tea leaves onto the now sparkling-clean display shelf behind the counter.

"Because women used its oil to dilate and enlarge their pupils for a seductive effect. They thought the wide-eyed, innocent look made them appear more attractive to men. Of course, that was before anyone figured out why beautiful rich women always seemed to die young." Shay examined her and Jen's morning we-have-no-customers work and smiled at their cleaning accomplishments.

"After Dean told me Cora died from a belladonna overdose, I was up half the night researching its uses. I tell you, I was amazed at what I found out about the makeup and beauty creams our ancestors used. It's downright scary and surprising that any of them lived past twenty."

"You mean scarier than that clay mask Aunt Elsie used to slather on her face when she came to live with us?"

"Oh yeah. Makeup used to be filled with lead and mercury. As a matter of fact, it was a certain kind of red mercury that gave women rosy cheeks, and they didn't have to pinch them anymore to achieve the result." Shay shivered. "Scary stuff that women used to do to make themselves look more appealing to the opposite sex."

"Speaking of." Jen nudged Shay in the ribs when the door flew open, sending the overhead bell into a frenzied jingle.

"*A chara!*" hollered Liam as he burst through the door. "We need to talk."

His electric-blue eyes were dark with fear and sent a tidal wave of uneasiness rushing through Shay, especially when his cousin, Conor Madigan, close behind him, had the same deep-seated panic in his blue eyes.

"What is it?" She looked from one nearly identical Madigan to the other. "What's wrong? Is it Gran?"

"No, it's Doyle," said Conor. "I've just seen 'im."

"What?" She stared blankly at him. "I don't understand. You saw him here . . . in Bray Harbor?"

"Aye, I did."

"Liam?" Shay turned to him, not certain if she could believe his cousin, who had proved to be a real jokester at times, and she mentally crossed her fingers that this was one of those times. As much as she wanted the man who was possibly her father to show up in Bray Harbor, so she could confront him and find out what had happened between him and Bridget, her biological mother, she also knew he had vowed to do whatever it took to get his hands on the blue bottle she wore around her neck. He had proven more than once that he was willing to kill for it.

"So he says." Liam gestured toward Conor and gave her an awkward smile. "But we don't know for sure yet, if it's—"

"I tell ye, it was him," said Conor. "I saw him when I went to the bank just past ten. I swear on me life it was Doyle."

"Then you're positive it was him." Shay's legs wobbled, and she gripped the counter for support.

"Aye, as best as I can be. He was in disguise, of course. He is famous all over Europe as being a master of disguise. But I swear it was him. He must have been wearing one of them head caps they wear in plays and stuff, like he was bald or something, and he was dressed older than his years. But, no matter how he's dressed now, I know him well enough from running in his gang back in Ireland to be able to pick out the telltale hip tic from when he was a wee lad and shattered his leg falling out of a tree."

"Whether it's really him or not," said Liam, "I think it's a good reminder that what went on last year is far from over, and we had better all be careful."

"It's him. As soon as I saw him come out of the hotel down there on the beach, I spotted him. He can change his looks all he wants, but he can't change that slight limp he's had most of his life. But, just to be sure, I followed him when he went up on the boardwalk until he turned in to that Madam Malvina's shop."

"In to Madam Malvina's shop?" Shay echoed, and gripped the now-burning amulet.

"What is it, *a chara*?" asked Liam. "Yer as white as snow, like ye just walked across someone's grave."

"I think I may have . . ." Fear gripped her chest; wide-eyed, she looked at Liam. "You're right. We do need to talk." She gestured to the back room and glanced apologetically at Jen. "Can you look after things while we go in the back and Conor tells me everything he knows about . . ." Shay swallowed hard. "Doyle, my maybe father," she whispered.

Shay hated keeping a secret from Jen, who didn't know about the diamond inside the bottle. But if Jen knew and put two and two together that a killer was in pursuit of the precious gem, she'd never let Shay out of her sight, and she'd smother her, all in the name of protecting her. Besides, if Jen ever found out that Dean knew and not her, she wouldn't understand she'd been kept in the dark for her own safety, and she'd take it as a slight that they hadn't trusted her with the secret.

Jen squeezed her hands. "Of course, take as long as you need. I hope him being here will give you the closure you need."

Not if you knew the whole story, you wouldn't. Shay gave her sister a weak smile and ushered Liam and Conor into the back room and told them everything relating to Cora's familial history and her possession of a blue-bottle replica.

"On inspection, I concluded it's probably a mass-produced souvenir that her mother or someone picked up on a trip to Ireland. Of course, she didn't really credit me because she wanted so badly to believe she was related to Biddy Early and that the bottle was the real thing. I guess when I didn't promote the idea, she took it to Madam Malvina, who, according to Tassi, seemed to encourage that idea, as they had been meeting every morning over the past week. I can only guess that the fake amulet had something to do with that."

"And now Doyle is in town," said Conor, shaking his head.

"And Cora is dead from a belladonna overdose," added Shay.

"Small world, don't ye think?" Conor looked questioningly from Shay to Liam.

"Is it?" said Liam, his eyes darkening.

"Wait, you don't think Madam Malvina and Doyle are actually working together, do you?" asked Shay.

"I know what I saw and where he went, so ye tell me,"

added Conor, giving Shay a side glance. "In the off chance I'm wrong about that feller being Doyle, I'll keep an eye on him. I'll let ye know if I discover anything else. But if it is Doyle, as I suspect, there would only be one reason why he would come to Bray Harbor." He gestured to the leather cord fastened around her neck.

"And by now," said Liam, "if he's involved with Cora's death, he must know that the stone inside her bottle isn't a real diamond and that her bottle isn't the real Early blue bottle."

When Shay checked the clock for the hundredth time, Jen gave her the disapproving mother look she'd learned so well when she'd had to take on that role after her and Shay's adoptive parents died in a boating accident when Shay was just eighteen and Jen twenty.

"What?" Shay instantly regretted her tone, knowing it was a little more snappish than she'd intended. *But really, shouldn't Tassi be here by now?* She glanced up at the clock again.

"You're checking the clock every two minutes," Jen whispered, eyeing the group at a nearby table. "Do you have someplace else to be, or are you waiting for someone? All I know is you messed up the last two orders, and the seniors' travel group are starting to talk about trying a new tea shop, and you know who they're talking about."

"I can't help it," said Shay, closing the till. "I really need to talk to Tassi. This whole thing about Doyle being in town has really thrown me."

"What's she got to do with it?"

"It's just that last week she was keeping—Oh good, there she is." Shay darted from behind the counter and met Tassi halfway across the tea shop. "We need to talk, now." Shay clasped Tassi's hand and pulled her toward the back room.

Tassi flinched and pulled back, stopping Shay. "Have I done something wrong?"

"No, of course not. It's just that we really need to talk. Sorry if I scared you, but"—she eyed the seniors' group, who now had their full attention on her—"something has happened, and I need to ask you about it."

"Something I did?" Tassi's eyes filled with confusion.

"No, not you, but you might have the answer. Please, I know I came on strong, but . . ." She glanced at Jen, whose disapproving mother look was now throwing daggers.

Shay closed the back-room door behind her and leaned her back against it for fear her legs would give out. "Last week, when you were keeping an eye on Cora—"

"I'm still watching the shop in the mornings."

"You are?"

"Yeah. In the mornings, I wait at the coffee shop close by Madam Malvina's for my friend Lori, so we can ride the college bus together. It's great because I still want to know what that woman has up her sleeve, so we can stay a step ahead of her."

"Good thinking," said Shay. "I had no idea, but that's fantastic. Then you'd know if an older balding man has been hanging around or frequenting her shop?"

"Every day."

Shay gripped the door handle at her back to steady her wobbling knees. "Was it when Cora was there last week?"

"Um . . . let me think . . . the first two days, no, but last Thursday and Friday he went in, and then again today. He came right after I did, about seven. He usually only stays for a few minutes, but today when he left, I heard him say, 'I'll be back later,' and then he headed down the board-walk toward the hotel, carrying a small bag with him."

"Did you hear Madam Malvina call him by name?"

Tassi shook her head. "Why, who is he?"

"He might . . ." Shay swallowed hard. "He might be Doyle."

"Is he here for you or the amulet?"

"When he discovers the one Cora had isn't real . . ." Shay couldn't stop the shaking in her knees and barely made it to a chair at the table before they gave way.

"Are you okay?"

"Yeah, but can you get me a glass of water? I just suddenly feel dizzy."

"Sure," said Tassi, dashing to the sink. "I know I wasn't around last year when there was all that talk about this Doyle guy, but from the bits and pieces I've managed to pick up, he sounds like he's a pretty nasty person."

"He is, and when he finds out that the amulet Cora had is nothing but a cheap souvenir, he'll be even nastier." Shay took the glass of water from Tassi and downed it in a long series of gulps. "Now, I have to think." Shay set the glass down with a thud.

"What is it about this Doyle that makes him so scary and nasty?" asked Tassi, her eyes filling with concern. "I've never seen you in this state before."

Shay looked into her young friend's eyes, and her heart swelled with pride at how far the once-lost and rebellious girl had come in the last few years. "I guess you're eighteen now. You're old enough to hear the whole sordid tale."

She took a deep breath and gave Tassi a mildly edited, young-adult version of how Bridget had received a special amulet as a gift from her mother for her sixteenth birthday, the same one Tassi had seen Bridget wearing. "Bridget was told it was special and had been passed down through generations of Early women. Excited, and wanting to know how the blue bottle worked, she went into the forest to try to figure out what made it so special."

"I sense something bad is about to happen."

"You're not wrong. While there, she came across a handsome fairy man, or that's what she called him, who took advantage of her girlish innocence. He seduced her and then tried to rob her of the amulet and nearly killed her for it. She escaped and ran home, only to find her mother badly beaten, having been attacked by this same man earlier. She sent Bridget, with the amulet, far away to live in America, where he could never find her or the Early blue bottle again."

"Wow! How awful."

"It gets worse. Bridget later discovered she was pregnant, and because her family said she brought shame on them, she fled to America."

"By herself? At sixteen?"

"Yes," said Shay, "and because she was so young and depended on the only skills she had—reading tea leaves—she knew she couldn't care for a child." Shay swallowed a lump of emotion stuck in her throat. "My parents were living in San Francisco at the time, while my father taught at Berkeley. My mother met Bridget at the tea shop where she worked, and they became friends. My parents already had Jen, but something happened during the delivery that left my mother unable to have any more children—"

"I knew Bridget was your real mother, but that also means . . ." She stared at Shay with horror-filled eyes. "This Doyle fellow is your—"

"Don't say it." Shay shook her head. "He has no interest in me as a person, especially as a daughter, except maybe to use it in some way to get his hands on this." She pulled the pouch out from under her blouse.

The door burst open. "We got him," Conor yelled. "He's at the tea shop now. Come on. Liam's meeting us there, and we can finally end all this."

Chapter 13

Shay and Conor raced across the street, around the corner, and flew up the beach-access stairs to the boardwalk. When they reached the top, Shay gasped and rested her hands on her knees. "Whoa, am I ever out of running form. I need a second."

Conor glanced at Madam Malvina's shop. "There, that's him. He's heading north. Quick," he called over his shoulder to a still recovering Shay.

"Ugh, it looks like we're running again," she muttered as she dashed after him.

Conor tripped over a sidewalk sign and stumbled to the ground.

"Are you okay?" she asked breathlessly, pausing at his side.

"Yes, just catch him. I'm right behind you," he replied, slowly getting to his feet.

Liam headed in their direction, directly in the path of Doyle, and Shay ran with all she had left to reach the bald man at the same time. When she was within arm's reach, she grabbed the man's arm. "Doyle, I presume?" she puffed, swinging him toward her. "Mr. Carlyle?" She released her grip and met his distressed gaze. "I'm so sorry." She brushed off his shirt sleeve. "I thought you were someone else."

Liam and Conor closed ranks around him.

Conor scanned the man from head to toe and frowned. "No, that's not him."

"I know it's not," said Shay. "This is Mr. Carlyle. He owns the butcher shop on Fifth Avenue. He bought it last year when Mr. McLaren retired."

"Aye," said Liam. "I thought ye looked familiar. Welcome to Bray Harbor." He straightened the man's shirt collar and smoothed out imaginary wrinkles from across his shoulders. "There, no harm done. Just a case of mistaken identity."

"Really?" said Mr. Carlyle. "So, you're looking for someone in particular?" He eyed them and stroked his graying goatee.

"Yes, a gentleman who looks a lot like ye actually," said Conor. "Ye didn't happen to see anyone like that in the tea shop just now, did ye?"

"No, no, I didn't, but funny you say that."

"Why?" Liam narrowed his eyes and studied the butcher.

"As it happens, someone left an envelope in my shop on Friday, along with a thousand dollars tucked inside it."

"A thousand dollars?" Shay gasped. "For what, did it say?"

"It said to go to Madam Malvina's tea shop today at four."

"Someone asked you to go there today?" she asked.

"Yeah, I was to walk as though I had a slight limp from an old injury to my left leg. Then I was to go in, order a cup of tea, stay for about half an hour, and leave. That's all I had to do for the money. So, I thought, no one is getting hurt, and business has been down with all these vegan types around lately, so . . ." He shrugged his shoulders. "Why not? Easiest money I ever made, I'll tell you."

"Did you see who left the note for you?" asked Liam.

"No, it was on the counter after a bit of a customer rush. But I will tell you that I'm not the only one in town that gift was given to. I heard that Old Jack from the storage facility up by the highway also received this mysterious message along with a thousand dollars. A few others too, they say."

"Are they all of a certain age and build?" Shay asked hesitantly.

"Yup, we're all pudgy"—he rubbed his stomach and chuckled—"and getting on in years and have lost most of our hair."

"Do you still have this note?" asked Liam.

"I do. I brought it with me so I could check to make sure I followed all the instructions. Didn't want anyone tapping me on the shoulder and telling me I had to give the money back because it's gone already. I used it toward the rent on the shop for the next month."

"Would it be possible for us to see it?" asked Shay.

"Just in case there are any markings on it that might tell us who left it for you," Liam added.

"When you grabbed my arm, I thought it was you telling me to give the money back because I messed up somehow." Mr. Carlyle dug a card-sized white envelope out of the back pocket of his trousers.

"Anyone have a tissue or something on them?" asked Liam, looking from Conor to Shay, who both shook their heads. He glanced around at the shops in close vicinity and dashed over to a table at a coffee shop, grabbed some serviettes from the dispenser, and hurried back. "There," he said, opening the napkin and gently clutching it around the envelope. "If it comes to it, Mr. Carlyle, you might have to give the police a set of prints so they can rule them out when they check this for prints."

"They already have them."

Shay's skin bristled with his words. "Oh, I see, well, um—"

Mr. Carlyle's eyes glinted with amusement. "Don't worry, Shay, I'm not this criminal you're looking for, or any other for that matter. My shop was broken into a few months ago, and I had to give them a sample set."

Mr. Carlyle limped down the boardwalk. Shay hoped her relief about him not being a criminal but a victim of crime hadn't shown too much on her face. She wasn't heartless, and as much as she liked him, she wasn't sure she was ready to find out he was really Doyle and her father.

"Do you believe him?" asked Liam, his gaze following the man's movements.

"What do you mean?" asked Shay.

"Do you think he is who he says he is?" Liam studied Mr. Carlyle as he disappeared into the crowd. "That's a pretty wild tale he had about some unknown person leaving him a thousand dollars to pretend to be someone else."

"You think he's Doyle? Yer daft, man. I know Doyle, and after seeing him close up now, I can tell ye that's not him." Conor shook his head emphatically.

"So ye say." Liam tilted his head and studied his cousin. "How do we know this isn't a setup and yer working with him to get your hands on—"

"Why you . . ." Conor lined his fist up with Liam's jaw and pulled back his arm.

Shay grabbed his arm. "Stop it, both of you! Let's talk this through. I think we're all wondering the same thing, and there's only one way to find out if what he said is true or not. Let's check his story out with the other names he mentioned. If he lied, then I give you permission to beat each other senseless if that's what's going to make you happy. Until then, we work as a team. We've got a lot of ground to cover. Let's go." She marched toward the stairs leading down to the beach.

Shay, Liam, Conor, and Spirit descended upon the owner of the storage facility, Old Jack, as he was known around town. After some pointed questions from ex-detective Liam, Old Jack's story lined up with what the butcher had shared. Old Jack led them to Duncan Bradley, editor in chief of the *Bray Harbor News*, who then led them to Bert Boyer, the owner of the Beehive Hardware Store. After some persuading, Bert finally gave them the name of Bill Fry, the owner of Wooden Relics–Furniture Restorations and an old friend of Shay's, as another person who might have received the same cash payment and letter. After some convincing again by Liam and after an assurance that he wouldn't have to return the money, Bill showed them his note, along with a bank deposit receipt for his thousand-dollar payment.

Doyle obviously knew he was being watched and was playing his own version of a sleight-of-hand or cat-and-mouse game.

"So where's the real Doyle?" Liam asked.

Shay took a deep breath to still her nerves. "All these aging men have the same tale. The mysterious envelope appeared in their shops during a flurry of customer activity, and the person delivering it went unseen."

"Which means we aren't any closer to discovering Doyle's current appearance." Conor punched his left palm with his right fist. "I don't know about you two, but I need a pint after this wild goose chase."

Once they'd settled into one of the rooftop patio tables at Liam's pub, Shay eyed every male of a certain age in her vicinity, and her brain kept firing questions that all sounded the same: Is that Doyle? No, is *that* Doyle? Is he wearing a different disguise or no disguise at all? Shay rubbed her temples as her head spun with unanswerable questions.

Even Conor eventually admitted that, after working years for the man, he wasn't really positive what Doyle actually looked like. "After all, he is famous for being a master of disguise, and if I, who have spent time with him, can stand face-to-face with him and not recognize him, we might be in a lot of trouble."

"What about his telltale limp? That's out the window too now, as he—or someone working for him—is asking the look-alikes to assume this characteristic. He's made his living primarily with his ability to be a chameleon." Shay stared down into her draft beer and watched the bubbles bouncing around inside the amber liquid. Beer wasn't her favorite drink of refreshment, but after the day they'd had, her tall beverage seemed fitting. "I'm going to go insane if I go around suspecting every man of a certain age and body proportion as Doyle. I'm already halfway there trying to keep myself and the Early family legacy safe."

Conor patted her shoulder. "I could be wrong, you know. Maybe Doyle's not really here at all, and he's only hired a henchman to do his dirty work for him."

Liam glared at Conor's hand on Shay's shoulder, and a low growl emanated from his throat. "Finally, you admit you could be wrong. Are ye feeling okay, cousin?" Liam held his glare on Conor's hand and only let up after Conor slipped his hand off Shay's shoulder. "Doyle enjoys creating this very atmosphere of confusion and mistrust. From what ye've said, Conor, he's probably getting a kick out of this. And if he did have anything to do with Cora's death, he'd be sure to keep his hands clean."

Shay took a long drink and set the glass down with a thump.

Liam's eyes darkened. "What is it, *a chara*?"

"I give up," she said. "I don't think Doyle is even in Bray Harbor. Like you said, he's too smart, and if he is behind Cora's death, he wouldn't dirty his own hands. We have to stop running in circles, trying to find him, and figure out who is working with him instead."

Conor set his glass of Guinness on the table and shook his head. "Nah, he's here. I'd bet me life on it."

"You just might be doing that if we don't figure out who he really is," said Liam. "With Cora dead, he knows she didn't have the real blue bottle, and if he thinks he's been crossed by a member of his gang, he'll be looking for revenge."

"Wait." Conor eyed his cousin. "Do ye think I led him here with the promise of the rare blue diamond? He's known about that fer years. It was only his discovery of where it was that made him focus on our Shay here and Bray Harbor. So I doubt he would have anything to do with Cora's murder. He knows who Shay is and that she holds the Early magic in her hands. I never told him that. He knew it, and he's the one who told me." Conor rose to his feet and glared down at Liam. With a sneer, he threw a twenty-dollar bill on the table and stormed off.

A few days later, Shay settled next to Gran in the back room of the tea shop, two half-empty teacups before them.

Gran sighed and drummed her gnarled fingers on the table. "I'm at my wit's end with those boys. I love the bones of dem, but they make it so hard sometimes."

"What are they doing now?" Shay refilled Gran's teacup with an aromatic blend of chamomile and mint green tea.

"Fisticuffs every time they're in the same room together.

I dunno know what's gotten into dem lately. I thought we'd got past all that rivalry, but out of the blue, they're at each other like two old badgers."

"I think that's because we've hit one dead end after another in Cora's murder, and they are feeling the frustration. It doesn't help that Liam thinks Conor's been working with Doyle behind our backs this whole time. Something about a leopard not being able to change its spots."

"He's not. I know me boy. If he says he's done with that life, then he's done. He's turned the clover over and is living the life here in Bray Harbor that I always knew he would once he got his head on straight." She set her cup down on the saucer with a clang. "What do the police say about the case?"

"They're in the same place as we are. Nothing's turned up. There are no leads, and they're still waiting for the final toxicology report."

"I thought ye said it appeared to be a derivative of belladonna?" Gran sipped at her tea and eyed Shay quizzically over the rim.

"Initially, yes, because of what Mia—"

"Who?" asked Gran.

"The botany professor I gave my poisonous plants to last year. She's married to Adam, the coroner.

"Aye, now I recall her. Has she not been well? We don't see her much these days. I hope she hasn't become the victim of some of those plants. Even the scent of a few of them can be toxic." She tsked and shook her head.

"I know she's not in the tea shop as much as she used to be." Shay smiled. "She said it's because they are expecting their first child, and she's running out of energy with teaching up until her due date next month. I think it has more to do with last year's events and the fallout that led back to her from that."

"Aye." Gran nodded. "I remember, and you might be right. She feels like she lost face."

"I know, but it wasn't Mia's fault. She was taken in, just like—"

Jen poked her head into the back room. "Sorry to interrupt, but Mayor Sutton is here and demanding to see you. And I'm afraid his agitation is drawing some unwanted attention from a few of our customers."

"Yeah, send him back, or do you and Tassi need help out there too?"

"No, we're fine."

"Good, because Gran and I are almost done with our conversation, and then I'll be out."

"No need to rush, but I'll send him back now before he clears the room with his pacing."

Shay nodded, and within seconds, Mayor Cliff Sutton barged into the back room. "Look what I found." He shoved a paperback book under her nose.

Shay tilted her head back and focused her eyes on the title. "*A Layman's Guide to Poison.*" She pursed her lips, flipped open the cover, and scanned the table of contents. "It says recipes included. I can't believe this. Someone actually wrote a book telling people how to grow and make poison." She flipped to the back cover and glared at the smiling author sporting a blond pixie haircut.

Gran snatched the book from her hands and glared at the author. "Ach, from the twinkle in dis woman's eyes, she's having a right laugh at all the poor suckers buying dis trash. She's probably getting a proper giggle knowing the police have their hands tied, knowing ders nothing they can do about the dangerous content in it." Gran tsked and shook her head. "How publishing anything like dis is even legal is beyond me."

"Where did you find this?" Shay eased the book from Gran's timeworn hands and waved it in the mayor's face.

"When I was cleaning out Cora's closet, I came across this in a box tucked behind some shoeboxes. There were a whole bunch of other strange-looking trinkets in there that I didn't recognize, but I took a closer look at this book." He opened the book to a dog-eared page. "Read this."

Shay skimmed the page and gasped. "This whole section about belladonna has been highlighted." Confused, she looked up at him. "Are these notations in the margins Cora's handwriting?"

He shook his head.

Shay focused on the highlighted passages and the handwritten notes. It appeared to be a homemade recipe, with instructions about increasing the dosage of belladonna so rebirth and entrance to the fairy realm could happen. Shay traced her fingers over the phrases, "Ingest hybrid tea," "enter fairy ring," and "Samhain Eve."

"Oh no." She looked at Gran. "This must be why I found Cora laid out in a ritualistic pose. She was copying these instructions."

She held the open page under Gran's nose. "Do you recognize this handwriting?"

Gran pulled a pair of blue, plastic-framed glasses from her handbag, adjusted them on the bridge of her nose, squinted at the page, and shook her head.

Shay sighed. "Well, we know she was seeing Madam Malvina, and I bet two-to-one it's hers."

Gran slipped her reading glasses onto the top of her head. "Aye, that's most likely, given this is the meaning of the elements you saw in Cora's tea leaves. Since Madam Malvina knows toss about anything, I'm guessing she did a reading too, but had no idea what she was looking at, only going along with what Cora told ye saw. Then she used that information for her own benefit."

"You're right. Cora's story about the amulet added to what Madam Malvina knows about folklore . . ." Shay's voice drifted off in thought. "We just need to figure out a way to get a copy of her handwriting."

"Shouldn't we take this to the police so they can question Madam Malvina?" Mayor Sutton reached for the book.

Shay hugged the book to her chest. "We need proof first. Dean is always talking about finding proof. Hunches aren't enough to build a case on."

"But I feel it in my bones dat's her writing," Gran said.

"So do I, Gran." Shay patted her hand. "But the law doesn't give a hoot about what you and I feel. We need hard evidence to show beyond a reasonable doubt it's hers, because I don't think, based on what we tell him now, that Dean can get a warrant for her handwriting sample. The DA will want just cause to issue one, and a hunch from us won't cut it."

"Yes, yes, you're right, of course." Gran scowled. "But we can't walk up to her and ask her to write something down. She'll be suspicious, especially if she is guilty, like me bones say she is."

"No, we can't," Shay said. "But Tassi can."

"Why would her asking for a handwriting sample be any different?" asked Mayor Sutton.

"Because she's the perfect Trojan horse." Shay grinned. "Orion, Madam Malvina's son, is our in." Shay's mind raced with ideas. "Tassi could ask her if she would like her to do any baking for her shop. Since we won the best booth award, people have been talking about our desserts, and Tassi and Jen's baking had a lot to do with that."

"Yes!" Gran clapped her hands gleefully, like a small child on Christmas morning. "Then she could ask her to write out a list of what she would like her to make. It's perfect!"

"But what if Madam Malvina doesn't want Tassi to bake for her? Maybe she's happy to continue to sell the Muffin Top's baked goods."

"Good point," said Gran thoughtfully. "Tassi will just have to make it an offer Madam Malvina can't refuse by saying—"

"What offer?" asked Tassi, pushing an empty tea cart into the back room. She glanced from the mayor to Gran, and finally to Shay. Horror filled her eyes. "Are you selling? Did you get an offer from Madam Malvina to buy the shop?"

"No, why would you say that?" asked Shay. "Have you overheard something about her wanting to buy my store?"

Tassi shuffled from one foot to the other as she closed the door behind her. "Well, not exactly . . . but . . ."

"But what? What exactly did she say?"

"She said if she had her way, she wouldn't have any competition in town."

Chapter 14

Shay took a series of deep, soul-cleansing breaths. The heat from the amulet waned more and more with every exhale. This was worse than she thought. "She actually said that to you, Tassi?" She pressed a hand to her chest to ease the pain clawing at her lungs.

Tassi meekly nodded.

A burning lump caught at the back of Shay's throat, and she coughed. Just one more betrayal from a person who'd squirmed her way into Shay's life under the guise of being a friend, only to betray her in the end. Shay smiled slyly, and she looked pointedly at her young protégé. "That's it, then! We'll have to give it a try."

"Okay, what's *it*?" Tassi eyed Shay.

Shay reorganized her thoughts. Tassi as the Trojan horse was her only option. It had to work, and she crossed her fingers behind her back that her young friend would agree.

Shay stilled her spiraling thoughts and shored up her hurt feelings. "I was thinking that if we can prove she had something to do with Cora's death, then . . ." The amulet warmed against her skin. "Then we can stop her latest underhandedness, along with whatever vendetta she has against me or had with Bridget right from the beginning."

Tassi's raised brow indicated she was just as confused as Shay was with her own words.

In her own mind, Shay knew she'd stopped making sense ever since finding Cora's body. She stretched out her shoulders and took a grounding breath. "Tassi, I know you are a young woman of many talents. You've proven that many times with your skill at quickly learning the tea industry, including harvesting and brewing. Not to mention, you're an excellent baker, and you picked up baking techniques from Jen that even professionals are jealous of." Shay held up three fingers. "On top of all that, you have other abilities and your uncanny connection with Spirit, and—"

"Just come out and ask her, lass," Gran chirped and focused on Tassi's pale face. "Tell us, Tassi dear, where does acting fall on your list of accomplishments?"

Shay grinned. The old woman really could read her mind.

"What we need to ask ye to do will be less suspicious coming from you than us." Gran waggled her thumb, indicating herself, the mayor, and Shay. "A request like this wouldn't seem as random since you and Orion are . . . well . . . what do ye young folk call it? Hanging out?"

Tassi's forehead creased. "Would one of you please tell me what exactly you are all trying to say and stop speaking in riddles?"

"They want you to be the Trojan horse and try to get a copy of Madam Malvina's handwriting so they can see if it's a match to the writing in this book." Mayor Sutton grabbed the book from Shay, and with a trembling hand, he gave it to Tassi.

Tassi opened the book and read the handwritten notes. "I can tell you right now that this is her handwriting. I've seen it a hundred times on sales receipts and on supply order requisitions and on all the little sticky notes she leaves for Orion."

"That's good," said Shay. "How easy would it be for you to get a sample of her handwriting so we can take it and the book to Dean?"

"Piece of cake, I think, but what do I say if she catches me taking a sample?"

"That's why we"—Shay jerked her thumb at Gran and the mayor—"were thinking you could tell her you want to expand your baking business and were wondering if she wanted you to make any goodies for her shop too. You could have her write out a list of what she'd like you to make. She'd have no suspicions about writing out a list for you."

"That's the part that confused me earlier. That cover story sounds pretty elaborate and not really plausible. Sounds a bit contrived, in my opinion," Tassi said.

"Maybe, but we were trying to think of something that wouldn't raise any suspicions." Shay smiled weakly. "You spend more time in her shop than any of us do. Do you have any other ideas?"

"Something will come up when the time is right. Let me play it by ear. I could always fish one of her notes out of the trash can. Orion just reads them, rolls his eyes, and tosses them out. Don't worry, I got this." She grinned mischievously. "There is no way that woman is going to run you or this tea shop out of town. We've all worked too hard to keep Bridget's dream alive." Tassi brushed her hands together. "Well, I best be getting fresh baked goods to the customers, who are loving them, by the way." With a newfound air of someone taking command, Tassi loaded up the cart with a tray of scones and other goodies and wheeled it out the door.

"That went better than I thought it would," said the

mayor. "Do you think she'll follow through so we can take this to the police? The sooner they can get some answers, the sooner I can find out who killed my wife."

"Yes," said Shay. "She's good for her word. Now, you stop worrying and leave this to us. We'll get what we need and make sure Dean sees it."

The stress lines etched into the mayor's face eased a little, and with a weak smile and nod, he left.

Shay checked the time. "I really should get out there and help Jen and Tassi. But, first, tell me again exactly what you saw in Cora's teacup."

"The same as ye did, dear."

"I know, but I need to see it written in black and white so that I can compare what we both saw with what I spotted in the clearing when I found her body. The whole scene seemed staged. It makes me wonder if Madam Malvina really saw the same symbols as we did when she did Cora's reading. Or, if she could have used the belladonna along with her uncanny methods of subtly extracting information from clients in order to get them to reveal specifics about themselves without them even knowing."

"Aye, only ta use the information in a later reading."

"Yes, making the client think she was legit, like Cora did. So, my thought is Madam Malvina could have used her tried and true tactics to get Cora to tell her what we told her and between the effects of the belladonna and the insider knowledge she'd obtained, she gave her the same reading, which made Cora believe Madam Malvina really had special powers."

"Which we know now she doesn't really have."

"No, but Cora did believe in her, and that would make her more susceptible to Madam Malvina's suggestions, especially if she was kept under the influence of belladonna, right?" Shay gathered writing supplies and poised the pen over the notepad. "We can start with what we both saw in her cup at our different readings." She wrote *black butter-fly* on the pad.

"Black butterflies, as I explained before, are associated in Irish folklore with the spirits of passed loved ones and can often be seen at funerals."

"Really? At funerals too?"

"Aye, dat can only be taken as a good sign because it means that the deceased is moving through the vale to the spirit world. The black butterfly is a symbol of rebirth, re-creation, and, more importantly, the 'death' of a misfortunate. It represents the ability of the mind, the body, and the spirit to be free of all restrictions and to go to the other side."

"I never told Cora it was a symbol of death. Did you?"

"Nah, because it doesn't always mean physical death. Sometimes it's the death of an idea or a belief, and the person is free to move forward from it and—"

"Except, in this case, it did mean physical death, didn't it?"

The only sound that could be heard in the room was the unbroken ticking of the clock over the sink. "I wonder," whispered Shay, "what Madam Malvina told her. Certainly, Cora wouldn't have followed the ritual instructions if she knew it would mean she could die."

"Unless," Gran's equally hushed tone matched Shay's, "Madam Malvina sugarcoated it by telling her the fairy ring represented a spiritual portal, which is why ye found her laid out in the center of it."

"According to legend, isn't doing that bringing misfortune and death, especially given the black butterfly image too."

"Exactly," said Gran, "and belladonna can also cause hallucinations. Ye said yourself she couldn't have possibly gotten into the center of the fairy ring without help."

"Yes, and there were no traces of footprints, at least none the police could find. The area had been swept, by the look of it, which means someone else had to have been there."

"Aye, and Cora, under the influence of the drug, allowed someone to walk her through the ritual. Perhaps the person involved didn't know poisons all that well and wasn't aware the poor woman had already taken enough to build it up in her system and accidentally killed her with the dose they gave her." Gran patted Shay's hand. "I best let ye get back to work or Jen will have me hide and yours."

Shay smiled and then frowned. "What if Cora's death was part of the plan to get the amulet from her?"

Gran wheezed as she struggled to her feet. "Let's hope our wee Tassi child is up to the task we have given her."

"Are you okay, Gran?" Shay shot to her feet and steadied the older woman.

"Aye, lass, I'm fit as a fiddle." Gran waved off Shay's help and clutched the back of the chair. "Just thinking that someone—someone we know—would lead another human to their death by way of a lie for personal gain. It goes against the ancient ones' ways and has me old bones a bit rattled, that's all."

If what Gran said about the ancient ones was true, it was no wonder Shay's instincts always told her to hold back and not outright accept Madam Malvina and her offered friendship. "Are you saying that the seer powers we have should never be used for personal gain?" Shay's mind raced to all the times she had charged people for a tea-leaf reading when she was reading their energy and seeing into their future with the help of her amulet. Guilt punched her in the gut.

"If the seer has something to gain personally by the information they give the seeker, aye, it goes against the oath of the ancient ones and the Early family too."

"But didn't Bridget and all the women in her family, right back to Biddy and before, charge for their services?"

"Aye, so they could eat and keep a roof over their heads, but never for personal gain by someone else's misfortune. That's a different kind of magic, a dark magic, and we don't go there. Ever!" Gran's strangled voice hissed out the last word.

"We don't." A chill shot up Shay's spine, and iciness settled at the base of her skull. "But someone else did."

"Aye." Gran's hands strangled the back of the chair until her knuckles whitened. "Someone who knows the dark arts."

"Madam Malvina doesn't have the gift of a seer, we know that, but could she have other powers we aren't aware of?" Shay's eyes widened. "Oh no, Tassi!"

"Tassi?"

"What if Madam Malvina catches her trying to take a sample note?"

Gran shook her head. "No, Madam Malvina doesn't possess any magic or other worldly powers. Only the dark powers of this world, like greed."

"I guess that's what I sensed about her from the beginning and why I always held her at a distance."

"Aye, because ye knew in your soul she was a fraud. If she held the dark secrets within her, ye would have felt a shock wave to the core of yer bones, to yer very being." She shook her head and stared at Bridget's crystal collection on the shelves at the back of the room. "'Tis someone else."

Chapter 15

"Spirit, are you slowing down in your old age?" Shay laughed over her shoulder as she eased up on the pedals and sailed around the corner to the back road that led to Crystal Beach Cottages. When she arrived at the top of the multi-level, wood-terraced stairway that led down to the beach and her cottage, she glanced back and hesitated. "Spirit? Where are you?"

He had been slightly lagging on their way home, but he was nowhere to be seen. Usually, he raced ahead of her and was already on the porch waiting for her, but she scanned the road and glanced down the lane that led between the upper row and lower row of cottages. No sign of him.

Her heart sank. She had been joking when she laughed at his slowness, but the thought that he could be feeling his age—whatever it was—didn't settle well with her. She only knew he'd been with her for over two years and had been with Bridget for as long as anyone in town could remember. *Wow! He must be ancient in dog years.*

Off to her left, a low growl, followed by a series of a sharp, quick barks, caught her attention, and a dark figure hopped over her back garden fence and disappeared into the wooded hill behind her cottage.

"Not another break-in!" She dropped her bike, raced down the steps, and sprinted down the wooden sidewalk to her home at the far end of the five cottages in the seaside row. She skidded to a stop at the sight of Dean on her front porch. "Dean?"

"Hi, Shay, we were hoping you'd be along soon."

"Was that one of your officers I saw around the back, or was that someone who took off when you arrived?" She jerked her thumb at Pearl Hammond's cottage next door. "Did she call in suspicious activity? I'll have to thank her if she—"

"No, nothing like that, don't worry. That was one of my men, but we are here on other official business."

"Official business?" she robotically echoed and stepped up onto the porch. "I really don't know anything more than I did before." Her hand tightened around the strap of her backpack, and her mind flashed images of the jotted notes in the margins of the book on poison. Surely, the mayor hadn't told Dean about it already. He said he'd wait until they had proof.

"No." Dean sat in one of the two wicker chairs. He motioned for her to sit in the chair opposite the small table beside him. "It's more what we know. The final autopsy report came back, and it seems the preliminary exam was correct. Cora died of a belladonna overdose."

"I see," Shay said, taking a seat. "Does that mean you're now looking for someone growing the plant in their garden or a greenhouse?"

"And a lab," he muttered meeting her quizzical gaze.

"What do you mean?"

"It seems the belladonna found built up in her system, which eventually caused the overdose, was a pharmaceutical grade used in doctor's offices."

"What doctors would prescribe one of the most toxic plants known to man to their patients?"

"According to the coroner's report, it's sometimes used in homeopathic treatments. Despite the known safety concerns and warnings put out by the FDA, belladonna is still sometimes used in the treatment of asthma, hemorrhoids, the common cold, and lots of other conditions, even though there is no scientific evidence to support its use in medical treatments of any of those disorders."

"Even though it was medical grade, anyone with a medical connection could have poisoned Cora. This doesn't mean the suspect is anyone *in* the medical field. Doctors, pharmacists, and naturopaths, who would have access to it, are all professionals, and their positions require state licensing. I can't believe they would jeopardize their career by purposely overdosing a patient."

"Even for a rare blue diamond?"

"I don't think so." She stared over the porch railing, with unseeing eyes, in the direction of the ocean. A dark figure flashed through her mind, and she closed her eyes and focused on it. A black flowing cape flapped wildly in the corner of her mind, and the amulet around her neck grew hot against her skin as the black cloak flew toward her, blocking out her mind's eye's shining light. Then everything went black. Her eyes flew open, and she stared at Dean. "No, you have to question Madam Malvina."

"We already have, and she denies any knowledge of having given Cora any belladonna or even suggesting she use it. She did admit that she sold Cora a book about herbs, which might mention it."

"Herbs?" Shay leaned forward in her chair. "Is that what she called it?"

"Shay?" Dean pinned her with a probing gaze. "Is there something you're not telling me?"

Shay glanced at her backpack by the door, where she'd dropped it. She couldn't come right out and lie to her brother-in-law about having the book, so she needed to bend the truth. "It's just that she was the one who told Cora about the conjuring ritual. According to Gran, who knows about these things, the crime scene fits the steps and finality of the ritual. By what you just said, Madam Malvina admits giving her a book that might have contained information about belladonna, so"—she shifted uncomfortably—"it stands to reason she is your main suspect."

"Maybe so, but as you know, I need proof, which brings me to the reason for our visit. When you found the body, do you recall seeing a small vial or bottle that could have contained a liquid solution of belladonna?"

"No, and besides trying to find a pulse, I never touched anything. When you arrived, everything was exactly as I found it. Why?"

"The report stated that a large amount, the fatal dose, had recently been ingested due to the amount still found in her stomach contents that had not been absorbed yet—"

"Not been absorbed yet?" Shay said thoughtfully. "That means the fatal dose must have been administered right before she died." She looked at Dean. "That dose must have been drunk as part of the ritual. You also need to be looking for a glass or cup, something that would have held it for her to drink from."

"You're right. That's what I was thinking, but I never thought of a cup or mug." He sat back, tapping his fingers on the arms of the chair. "And if it's, as you suggest, part of a ritual, then there must be some kind of vessel close to where the body was found." He rose to his feet and pinned his gaze on Shay. "Thanks, but we have to get back up there."

"But if someone did murder Cora, wouldn't they have taken it with them? They'd have to be pretty stupid to leave it lying around, especially if they wanted to maintain the illusion that Cora either took her own life or that a conjuring spell went wrong, right?"

Dean blew out a frustrated breath. "You're right again." He sat back down. "I guess I'm just hoping that if we can find something with identifying marks on it, we'll be able to trace it and get a lead. As of right now, I have nothing, and it's starting to look more like—"

"The fairies did it?"

Dean tsked and rose to his feet. "Just give me a call if anything credible comes to mind, will ya?"

"Of course, if any . . ." She swallowed hard. *It isn't a lie if I word this correctly, right?* "If actual proof comes to light, you'll be the first to know." She attempted an innocent smile and rose to meet his searching gaze. "What?"

"You are telling me everything you know, aren't you?"

As far as Shay knew, Dean wasn't a seer, but he seemed to have more insight than she did. "When I have proof of anything, I guarantee I will tell you everything I know." She smiled. Yes, *proof* was the key word and one she could use to not lose face with her brother-in-law and jeopardize their relationship.

"Okay, I'm going to hold you to that," he said, as he descended the porch steps. "And I trust you won't be out there investigating on your own."

"I promise not by myself." She crossed her heart and hoped taking Spirit along as her companion counted.

He nodded and started back toward the beach stairs. "Or . . ." He turned back to her. "If you feel the need to check something out, at least make sure Liam is with you."

"Liam?" Her head snapped back at his words. Dean knew her and what she was capable of, based on past experience—or, at least, she thought he did. "You think I need police protection? That I'm not capable of looking after myself?"

"No, I didn't mean it that way. It's just that, since he used to be a detective—"

"Don't bother trying to dig yourself out of that one." She laughed. "Besides, I think he's too busy with his new girlfriend, isn't he?"

Except for the day she, Liam, and Conor had tracked down the Doyle look-alikes, she hadn't seen Liam around much and hadn't even got a glimpse of him coming home to his cottage, which was right behind hers. Not that she had been spying on him, but she couldn't help noticing that, ever since the Monster Mash dance on Halloween night and his first date with Maggie Somers, he hadn't been around.

"I'd say that date he had with Maggie must have worked out well for him." She flashed a sheepish glance at Dean and caught his confused expression. "What?" Her chest constricted, and her breaths came short and fast in anticipation of what he might say. Had Liam moved in with Maggie and left Gran to the cottage? *No, Gran would have mentioned that, wouldn't she?* Her eyes widened, and her hand flew to her tightening throat. "What are you not telling me?"

"I thought you knew."

"Knew what?" She clutched at her throat.

"The Halloween dance was their one and only date—"

"It was?"

"Yes, it turned out she was just trying to make her ex-boyfriend jealous that night, and apparently it worked because now they're back together and planning their wedding."

Shay was confused. "Then where's he been lately?"

He wasn't with Maggie. Why hadn't he told her and asked her for advice on who he should date next, something he'd been doing for as long as she had known him? Then she recalled their encounter in the greenhouse before the carnival, when she had told him—no, shouted at him—

to get out and not come back. She'd even asked if he'd heard her, to make sure he'd understood her demand. Her chest heaved. He had never listened to her before, so why had he this time? The last thing she recalled from that argument was him saying he was going to see Madam Malvina.

Did that mean he and she were . . . No, she couldn't even go there, or should she? Shay shuddered at the thought. No, Liam wouldn't be so desperate as to date someone nearly as old as his mother. However, he had made worse matches in the past, and knowing the hard truth was better than wallowing in doubtful guesses.

"Is he seeing someone else?" she coyly asked, fighting to keep her voice even.

"I have no idea. I haven't seen him lately, but I'm sure if you called him and asked him to accompany you on any . . . unauthorized sleuthing adventures you decide to embark on, he'd help you out." Dean grinned and sauntered down the sidewalk, meeting up with his deputy waiting at the top of the terraced stairs by the upper roadway.

"Did you hear that, Spirit?" She turned her attention to the white shepherd when he bounded up the steps and sat panting at her feet. "Dean hasn't seen Liam either. You don't think Madam Malvina and he are—" She gulped. "You know . . ."

Spirit let out a series of short, sharp yips.

"No, you're right. He's probably doing surveillance since she seems to be our only suspect besides an invisible Doyle right now."

Spirit let out what sounded like an approving yap.

"Alright, I'm trusting your instincts right now and won't head down the jealousy path until we get some proof. Proof . . . yes, we need proof for a lot of things right now, don't we?" She leaned over and ruffled the soft fur on his head. "Nothing I see in the bottle will fly in court, but perhaps it will show me where to look for all this elusive proof Dean needs to find Cora's killer and close the case."

Spirit yipped.

"Yes, the proof is out there, and we have a way to find it, so why not use it?"

Chapter 16

Despite the cool ocean breeze, sweat beaded on Shay's skin at the thought of Liam in danger. If he had gone to Madam Malvina's after their argument in the greenhouse, maybe he had sensed something off, but didn't know what it was until the Doyle puzzle piece clicked into place. With his instinctive cop gut and tendency for wanting to protect Shay, she didn't put it past him to go off half-cocked and investigate on his own. With him and Conor on the outs, he could have gone off alone in a hunt for someone who was a killer, and that someone could be Doyle, the man who wouldn't stop until he had the amulet.

Shay looked over her shoulder. She was tired of feeling hunted. If only she knew for sure if Doyle was in town or not. But with the look-alike stunt, he proved he didn't need to be in order to wreak havoc and chaos. He only needed eyes and ears in the vicinity to keep him informed. A shiver of dread snaked down her spine, and she pulled her sweater tighter about her. If only she knew where Liam was. If anything ever happened to him and in the pursuit of helping her, she'd— Shay shut down that thought. She needed to think clearly and not panic.

She focused on the waves tumbling onto the beach, adjusted her breathing to match their rhythm, and cleared her mind of all distractions. "Okay, Bridget, I think I'm going to need a bit of help here," she whispered as a gentle breeze caressed her cheek.

She closed her eyes and smiled. There it all was, she could see it. Cora dead from a belladonna overdose. No footsteps leading to her ritualistically laid out body. Someone had planted her there and covered their tracks. The handwritten notes in the poison book. The teacup images.

Spirit growled, snapping her out of her trance.

"What is it, boy?" she cried when he leapt off the porch and took off down the path running alongside the cottage to the back garden.

"Where are you going?" she called, hurrying after him. "What did you hear?" She caught up to him at the end of the garden, squinted into the fading evening light, and gasped. *What the heck . . . ?*

Brad hoisted a cardboard box in his arms and said something to Angela. She laughed in return and wrestled a suitcase out of the trunk of her car.

Spirit growled low in his throat, and he barked.

Shay placed her hand on his head to silence him, but it was too late. Brad and Angela whirled in their direction.

Angela gave a cheery wave and a saccharine smile so overly sweet it made Shay's teeth ache. "Why, hello. Fancy us being neighbors." Without another word, Angela used her hip to open the front door of the cottage and disappeared inside.

"Remember, neighbor, if you ever need to borrow some sugar, you know who to come to." Brad mockingly winked at her over the top of the carboard box he still carried, and he too disappeared inside the cottage without another word.

Shay's heart sank. Tears clogged her throat, and she coughed. "No, you will not," she hoarsely whispered.

She bit the inside of her cheek. She would not give Brad

the satisfaction of seeing her cry. Not anymore. Not ever again would she shed a tear for that man. So many questions raced through her mind as she hurried back into her cottage, Spirit hot on her heels.

She sank to the couch. "No! Not that cottage. It can't be. Brad and Angela?"

Spirit whimpered and nudged her knee.

Shay played with his soft ears. "I don't suppose you could figure out how those two ended up in my backyard and right across the lane and next door to Liam and Gran? When he told me they were buying a winery, I just assumed it came with a house or something, but it seems not." She shivered at the thought of them being neighbors, and tears threatened to rise up behind her burning eyes.

Spirit rested his chin on her thigh and whimpered.

Shay smiled. "What would I do without you?"

Hoisting herself to her feet, she made her way to the kitchen on wobbly legs. It was clear she needed comfort food, and she quickly set about preparing a snack and brewing a pot of chamomile tea.

A soft tap on her back door interrupted her last blissful bite of a peanut butter and jelly sandwich. With a growl, she swiped at the crumbs on her sweater and opened the door.

"Liam?"

"Receiving company?" he asked, wincing.

Shay fought the urge to slam the door in his face, and if he had displayed his normal devil-may-care grin, she would have, but there was an unease about his aura that pricked her senses. She stepped back and gestured to a chair at the kitchen table. "Care for a PB&J sandwich? Tea's almost steeped. Want a cup?"

Liam waved off both and folded his hands in front of him. The only sound in the room was the ticking of the clock on the wall as Liam sat in silence, studying his clenched, interlocked fingers. "I saw Madam Malvina again today," he muttered quietly.

Her hand shook when she reached for a teacup. Jealousy reared its ugly head. So he hadn't been in danger. He had been seeing that . . . that . . . black-cloaked . . . Shay inhaled and steadied her hand as she poured her tea. Liam had a bad habit of oversharing some of the details of his previous dates with her, and she wasn't sure if she could stomach hearing even the slightest details of this particular relationship. She shivered. To judge by the drawn expression on his face, he was grappling with something, and if it involved what to tell her about him and Madam Malvina, she hoped he would choke on his words and keep whatever else he had to say to himself.

"I suppose you want to know why?" he asked.

Shay paused mid-pour. "Not really," she said coolly and took her seat.

"What do you mean?" He traced the wood-grain pattern of the kitchen table, and his gaze followed every movement his fingers made.

Since she had no real proof, a shot in the dark couldn't hurt, could it? At least then she'd know what she suspected. "I heard through the town grapevine that you and she were spending time together and, well . . . it's none of my business who you choose to spend time with, so I don't want to hear anything about your . . . whatever you and she do."

"What we do?" He stopped his tracing and laughed so hard that she did get her wish when he started choking.

"Are you okay?" She jumped to her feet and patted his back.

"Yes." He coughed. "I'm fine." He took a deep breath and smiled up at her. "Are you actually jealous of the time I spent with her?"

"Me, jealous? No, of course not." She glanced at Spirit,

whose ears perked up, and he lifted his large head, whined, laid his head back down on his dog bed, and covered his eyes with his giant paw.

"I'm just surprised," she said. "Because I thought we were working together to find out who killed Cora, and Madam Malvina is on our list of suspects. That's all." She shrugged nonchalantly, raising her cup to her lips. She felt stupid that she'd worried about his safety. It appeared she'd never learn when it came to matters of the heart with Liam.

"Which is exactly why I have been spending time with her."

The tightness in Shay's chest released like a popping balloon. Her fingers fumbled, and the cup tipped, spilling hot tea over her hand.

"*A chara*, ye've burned your hand." He jumped up, wetted a cloth, and rushed back, pressing the cool, damp cloth to her singed hand. "I wanted to get some answers. The night of the bonfire, I caught a glimpse of her having a heated conversation with someone. Someone who looked remarkably like what Conor described as Doyle."

So she had been right. He had put himself in danger for her sake. Shame at thinking Liam would be foolish enough to get involved with a woman like Madam Malvina heated her cheeks. Shay placed the cool cloth against her hot cheeks and hoped Liam hadn't noticed her blush. "But as we've come to find, there are a lot of men who look like Doyle."

"That's why I wanted to talk with her." He reached across the table toward her hand, but quickly retracted his and tucked it in his lap. "She denied the accusation. Said she'd never heard of a man named Doyle, and that it was none of my business who she had disagreements with."

"Do you believe her?" Shay asked.

Liam's sixth sense with women was off-kilter, but she'd never had cause to doubt his cop gut.

"No. I think she's hiding something, and if I were a betting man, I'd say she knows exactly who Doyle is."

"I wonder what she'll say when we confront her about the handwriting in the poison book?"

"Nothing but lies. But promise me you won't confront her alone."

Shay squared her shoulders and lifted her chin. "I don't need—"

Liam gripped her hand in his and squeezed lightly. "Shay, I get the sense the Madam Malvina is a very dangerous woman, who, if she did guide poor Cora in all this nonsense, is responsible for her death. And if she knows Doyle, that means there's a connection between the two, and he wants nothing more than to kill you to get the treasure he knows you wear." Liam's gaze dipped to where Shay hid the pouch under her shirt. "I don't know what I would do if something—" His throat worked for several minutes as he composed himself. "Please. It doesn't need to be me if that thought bothers you so much, but please do not confront Madam Malvina on your own."

With his warm grip heating her from the inside out and his soft gaze studying her face, Shay had no choice but to agree. "I promise."

Chapter 17

Shay needed to move, to escape the feelings rushing through her, and sprang to her feet. "Well, what are you waiting for? Let's go have a chat with Madam Malvina."

"Right now?" asked Liam.

"Why not?" She quickly cleared the table, and after grabbing her purse, she stood at the door. "Let's go. I'm not getting any younger waiting for you two slow pokes, you know."

Spirit cocked his head and yipped. Liam rolled his eyes. "There isn't anything slow about either of us, *a chara*. In fact, I bet I can beat you in a footrace to my Bronco."

"In your dreams," she scoffed and started down the back steps.

"Loser buys a round at my pub. How does that sound?"

"Why would I pay for you to drink your own beer?" Shay asked.

"You better not lose then." Before she could offer a retort, Liam and Spirit sprinted across her back garden to Liam's driveway.

She panted when she reached them and narrowed her eyes at Spirit. "Traitor." Then flashed Liam the same rebuking look.

Liam chuckled and opened the passenger door for her. "Losers first." He ducked her well-aimed swat just in time and sauntered around to the driver's side, a grin on his face.

By the time Liam parked behind the pub and they walked around to the front of High Street, Shay realized by the sparse traffic that it was getting late, and other than the pub, nothing appeared to be open. Not even Cuppa-Jo. She crossed her fingers that there would be more foot traffic over on the boardwalk and it wouldn't feel like she was stepping into every action-movie heroine's nightmare and confronting her nemesis on a dark, deserted street.

"There's no way Madam Malvina is going to still be there," said Shay, cupping her hand around her eyes and straining to see through the window and into the darkened tea shop. "There is no sign of life inside. She's definitely not here."

"Are ye certain?" Liam pressed his face to the glass.

"Yeah, and I changed my mind. Let's go." Shay glanced down the desolate boardwalk and involuntarily shivered.

"But she told me she had a reading late tonight and that's why she couldn't meet me."

"And you're heartbroken because she lied to you?"

"No."

"Really?" Shay laughed and nudged his shoulder. "I think you're hurt that Madam Malvina lied to a man of your caliber and dating prowess." Knowing Liam didn't fancy Madam Malvina made it easier to tease him about it and made her feel less foolish about dragging him out here this late because she was trying to avoid facing the feelings for him that he'd stirred up back at her cottage. "I'm thinking you're bothered by her not being where she told you she'd be more than you're letting on," she singsonged teasingly and placed her hand over her heart and sighed.

Instead of rolling his eyes, like she'd thought he would,

Liam placed his hands on her shoulders and spun her toward him. She gulped at his darkened gaze.

"*A chara*, are ye jealous?" Gone was the playful tone he'd used when he'd challenged her to a race just minutes before.

"No, what would make you think I am? You're the one pouting about how she lied to you." She weakly smiled. "In fact, if I didn't know any better, I'd think you were pining for—"

Liam's head descended, and his lips captured hers. He could have kissed her for seconds, minutes, or hours. Shay didn't know or care. Time ceased to exist, and all that mattered was Liam's lips on hers and his fingers entangled in her hair.

He slowly eased his lips from hers, leaving her wanting more. She had never been kissed like that before, and she fought to steady herself. "Well . . ." She swallowed hard. "That was unexpected."

"Exactly the effect I was going for," he whispered while he pulled away and gazed down at her. The reflection of his dilated pupils under the streetlight indicated to her that he hadn't been unaffected by their kiss. He cleared his throat and jerked his chin at Madam Malvina's tea shop window. "I told you I was working her, but she doesn't know that, and I'm hoping to make her think I'm interested in her . . . romantically."

He might as well have dumped ice water on her. Any residual heat still cruising through her veins from his kiss froze. "And how exactly is kissing me is going to help you prove that?"

"Turn and face the window," he said through clenched teeth. "Don't look around or look up, but there is a security camera up under the awning, and if she reviews the tape, I want her to see us kissing."

Shay's chest deflated, and a spasm of pain stabbed her

in the heart. *The kiss wasn't real?* "So, you used me?" Her voice faltered. Anger replaced heartache, and she stood toe-to-toe with him. "You used me!" She stabbed his chest with her finger. "And . . . how in the world is you using me . . . ahem . . . kissing me . . . going to prove you want her 'romantically'?" Shay hooked air quotes and sneered.

"I want to make her jealous, because maybe I can push her into revealing more to me than she has been."

"What? You really are an egotistical jerk, aren't you?"

"What do ye mean?"

"I mean you think she's going to be so upset about you kissing me when you're supposed to be going out with her that she's going to admit to killing Cora?"

"No, don't be silly. I'm hoping that if I can gain her trust, make her think I'm madly in love with her, or whatever some such nonsense she might think, then she'll slip up, accidentally give a clue she wouldn't otherwise."

Shay spun on her heel and stomped off down the deserted boardwalk.

"Shay, my car's parked the other way."

Shay ignored him and continued speed-walking in the opposite direction.

Liam ran after her and grabbed her arm, spinning her toward him. "Don't ye think she'll fall for it and slip up?"

"No, and that's the dumbest thing I ever heard." She yanked her arm from his light grasp and glared at him. "And you were a police detective in San Francisco?"

"Aye, yes, and setting up a perp to get a confession was something I was good at. People don't want to confess to a murder, so sometimes they have to be convinced to do that, and I'm good at getting people to confess. The closer I can get to them, the more I can gain their trust, the easier it is."

"You mean you're good at pushing people's buttons. I can attest to that!"

"What are you talking about?"

"Nothing."

He placed his hands on her heaving shoulders. "Listen to me. I only remembered after we got to her tea shop that she reviews the camera tapes every morning when she goes in. I decided it was a great way to set her up and push her toward opening up to me."

"Or slap your face." She shook her head. "I don't think you thought this scenario through very well, did you?"

"I admit it was on the fly, but what else was I supposed to do to cover up the fact you and I were looking through her shop window at night."

"But do you really think—"

He pressed his finger to his lips. "Shhh, let me finish. When I remembered about the CCTV, I knew she would see us peeking in the window and that would put a target on both of our backs if she's the killer. When she sees me kissing you, I can tell her that we were there because you suspected her of being the killer, and when we discovered no one was in the shop, you wanted to break in to see if we could find any evidence so . . . that's when I kissed you. To distract you from breaking in. Then I'll play dumb."

"Not a stretch," she muttered.

He rolled his eyes, and she shook her head and marched down the boardwalk in the direction of her cottage.

"Wait!" He caught up with her. "At least let me drive you back. I just wanted her to be upset about me kissing you, and maybe her jealousy would kickstart her thinking she's more in love with me than she thought."

"You really do think highly of yourself, don't you?"

Liam massaged the back of his neck and at least had the decency to blush. "Well, ye know . . . just a touch of acting and that sort of thing."

"No, I don't actually know." Shay hugged her arms around her middle, stared out into the night-cloaked sea and thought for a moment, then looked back at a sheepish-looking Liam. "I guess once I hear the whole plan and the reason for the kiss, it doesn't sound quite as dumb as I first thought."

"Ye know, I also kissed ye because . . ." He trailed his finger over her forearm.

Shay's chest heaved, and her silly schoolgirl, mutinous heart leapt. She hated it about as much as she was starting to hate Liam. "I swear, mister, if you kiss me again because there's some security camera you need to play up to, I'll smack you."

"Listen, I know when I kissed ye the first time, it was to protect my cover story, but I . . . ah . . . I really wanted to . . ."

Shay didn't want to look at him, afraid that his gaze would match the sudden longing in his voice. She wouldn't be able to resist, and she couldn't afford to make the same mistake with him under the influence of conflicting and confusing emotions. She avoided his eyes, glanced over his shoulder, and gasped.

"Did ye not like me kiss?" Liam tipped her chin back and forced her to look at him. Worry and something like regret swam in those electric-blue depths.

"It's not that. It's just that—" Shay halted his movement to turn around and look where she was staring. "No, don't turn around."

"What's wrong?" His gaze sharpened, and he drew himself up.

"Angela and Madam Malvina just went into her shop."

"Who's Angela?"

"Brad's new wife."

"She's here? In Bray Harbor?" He turned to look.

"No, don't—" She sighed and let go of his forearm. "Never mind, they went inside."

"Did they see us?"

"No, they were too busy talking." She laughed when

Spirit darted down the boardwalk toward them, barking and prancing at her feet.

"What do you want, boy?" Shay scratched between his ears.

He licked her hand and pointed his nose toward Madam Malvina's tea shop. "Well, we gotta go back and see what they're up too. Spirit says so."

"No." Liam gripped her arm. "We need a plan. Remember, she'll already see us on the surveillance camera. She's really going to wonder if we go back." A mischievous grin played over his lips. "Not that I don't want to, because then I'd have to kiss ye again."

With his words, her heart and mind fought over whether she really wanted another kiss from him. Who was she kidding? Of course she did, but this wasn't the time or place. *Keep it light. Keep it light.* "You're right. Kissing me again would be horrible, wouldn't it?"

Liam traced his index finger down her face and across her jaw. "I'm afraid we'll have to put the kiss discussion on the back burner for now, but sometime soon, we're having a nice long chat about it, okay?" He grinned shyly and tucked his hands in his pockets.

"You're right." Shay's fervour faded, as did her hopes of tasting his lips on hers one more time tonight, and she tried to refocus. "We need another plan now."

"Aye, we do," he said thoughtfully. "Can ye think of any reason yer ex's wife would be meeting with her? Are they old friends or something?"

"Not as far as I know." Shay frowned. "Unless Brad and Madam Malvina know each other."

"Where would they have crossed paths?"

"I'm not sure. Maybe they met on one of the many business trips he used to take to Monterey and Carmel to sell my jewelry. Knowing her could also be how he's kept tabs on me and why he ended up here."

"That would explain so much, wouldn't it?"

"Yeah," said Shay, "but the question is, how long have they been friends?"

"There is one way to find out," said Liam. "First, we need to find out where they're staying in town."

"Brad and Angela just moved into the vacant cottage next door to yours."

"They did?"

"Yes, today I saw them unloading and . . ."

"That's why ye haven't been yerself tonight."

She narrowed her eyes. She thought she'd been doing a great job covering up her wounded heart. Perhaps Liam had the gift of sight too. "I'm fine."

Spirit growled low in his throat and nuzzled her hand.

"Right." Liam smiled knowingly and squeezed her hand.

Chapter 18

"Now that I'm standing here, I'm rethinking this," Shay whispered.

"Just let me do the talking," Liam said, rapping on the door.

"Did you forget your key?" said Brad, as he opened the door. "Oh, you aren't Angela." His piercing gaze flicked from Liam to Shay and zeroed in on her. He leaned against the doorjamb. "Shay, what brings you by this time of night?" He casually raised a brow at Liam. "And I see you've brought another unannounced guest with you."

Liam stuck his hand out. "Liam Madigan, yer next-door neighbor." He jerked his thumb over his shoulder.

Brad ignored Liam's proffered handshake. "And Shay is with you because she's the head of the community welcome wagon?" Sarcasm rolled off his tongue, and his gaze flicked between Shay and Liam.

Shay's gut curdled at the suspicion lurking in Brad's eyes.

"No, she's my—"

"Girlfriend," she blurted. There, let Brad know she'd moved on and that she'd found a new and better man.

"Yes, my girlfriend." Liam circled his arm around her waist, pulled her close, and kissed the top of her head. He grinned at Brad. "She just agreed to my ever-long pleas. Probably got sick of me asking, didn't you, love?"

Shay's heart fluttered at his deep voice calling her "love," and no matter how much she demanded it to stop being foolish, it continued. "Wore me down, you did."

Spirit yipped what sounded like an agreement to Shay and Liam's farce. "And this"—Liam patted the large German shepherd's head—"is Spirit, our dog."

Spirit yipped again.

"Your dog?" Brad gaped at Shay. "Then it must be serious. You and I never even had a dog or a cat because you said you weren't ready to commit to looking after another living thing. Little did I know at the time that that statement included me." He winked at Liam and laughed. "Know what I mean?"

"No, I don't." Liam dropped his arm from Shay's waist and squared his shoulders. "I have no idea what you're talking about. I only know that—"

Shay stepped forward. "We only wanted to welcome you and Angela to the neighborhood," she said before the two bullheaded men started throwing punches. "It's a small community here, and we're bound to run into each other from time to time, so we wanted to say hello first, just so it won't be uncomfortable when we do cross paths in the future, like at the garbage bins or—"

"Right, we wouldn't want you to feel uncomfortable." Liam fixed an icy gaze on Brad, who met it with an equally cool glare.

"I just wish Angela was here too, so she knows there's no hard feelings." Shay faked a smile.

"I'll pass that along."

"Where is your lovely wife, by the way?" asked Liam. "I've heard so much about her that I was looking forward to meeting her."

"She went to the grocery store to pick up a few things we need."

"Oh, really? You should have just come and asked me if you could borrow some sugar," Shay said as sweetly as she could.

"I'll remember that." Brad stepped back into the doorway and began to close it. "If you'll excuse me, I have some unpacking to do so we at least have sheets and blankets tonight. I'm sure you understand."

Liam nodded, but Shay crossed her arms over her chest. "There is one thing I'm curious about, though."

"What's that?" Brad asked through the partially open door.

"When I saw you at the carnival, you said you were buying a winery. Did that deal fall through?"

"No, we bought it."

"It didn't come with a house?"

"Yes, but it's not to Angela's standards, so she refused to live in it until we renovated."

"How like her," muttered Shay.

"What was that?" Brad poked his head out the door and cocked his head.

"I said 'and is this cottage better?' "

"This cottage is free for the two months the renovations are going to take."

"Free? How did you swing that? These are much sought-after cottages."

"That's what I heard, but remember this is offseason, and the realtor we used—Julia, remember—she found us the winery. I had her throw this in as a bonus as long as we needed it. She owns most of these cottages, you know."

"Yes, I know," said Shay.

"I did try to get that lovely one at the base of the hill on the beach row, but—"

"She doesn't own that one." Shay straightened her back and raised her head high. "I do."

"So I understand. I really hope that's not going to be a problem. You know us, being neighbors and all?" he said, peering through the narrowing crack in the door. "After all, your friend Julia is a smart businesswoman and knew it was better to have us in here than have it sit vacant all winter and have to hire a caretaker to check in on it. But if that's all . . ." The door began closing in her face.

"No, it's not a problem at all. I was just . . ." Why, oh why, did he have to pop back up into her life—as her neighbor, no less—and turn her life upside down again, plus drive a wedge between her and Julia? "But thanks for Bradsplaining it to me," she said snarkily, as the door clicked shut.

She took the steps two at a time to get away from him and met up with Liam in the lane. The first thing on her to-do list was to talk to Julia, her supposed friend, about not only selling a local property to the man who had ruined Shay's life and stolen everything from her, but then turned around and rented a cottage right on her back door to that same man. Some friend Julia was.

Shay and Liam wandered back to her cottage in silence. She suspected Brad was watching them, so she slipped her hand into Liam's, wanting to make sure he saw that she had truly moved on from him. To her surprise he gently clasped it back and fit it comfortably into his.

When they stepped into her kitchen, Liam brought her warm hand to his lips and softly kissed her knuckles. "So, yer me girlfriend, are ye?" He chuckled, dropped her hand, leaned against the counter, and grinned like a Cheshire cat.

Shay's heart thudded. It seemed Liam was enjoying the game they were playing, but for her, this was no game. She had to shore up her heart against his flippant treatment of hers. "It was for show. Heaven knows I can't keep up with your revolving door of women."

"There's just one thing about that." He slipped his hand around her waist and pulled her close as she shimmied past him to put the kettle on.

"What's that?" Her face was mere inches from his, and his warm breath, caressing her cheek, started chipping away at the defenses she'd erected to protect her heart.

"Angela's appearance at the tea shop tonight might mean that she and Madam Malvina are friends, and woman friends talk about personal stuff, like who's seeing whom and all that, don't ye?"

"Oh no!" Shay's hand shot to her mouth. "I never thought of that."

"It's not that I mind ye calling yerself me girlfriend, but . . ." He twisted a coil of her red hair around his finger and let it gently fall down the side of her flushed cheek.

"No, but blurting out I was your girlfriend just blew your cover, didn't it?" Not that his answer would have mattered. With his hand on her waist and his finger twirling another curl, she couldn't think of anything else.

"Nah, I can work around that . . . somehow." His gaze met hers, and the air in the kitchen seemed to crackle with electricity. He blinked and released her so quickly she stumbled backward into the kitchen counter. "Sorry, back burner, remember." Liam rubbed the back of his neck and cleared his throat. "But there's something that's not sitting right about Madam Malvina and Angela."

"Just one thing?" Shay softly laughed, releasing the breath she'd been holding in anticipation of another kiss, got her bearings, and filled the kettle.

"I've been thinking about something you said earlier, and it makes me wonder about something."

Shay sank to a kitchen chair. "Okay, what are you thinking?"

"Madam Malvina is a rather private person, right? So she'd have to know Angela fairly well to meet up at her shop after hours."

"You're right, and Angela just got here days ago. There's no way she could have struck up such a quick friendship or even acquaintance with Madam Malvina already. So that does suggest that maybe I was on the right track when I said maybe Brad met her on a business trip."

Liam settled in a chair next to hers. "Exactly, meaning there is also the possibility that Brad and Angela and Madam Malvina have known each other for years. After he cheated you out of your business, he'd need knowledge of gems, right? Perhaps he used his connection with Madam Malvina in his search for answers. He couldn't or wouldn't ask you, would he?"

"No, he had Angela for that. She was my assistant and also a geology undergrad. It would have been for another reason."

"Well, what does she have that Brad or Angela would find worth befriending her for? Seems an odd relationship."

"She's an expert in hoodwinking people, betraying friends, and creating mischief—"

Liam grinned. "As much as I agree with you, what are her marketable skills? What is she knowledgeable in?"

Shay closed her eyes and rubbed her temples. *Think, Shay, think.* She replayed all the advice—which to Shay now seemed like a collection of twisted lies—the woman had given her. She was the one who had showed up on Shay's doorstep when Shay started to make changes in the tea shop after inheriting it from Bridget, and she had always appeared in Shay's life at the most momentous times. It was Madam Malvina herself who had pointed out Shay's poisonous plants.

She snapped her eyes open and clutched Liam's hand. "Poison. Madam Malvina knows her poisons."

"Why would Brad reach out to her about poisons?" Liam's eyes widened. "Describe to me exactly yer mental state during Brad's destruction of yer life?"

"Why hash that all out now? That was years ago."

"Humor me." He rubbed his thumb over the back of her hand. "Please."

Shay shivered. "I honestly don't remember much. The last two years with him were so blurry, and quite honestly, I still have no clue how I lost everything in court and was found guilty of embezzlement and fraud. I never did anything illegal in my life."

A muscle in Liam's jaw ticked. "When I worked in the field, I heard about schemes where such things happened. Could he have been poisoning ye, ye know, before it all came apart? That's why everything's a blur and—"

Shay's heart skipped a beat. "Do you think I was drugged? Poisoned? To allow him the freedom to pull off so much right under my nose." She fisted her hands and banged them on the table. "It all makes so much sense now. I didn't have a clue what was really going on. I was in a fog, a daze, the whole time."

Liam scooted his chair closer and cupped her hands in his. "All I can say is the Shay I know is way too perceptive and observant for anyone to take advantage of her like that. Something must have contributed to yer . . . foggy memory."

Shay's spine tingled at the memory of Brad surprising her with gifts of chocolate or her favorite blend of coffee. She hadn't suspected a thing. Until it was too late, and her life as she knew it was ripped from her.

"Why didn't I think of this?" Her gut churned. "All this time, I've been studying herbs and plants and their effects, especially the belladonna Cora had been taking, and I've missed all the cues." Her eyes widened. "Oh my goodness, I've been a part of all of this . . . from the beginning."

Liam squeezed her hand. "What do ye mean?"

"Madam Malvina. She must have had a hand in orchestrating everything because she knew about the blue bottle I stood to inherit from Bridget." She gasped. "Do you think she played a part in Bridget's death too and getting me to move back to Bray Harbor in the first place?"

"That's quite the—"

Shay pulled away. "I can't believe I never thought of that once I started working with various teas. Brad could very well have been working with Madam Malvina all along to try to get his hands on the blue bottle and the priceless blue diamond."

"You didn't know about it then. What makes you think Brad did?"

"If he had sought her help with a little something to slip me, Madam Malvina may have told him the folklore story about the bottle, once she found out who I was and my connection to Bridget Early. She could well have helped set the whole plan in motion. She knew the folklore. He was a direct link to me and her way of getting what she wanted. But," she said thoughtfully, "if that's the case, I'm pretty sure she had a backup plan that didn't include him, since she doesn't strike me as the sharing type." Her eyes widened, and she looked at Liam. "That means Brad and Angela could be in danger too."

"Whew, that's a lot of assumptions, but you might be right. We just need proof, so why don't I go talk to Dean about this, and we can start checking some police databases for anything that shows a definite connection between Brad and Madam Malvina before we get too far ahead of ourselves." He lightly squeezed her hand, opened his mouth, and then snapped it shut. "I'd better go."

He patted Spirit's head and flung the door open. "Conor?"

he cried. "What are ye doing here at this hour?" His gaze flicked between Conor and Shay. "Or is there something going on here that I don't know about?"

So jealousy was contagious.

"What?" Shay shrugged, enjoying Liam's obvious discomfort at the thought of her and Conor. After what he'd put her through with the idea of him and Madam Malvina, he deserved it. "And if there was, what business is it of yours?" She winked at Conor, who stood in the open doorway, his eyes narrowed in confusion. At Conor's outstretched arms and what-in-the-heck look, Shay rolled her eyes. "Never mind."

Shay was still taken aback at how much these cousins looked like they could be twins.

When Conor still stood in the doorway, his wary gaze locked on Liam, Shay stepped forward and nudged the territorial Liam out of the way. "What is it, Conor?"

"I just saw Doyle."

"Where?" Liam squared his shoulders.

"Going into cottage number 1," Conor said.

"Did you say cottage number 1?"

Conor nodded.

"That's Madam Malvina's." Shay winced when her amulet heated uncomfortably against her skin.

Chapter 19

Two identical sets of eyes gazed at her with concern. Shay's feeling of doom faded, and she dragged the two men to the kitchen table and ordered them to sit, as she paced.

Liam and Conor shared a looked, shrugged their shoulders, sat back, and watched.

"Shay, what has gotten into ye?" Liam asked, a grin tugging at the corner of his lips.

"Aye," added Conor, "as much as I enjoy watching you walk back and forth, we still have a criminal to catch."

Shay held her hand up, silencing them. "Liam, your cover is saved."

Conor quirked an eyebrow at his cousin. "Cover? Are you working someone?"

Liam ignored him and gestured for Shay to continue. "I'm with Conor on this one. What's going on in that head of yers?"

"Do you two realize how much you look alike?"

Conor scoffed. "So we've been told, but I know for a fact that I'm twice as handsome and have a better disposition."

Liam grunted, crossed his arms, and glared at Shay. "What's your point?"

"My point? Madam Malvina barely knows you and has hardly ever met Conor. She wouldn't be able to tell the difference between you. When Madam Malvina confronts you about our kiss—"

Conor scooted forward in his chair and rubbed his hands together, a cheeky grin on his face. "Kiss? You two? Finally, you two pull your heads out of your backsides. Maybe now Gran will quit fussing about you two."

"Hush," Shay pointed at Conor and locked gazes with Liam. "Think it through. You and Conor look alike. I may not be an experienced investigator, but I am experienced in unfaithfulness in a relationship. When Madam Malvina confronts you about kissing me on camera, you insist it wasn't you. Tell her that your cousin and I have recently hooked up, and that you and he often get mistaken for each other. Make up some story that one of your cronies will corroborate, if you need it, but I don't think you will. All you have to do is turn it around back on her. Deflect, deflect, deflect. That's what Brad always did to me when I got suspicious about where he had been and with whom. Just ask her about the man you saw going into her cottage late at night. If that doesn't turn the tables on her, I don't know what will."

"That's brilliant, Shay." Liam's grin faded at Conor's open stare. Liam cleared his throat. "What concerns me about that plan is I introduced myself to Brad, and he knows yer my girlfriend."

"Blimey," Conor said, laughing and slapped his knee. "Gran's gonna be planning yer wedding by morning."

Shay flashed him a look of reproach and looked over at Liam. "You're right, I forgot," said Shay, as she resumed her pacing. "Wait, if it comes up, just say your cousin is always telling people he's you because he thinks it's funny, and he thinks it will help him be accepted more in Bray

Harbor, blah blah blah or something. Don't you see, it's all about deflecting everything and taking no responsibility. Exactly what Brad did to me."

"Okay," Liam nodded, "but I won't bring up meeting Brad unless she does. That might just buy us some time until we can figure out what Madam Malvina's relationships with Brad, Angela, and now Doyle have in common."

"The only thing I can think of is the blue diamond."

"Don't forget the power the blue bottle has," said Conor.

"I'm not," said Liam. "The rare blue diamond could explain why Brad and Angela are mixed up with this."

"Right," said Shay. "They were willing to destroy my life to steal my humble gemstone and jewelry business in Santa Fe. I wouldn't put it past them to do something more extreme to gain what's inside the blue bottle."

"Perhaps access to the power of the blue bottle and the need to possess it would be why Madam Malvina is involved," Liam said.

Conor shook his head. "If she thinks a man like Doyle will share anything he's going to get, anymore than she would, we're going to end up with a whole passel of dead bodies on our hands before this is done."

The amulet grew warm against her skin. "Why don't I use the blue bottle now? I think we can use all the help we can get."

The glow from the candle on the table flickered on Liam and Conor's drawn faces, and Shay pulled the bottle out from her shirt.

"Do ye think this will work?" asked Conor.

"I hope so." Shay held the blue bottle over the flame and watched for the bubbles to form inside the bottle.

When they started dancing, she pulled her hand back,

clutched the bottle in her fist, and brought it to her fore-head.

"I didn't know there was a ritual for this," said Liam.

"There isn't. I'm just trying everything I've done in the past that made the bottle speak to me in visions." She closed her eyes and waited, fighting to clear her mind of every-thing around her. The muffled sounds of Liam and Conor's breaths, the scent of Liam's musky cologne, and the tick-ing of the kitchen clock distracted her. She concentrated on Spirit's tail thumping rhythmically on the floor. Her spiraling thoughts evaporated, and the fog lifted. She jerked when her visions came in a succession of snapshot images, arriving so quickly she struggled to comprehend what she saw.

A man's contorted face shot toward her through the dis-sipating mist. A snapshot of her face replaced the first one, and just as quickly another blurred image flew into her vi-sion. She squinted and tried to make out the swirling fea-tures. Before she could decipher it, a snapshot of a balding man's face loomed up, only to quickly be replaced by hers again. The man's face appeared again. Shay narrowed her eyes. *Who is that?*

"I see a man like the one you described, Conor. Short and balding, with graying hair."

"Doyle?"

"It must be." The snapshot image quickly flipped to the mysterious blurry one. "And me and someone else, but I can't make out . . . Wait, the image changed again. It's the fairy ring."

"The same one where you found Cora?" Liam asked.

"Yes," she whispered and opened her eyes. "We have to go back to the site."

"Not tonight," said Liam. "It's nearly ten."

"There's something there we're supposed to see."

"We can go at first light, but right now I suggest we all get some sleep." Liam rose to his feet.

Shay pulled her shoulders back. "But—"

Liam held his hand up, but there was a softness in his gaze, and he spoke gently. "If there is something we're supposed to see, we can't go stumbling around in the dark. We won't have any better luck than Dean and his deputies did the first night anyway. We need to wait until it's light out."

"Yes, I suppose you're right."

"But what if the vision was telling you Doyle was there now, performing another ritual or digging up something he stole from Cora when he killed her. Maybe we can catch him in the act." Conor jumped to his feet and headed toward the kitchen door.

"He wasn't in the image I saw of the fairy ring, though, so I doubt that's what it meant." Shay sighed.

Liam smiled gently and placed his warm hand on her shoulder. "Goodnight, *a chara*. We'll see ye in the morning, okay?"

Shay wanted nothing more than to nuzzle his hand, but that would prove she wasn't just pretending. "Good night."

After closing and locking the kitchen door behind Liam and Conor, Shay went through her nightly ritual. She robotically filled Spirit's water dish, turned off lights, locked the front door, and shut all the open windows. After ensuring all was secure, she readied herself for bed, snuggled in under her cozy duvet, and closed her eyes. Sleep evaded her, however, and the more she tried to empty her mind and drift off to sleep, the more she tossed and turned. After her tenth attempt at making herself more comfortable and multiple punching matches with her pillow, she sat up and threw her pillow across the room.

An image of the fairy ring, mingling with the three faces from her other visions, loomed before her.

"Conor might be right." She jumped out of bed. "Maybe Doyle is there right now, and that's what the vision is trying to tell me!" She shoved her feet into her slippers and got dressed.

Spirit lifted his head from where he lay on his bed and let out a howl that sent goose bumps down Shay's arms.

Chapter 20

Outside, those same goose bumps still prickled as Shay wound her way around her cottage. Sticking to the shadows, she made her way to the base of the cliff. A bristling sensation tingled in her neck and across her shoulders. She had no clue what she would find once she got to the fairy ring, but given that Spirit's ears were pinned back, made Shay look over her shoulder more than once. The sense of being watched brought with it an overpowering feeling of dread, and she jump at every little night sound.

She paused, took a deep shaky breath, put her head down and continued creeping through the low underbrush at the base of the hill, then started the arduous upward trek in the dark. Not wanting to draw any attention by using a flashlight, she relied on the moonlight to illuminate her path. This was not an easy task, as the clouds played peek-a-boo with the moon, which one second was lighting her path, and then suddenly plunged her back into darkness.

"I didn't think this through, did I, Spirit?" Shay grunted as she stretched, reaching for a large tree root protruding in front of her.

Spirit whimpered and nudged her hand with his wet nose.

Shay groaned and heaved herself up another whole foot while she kept low, scrambling crablike up the steep hill. "Now, if you were a person, you would have told me this was a bad idea to attempt in the middle of the night." She panted and gritted her teeth as she pulled herself up another foot or so. Her lungs screamed, and she paused to catch her breath. "At least you would have told me no one in their right mind would be wandering around the cottages at this time of night and that I should have taken the regular path like a normal person."

Spirit let out a whimper that sounded a lot like "I'm sorry."

"You better be sorry, mister." She grunted as she grabbed for another handhold on a protruding tree root and wiggled over the top of the incline. "Made it." She lay facedown, gasping. "Are you up yet, Spirit?" She flipped over and was met with a face wash from a lapping pink tongue. "Okay, enough." She laughed and pushed her furry companion away. "I'm fine and glad we survived."

Spirit's ears twitched, and he cocked his large head.

"What is it? What do you hear, boy?" Shay stayed low to the ground and scanned the darkness. The patchy moonlight through the shifting clouds created odd shadows, and Shay shivered.

Spirit tucked his tail under his rear and crept forward, paused, sniffed, and moved forward again. Not sure what she should do, Shay lay frozen on the cliff top. Once she couldn't make out Spirit's form in the moonlight, a chill raced through her, and on all fours, she scrambled in the direction he had gone and caught up with him quickly.

"Hear anything?"

Spirit edged forward again, and she crept along behind him. Her hands and knees stung, but there was no way she was going to stand up and make herself more visible to whoever might be around. Her gut convinced her that she and Spirit were not alone.

When they got closer to the meadow where the fairy ring was located, Shay's shoulders tightened. Whatever had initially set off her internal alarm bells sent fiery shots into the back of her head. She grasped the amulet around her neck and blinked in surprise. It was cold.

Spirit stopped, and his ears flattened. Through the wondering moonlight, Shay spotted a dark figure hunched close to the ground beside the large boulder she had sat on for hours after discovering the body. A low growl escaped Spirit's throat, and then he yipped, leapt forward, and shot off into the night. Shay froze and held her breath and waited for a scream.

Seconds later, it wasn't a scream but a familiar laugh.

"Tassi?" Shay said incredulously, rising to her feet. "What in the world are you doing up here?" She skirted around the fairy ring.

"Shay! Whoa, you scared the bejeezus out of me." Tassi pressed a hand over her heart.

"Likewise. I knew someone was up here, but I never guessed it was you."

"I had a weird dream about the fairy ring that woke me up, and a strong feeling that I had to come, that something was here I needed to find."

"Me too, but you're certainly not what I expected." Shay sat on the familiar boulder.

"Maybe something is trying to tell us there is a clue here that the police missed when they searched and that it's up to us to find it."

"I thought maybe Doyle was up here."

Tassi eyed here. "And you thought it best to come up here. In the dark. Alone?"

Spirit yipped and sat beside Tassi, resting his chin on her thigh.

"See?" Tassi petted his giant head. "Even Spirit agrees with me."

"Yes, he seems to have chosen every other person's side besides mine lately." She waved away Tassi's questioning look. "Never mind. Did you see something particular in your dream?"

"I dreamt there was something hidden by this rock."

"Maybe we're both right and Doyle hid something by it?" Shay jumped off the boulder and started patting the ground.

"Two can dig faster and cover more territory than one." Tassi held out a garden trowel.

"Look at you being prepared and everything."

"And I'm sure you prepared yourself with a defensive weapon in case you ran into Doyle, right?"

Shay's face burned with embarrassment. She hadn't even thought about arming herself. How stupid could she have been? What if it was Doyle up here and not Tassi?

Spirit woofed.

Shay scratched his chin. "Yes, I did have you, and you're all the protection I need, right, boy?"

He woofed again.

"Come on," said Tassi, returning to her digging. "In case your sixth sense was right and Doyle does make an appearance, I want to find what we're supposed to discover and get out of here."

Shay shoved her trowel into the hard, dry soil. "You might be right about Doyle showing up. When I was at the bottom of the hill, I sensed someone watching me. Conor saw him going to Madam Malvina's cottage earlier this evening."

"You're kidding." Tassi gaped at her.

"I wish I was."

"Does he know you live in one of the cottages?"

"Probably. If Conor's right and this guy is Doyle, he's been in town for a while. I'm sure he knows by now, especially if he and Madam Malvina are friends, which it seems they are since he's been going to her shop too."

"Wow, if it was him watching you, maybe he did follow you up?" Tassi looked over her shoulder and whispered to Spirit, "We can't see in the dark, but you can see and smell, so you keep watch while we dig, okay?"

Spirit whined his support.

After Shay hit bedrock with nothing but a pile of dirt as a reward, she tossed the trowel to the ground. "Well, if you're running into the same issues I am, it might take too long to dig all the way around the boulder."

"It's what I dreamed. Maybe it was just a dream and not a premonition." Tassi pouted and glared at the hole she'd made with equally unlucky results.

Shay attacked another spot with her trowel and, after a few minutes of digging, yelped in surprise. "It wasn't just a dream. Look what I found." Shay held up a dirt-covered shoe. She dug frantically beside where she'd unearthed it and grinned, holding up its mate. "Do you know what this means?"

"Someone buried Cora's shoes, and the police never found them?"

"It also means someone else was with Cora at the fairy ring. She was found barefoot, and the lack of dirt marks on her feet helped prove that. And here's the proof someone buried her shoes after she died, because there was no dirt or scratches on her feet, which there would have been if she'd made that same climb we just did. More importantly, the person who buried these could be the killer."

"It doesn't make sense, though," Tassi said, frustration clear by her tone. "Why wouldn't they have taken them? What's the symbolism of her appearing barefoot?"

Shay sat back on her haunches and studied the dirt-covered pair of Prada slide sandals. "Unless it's part of the ritual, the only reason I can think of is that there is something on these shoes that can help identify the killer."

"But there wasn't any blood on the body, was there?"

"No, but that's not to say there's no trace of saliva or maybe even fingerprints, or—"

Spirit let out a low growl, and his ears flattened against his head. He dropped into a low crouch, and Shay motioned for Tassi to do the same just as a branch snapped in the bushes on the other side of the fairy ring.

Chapter 21

A raccoon waddled out from the underbrush, caught sight of Shay, Tassi, and Spirit, and scurried back into the protection of the woods. Shay slammed her hand over her heart and inhaled. Tassi hissed a curse word and then slid Shay a side glance. "Sorry about that."

Shay waved away Tassi's apology, knowing that, while she hadn't verbalized one, curse words were swirling around in her head too.

Spirit whined and looked from one to the other, then at the brush where the raccoon had gone. He was clearly conflicted about whether or not he should run after the nighttime prowler or stay with Shay and Tassi.

Shay buried her fingers in the soft fur of his neck. "It's okay, boy."

Tassi slouched beside Shay, her face as pale and haggard-looking in the moonlight as Shay felt. Exhaustion seeped into her bones, and she wasn't sure she could make it back to the comfort of her cottage, but she had an obligation to keep Tassi safe. She hoisted herself to her feet and helped Tassi to hers. "Let's get you home."

Tassi followed Shay down the path, Spirit acting as guard from behind. "Why do I feel like we accomplished nothing?" said Tassi when they'd safely reached the bottom.

Despite finding the shoes, proving that someone had been on the hilltop with Cora, Shay nodded her head. They hadn't uncovered any answers. They had only exposed more questions. Questions that swarmed Shay's brain. Why would the potential killer bury the shoes instead of taking them with them to dispose of later? Most importantly, why leave evidence behind?

"There's so much that doesn't make sense," said Tassi, as they reached the bottom of the path and Tassi's bike.

"My thoughts exactly." Shay concentrated on the cottages when they came into view at the end of the treeline. A few lights twinkled, showing signs of life, but the majority of the cottages were shuttered in darkness.

"Shay?"

Shay smiled apologetically at Tassi. "Sorry. Lost in my own thoughts. Like I said, the only thing I can think of is, there is something on them that could connect the killer to the scene. It definitely is a reasonable answer to why the killer would leave evidence behind when he or she could have simply taken the shoes and then thrown them away later."

"Do you think they were removed before or after she was"—Tassi gulped, leaning her bike against her hip—"you know, dead?"

"Good question. If they were removed before she died, maybe Cora thought the burial of her shoes was part of the ceremony, an extra step to get her to commune with the fairies, which means she must have trusted whoever was up there with her, and I don't think she'd trust a stranger such as Doyle." The amulet warmed against Shay's chest at the mention of Doyle's name, and she hurried her steps down the path with Tassi until they reached Shay's cottage. "If you wait here, I'll grab my bike from the shed and make sure you get home safely."

Tassi waved her cell phone at Shay. "I'm good. It's not far, and I'll be careful."

"Are you sure, because I—"

"I'm good. Really. See you at the tea shop tomorrow; then we can talk more about our ideas, okay?" Tassi pushed off, and before Shay could tell Spirit to make sure Tassi got home safely, he bounded after her.

"Good dog," Shay whispered. Maybe Tassi could wait until tomorrow, but the warming of the amulet with the mere mention of Doyle's name had stirred an uneasiness that she knew wouldn't let her settle in for a much-needed night of sleep. A cup of sleep-inducing tea on the porch sounded like the perfect prescription to calm her erratic thoughts, and she made her way around to the front of her cottage and slowly climbed her front porch steps.

"Late night, me girl."

Shay yelped and stumbled back a step. Her pulse pounded in her ears, deafening her. Her hand flew to her racing heart, as she narrowed her eyes at the little old lady swaddled in a heavy gingham-print robe, her head haloed by pink curlers encasing snowy white hair.

"Gran, you have to quit scaring the daylights out of me."

Gran chuckled and motioned to the front door. "Mind letting me in? It's too cold out here for dese old bones."

Shay pulled her keys out of her pocket with shaking fingers, and once the door swung open, gestured for Gran to go through. "How long have you been waiting, and more to the point, why have you been waiting?" She glanced down at her phone, still in her hand from their walk back down the hill, and checked the time. "It's . . . it's almost two in the morning."

"I couldn't sleep."

Shay shook her head, filled a kettle with water, and dug her homemade sleepy-time blend from her tea supply.

"Did you try counting sheep?" Shay grinned over her shoulder but wavered. Gran's face, which had been obscured by the darkness of the porch, shone white, and the furrows etched with age looked deeper than normal.

Shay abandoned the teacups and sat next to Gran, taking her wrinkled hands in hers. "What is it?"

"I saw visions."

Shay shuddered. "What kind of visions?"

"I saw photographs. One with yer face. The other with the face of a balding man. And the fairy ring. I also sensed ye had used the blue bottle."

"I did." She swallowed. "Those were the visions I saw too. I . . . I couldn't sleep with those images dancing in my thoughts, and I thought that the bald man might be Doyle so I . . . ah . . ."—she shrank under Gran's gaze—"went up to the hilltop to see if he might be there." The last words came out in a rush to get the recapping of her foolish actions over as quickly as possible.

"Are ye saying ye went up to the fairy ring alone . . . in the middle of the night . . . to see if the man who wants ye dead was up there?" Gran eased her hands from Shay's grip and settled them in her lap. "Are ye daft, lass?"

"No." At Gran's lifted eyebrow, Shay sighed and dropped her gaze. "I wasn't alone," she said meekly. "Tassi was up there and—"

Gran snorted her disapproval.

"And Spirit went with me."

Gran shook her head, obviously unimpressed with Shay's companions. "And what would ye have done if Doyle had been up there? Ye and a waft of a girl and a dog? Albeit a special dog, but still he can be no match for a man with the powers Doyle is rumored to possess."

Shay opened her mouth and snapped it shut. "You're right, Gran. I am daft, but what else am I supposed to do. The blue bottle revealed only tantalizing strings to grasp hold of. I can't wait around for an elusive vision that may or may not come. Someone has killed for the blue bottle, and by now they must know it was fake." Shay's gut churned with unease. "Don't you see, Gran, I'm next. If I don't find them first, they'll find me."

The kettle screamed, and both women jumped.

Shay patted her erratically thumping chest, grabbed the kettle, eased out a calming breath, and poured the boiling water over the tea-leaf blend. "There," she said when her heart rate retuned to normal. "In about five minutes, we'll have a relaxing beverage that will hopefully bring both of us pleasant dreams and a restful sleep."

"Ye know, Liam and Conor visited me earlier this evening." From the twinkle in Gran's eyes, Shay suspected they hadn't held any information back.

"You know how they like to embellish a story, so you really shouldn't listen to everything they say, Gran."

Gran grinned mischievously. "I never do." She winked and tapped the side of her nose. "I listen to everything they say, and then I know the truth lies somewhere in the middle. That's my secret, ye know." Her eyes narrowed, and she waved her finger back and forth. "But I warn ye, lass, if dat Madam Malvina does have past connections with yer Brad and dat Angela that preceded ye comin' to Bray Harbor, there's malice that is truly evil. Perhaps even more so than Doyle's. Be careful, lass. Be very, very careful."

With Gran's warnings echoing in her ears and unease slinking up and down her spine, Shay poured the tea into cups, wishing she had something stronger to spike her sleepy-time blend.

Shay woke before her alarm, and while she had a dreamless sleep, she was still filled with the unease from yesterday. She pushed aside the unsettled churning in her belly as she readied herself for the day and then fed and watered Spirit. After checking that all entrance points to her cottage were locked, she hopped on her bike and peddled off toward Crystals & CuriosiTEAS.

The cool briny ocean breeze whipped at her cheeks, and by the time she parked in front of her tea shop, the sea winds had numbed her face. She pressed her hands to her cheeks to help stop the stinging and used her elbow to press down on the door handle, then her hip to push the door open. The cooler autumn morning had snuck up on her, and she put "dig out cooler-weather gear" on her ever-growing to-do list.

"Hey, Shay." Jen's grin slipped as she rounded the sales counter and was quicky replaced by a frown. "What's wrong?"

"Nothing." Shay smiled shakily. "Didn't sleep well is all."

Shay didn't dare mention her nighttime adventures to Jen. It had been bad enough to have received Gran's disapproval last night, but Jen had mother-henned her most of her life, and Shay knew she wouldn't be any different now. Shay was too emotionally exhausted to hear another sermon on safety and the dangers of an unsupervised evening outing. In Jen's eyes, like Gran's, Tassi and Spirit as her only companions with a murderer on the loose wouldn't have been enough. Jen would only point out that they would have added to the collateral damage of a killer. So there was definitely no need to get Tassi in trouble too. Gran was hard on her enough as it was.

"Well, I hope that, with our increased customers, you'll be too busy to be tired." Jen patted her shoulder and went back to busying herself with sorting tea products.

If only Shay's problem was simple fatigue. She could fight through that. She had done so before. The psychological fatigue was wearing her down, and the fear of something lurking just out of sight had her jaw aching from constantly clenching her teeth.

"Too busy to be tired, that sounds perfect." Shay stretched her taut jaw, forced a smile, and grabbed her apron. "But if you don't need me right now, I think I'll go and harvest some herbs. Just call me the moment you need me, okay?" Shay shifted under Jen's worried gaze and made her way to the back room to ascend the steps to the greenhouse.

A sliver of guilt worked its way through her. Jen had never been anything but kind to her, and after finding out they were not blood-related sisters, Jen still accepted Shay with open arms. Yet Shay repaid her by closing her off to the things that truly mattered in her life. Some sister she was. When this was all over, she'd make it up to Jen somehow.

Shay reached the top of the spiral staircase, closed her eyes, and breathed in the comforting aroma of freshly watered earth, mixed with the sweet scents of herbs and flowers. She settled herself on the bench by the potting table, closed her eyes, and attempted to clear her head. Instead of clarity, though, she couldn't see past the people and events of the past few days. Brad and Angela. Cora. Madam Malvina and Doyle. Poisons. Then there was Liam's face so close, then his lips on hers, only to be replaced by the stabbing in her chest when he confessed it was all in the name of duty.

She shook herself, inhaled deeply, and focused on the good in her life. Gran. Jen. Her niece, Maddie, her nephew Hunter. Her true friends Tassi and Spirit. Her tea shop. The amulet. Bridget.

With that, her chest warmed, and not only from the amulet hanging around her neck; her mind had cleared. For a moment, all she saw was a bright light that provided warmth instead of blinding her with its fiery intensity. She held her breath and waited. Waited for the voice of her biological mother. The woman who had given her life and second sight.

Like a warm caress, Bridget's voice flitted over her cheek and across her ear. *Not all that ends ill began with evil intentions.*

Shay opened her eyes and a sense of calm spread through her body. As if someone else was moving her legs, she meandered around the raised beds of assorted herbs and flowers and stopped in front of a plant she normally ignored and only kept because of the green foliage winding up its trellis, the pretty yellow, bell-shaped flowers when in bloom, and the purplish-red bracts surrounding black berries during its harvesting season. She eyed the wooden stake at the base of the plant: *Lonicera involucrata*, aka twinberry honeysuckle.

Shay wrinkled her nose. "Bridget, why would you lead me to this plant? I'm not even sure what it's used for." Confused, but driven by a renewed sense of purpose, Shay grabbed her plant almanac from the shelf on her potting table and thumbed through the pages until she came to the page dedicated to the twinberry honeysuckle.

Her fingers followed the words as she read out loud, "*Lonicera involucrata*, otherwise known as twinberry honeysuckle, is native to Alaska, the West coast, and Canada. Native Americans used various parts of the plant to treat a variety of ailments, including sore feet and legs, coughs, and itchy skin, and it was even used to prevent dandruff and to keep hair from going gray." Shay chuckled. "If that's true, I could make a fortune selling it." She shook her head, still laughing, and continued to trace her finger through the long paragraph, her lips moving silently. "What?" She reread the line again out loud. "At times, the plant is mistaken for *Atropa belladonna*, otherwise known as deadly nightshade." Shay's heart skipped a beat, and she sank onto the nearby bench. "What does this mean?" she whispered and listened carefully for her mother's voice.

Silence.

Shay sighed and began tracing her fingers under the words and reading out loud again in the hope that hearing the words as well as seeing them would trigger something other than confusion. "Although Indigenous peoples considered the berries poisonous and refrained from eating them, at times the fruit or leaves of the twinberry honeysuckle were used to purge the stomach for purification ceremonies or to induce vomiting from suspected poisoning . . ." Shay furrowed her brow at the irony and read on. "The plant is not used much or at all in modern homeopathic practices, and the USDA considers the plant mildly toxic and poisonous to both humans and cattle."

Shay closed the book, laid it in her lap, and folded her hands on the cover. There had to be a reason Bridget had guided her to a plant that looked like deadly nightshade, the plant proven to be what had killed Cora. Bridget's whispered advice from beyond created goose bumps on Shay's arms. Add to all that the slightly poisonous plant masquerading as a far deadlier one, one that did not kill Cora, and Shay got the impression that Bridget was telling her that not all was as it seemed. What any of that was, Shay had no clue. She would have to talk with Gran as soon as she could. If anyone knew what to do, it was the uncanny old woman.

"Shay?" Jen's voice called up the staircase. "Joanne's here."

Shay sniffed and swore she could detect the illicit smell of coffee. She used to revere that beverage as the elixir of the gods, but since opening the tea shop, she only dared to indulge in it during the mornings with her sister. It was one secret they did share with no guilt on either part. However, since they had missed their morning ritual, Jen's words made Shay nearly trip racing down the stairs to greet her friend and enjoy a much-need beverage from Joanne's coffee shop, Cuppa-Jo.

Chapter 22

"Joanne, it's so good to see you." Shay smiled and took the proffered to-go cup from her.

"I've caught glimpses of you coming and going, but I almost don't recognize you, it's been so long since you've been in to the café and we've chatted." Joanne grinned, settled in a chair, and patted the white tablecloth-covered table. "Have some time now?"

"Uh, sure." Shay checked the time on the wall clock and took a seat. "Yeah, sorry, I didn't mean to make you have to run after me to catch up. Jen's been picking up the coffee lately, and I was swamped with the carnival preparations. Then there's the matter of the dead body." She took a sip and locked her gaze on Jo's wide eyes. From the light clicking and clanking of teacups and saucers, Shay figured Jen was setting up for tea service. She really should be out front helping her sister, but from the drawn expression on Joanne's face, just catching up wasn't what was on her mind. "What's the matter?"

"You can tell, huh?"

"Yeah, we've known each other for years. I can tell when something's bothering you." Shay sipped her coffee and sighed. "Look," Shay reached over and touched her cool hand, "Jen told me you were really upset about Tassi being up on the ridge with me when we"—she drew in a breath—"found Cora's body, but I swear if I'd had an idea any of that was going to—"

"No." She waved her hand. "I was upset, of course. That's not something anyone wants a child to see, but after Tassi calmed me down and explained everything, I'm fine." She shook her head of cropped brown hair.

"Good." Shay patted Jo's hand. "Enough of that then. What's going on?"

Jo sighed. "It is about Tassi. I'm worried about her, and she's way closer to you than me, so I'm hoping you can give me some insight."

Shay clutched her to-go cup. "Why? What's happening?"

"That's the thing. I don't know. She went from being a successful college student dedicated to her studies to walking around as if she's in a daze. She seems preoccupied by something, and whenever I ask her about it, she spouts some weird slang from this new generation that I don't get, shrugs her shoulders, and finds an excuse—usually a terrible one—to leave the house. That's not like her. It's almost like she's reverting to her old sassy teenage self." Jo shuddered. "And no one wants that again. Which makes me think it's Orion's influence on her. My son, Caden, says that Orion's always been an odd one. I mean, really, look at the life he lives with that scary mother he has." Jo looked pleadingly at Shay. "I just figured, since you and she are so close, that you might know what's up with Tassi."

"Ooh, well . . ." Shay shifted on her chair as she struggled to find the words that would alleviate Jo's fears. "First, Madam Malvina isn't as scary as she appears."

"She's not?"

"No, it's an act. You know, to give off the aura of magic and mystery. That's how she makes her living." Shay hoped Joanne bought the nonchalant lilt with which she tried to color her words. If only Shay could tell her the truth. Even though she trusted Joanne, the Cora situation was too perilously balanced. One misspoken word, even innocently said, could bring her sleuthing to a screeching halt, not to mention put a target on her and Tassi's backs. It was bad enough the mayor knew about their plans and the book of poisons. The less people who knew, the better.

With that mantra going through her head, Shay forced a smile she didn't feel. "I really haven't noticed anything. Do you think it could be boy problems? Maybe she and Orion are going through a rough patch." Tassi had been sending the boy puppy-dog eyes during the Halloween carnival. Maybe that had more to do with heartbreak than longing. Shay hadn't asked. Her life had been too busy spiraling out of control for her to take notice or interest in her young friend's problems. Just another thing for her to do some type of penance for.

"That's that last thing I need in my life. College romance drama." A gleam of hope flickered in Joanne's eyes. "Do you think that's it, though? You don't think she's failing classes or getting sick or—"

Shay laid her hand over Jo's trembling one. "I think Tassi's probably going through things the typical eighteen-year-old does. Whatever she's dealing with will pass. If you'd like me to speak to her, I can." Her chest tightened at her evasion of the truth. While she wasn't outright lying to her friend, she was certainly not being truthful, and her gut churned at the idea.

"Would you?" Joanne grinned. "Thank you. She'll probably listen to you more anyway. I'm just the boring old aunt who likes to nag. You, on the other hand, are hip and cool, according to Tassi, and someone whom she respects very much."

A warmth spread throughout Shay's body. "That's nice to know, although don't tell Tassi that the only way I'm hip"—she hooked air quotes—"is in reference to hip pain from just sleeping wrong."

"Tell me about it. I best be going. Thanks for the chat."

Shay walked Joanne to the door, and after she left, Shay turned the CLOSED sign to OPEN, letting in the handful of people waiting outside the door. A few of the regulars who had come back to Shay after her success at the carnival smiled at her, the go-to cup still clutched in her hands.

One lady, who was so short Shay wondered if she had surpassed five feet before shrinking with age, pointed at the cup, and winked. "Your secret is safe with me, dearie. But I warn you, that stuff will stunt your growth. Just look at me."

Shay laughed. "Your advice is solid, Mrs. Bird. But some bad habits are hard to break."

The next few hours flew by. Customers continued flowing in, and for a blissful moment, Shay was able to forget her troubles, forget that someone had killed Cora, forget that Brad and Angela had remerged like some nightmare back into her life, forget that Liam probably would never feel toward her what she felt toward him.

With the after-tea-service lull and her tea shop relatively empty—except for a few regulars who she knew would sit and chat for another hour or so—those buried problems began to unearth themselves. Shay left the tea shop in the capable hands of her sister and went in search of Gran next door.

The bartender at Madigan's Pub took one look at her and jerked his head in the direction of the office upstairs. When Shay reached the top, before entering the office, she bent over and rested her hands on her knees, wondering how in the world Gran did these steps several times every day. Once was enough to leave Shay feeling breathless and in need of a more strenuous exercise regimen beyond riding her bike.

"Once yer done huffing and puffing outside me door, ye can come in." Gran's voice sifted through the half-closed office door, a hint of amusement putting an extra lilt in her voice.

Shay shook her head and grinned guiltily, and was thankful, for once, that the wily Irish born and raised woman had never been her mother. She couldn't have gotten away with half the things she did in her teen years with Gran around. Shay inhaled deeply to get her heart rate under control, evened her breathing, and stepped into the office. The afternoon sunrays spilling in the windows created a halo effect around Gran's head, giving the impression she was crowned with light. Gone was the wan and pale complexion that had alarmed Shay earlier that morning. Gran's skin nearly glowed with pink health.

Shay grinned and made a circling motion at Gran's head. "You look like a grand fairy crowned with clouds."

"Pfft." Gran waved Shay's words away and gestured to the chair on the opposite side of the walnut desk. "Have a seat, lass."

Shay sat in silence for a moment, unsure of what exactly she'd come for. She needed so much from the wise woman across from her that all her problems muddled into one messy mass. "Do you know anything about the twinberry honeysuckle?"

Gran's eyebrows rose, and she steepled her fingers under her chin. "Aye."

"Well, what's it used for? I read up on it, and it doesn't seem to have a purpose beyond traditional Native medicine, and I'm not even sure it's used that way anymore."

"The plant's usefulness depends on who ye talk to. Some say it's toxic, while others claim there's medicinal or even edible value in it. Why'd ye ask?"

"I found it—well, Bridget led me to it this morning—in

the greenhouse. I always knew I had it, but as I don't use it in any of my tea blends, I forgot about it."

"Bridget's spirit led ye, then?"

"Yeah, after her voice told me that something that ends badly didn't necessarily start with bad intentions." Shay leaned forward and placed her elbows on the desk. "What does all that have to do with a rather innocent plant that looks like a killer one? Do you think it all has something to do with Brad and Angela? Perhaps their intention in moving to Bray Harbor has nothing to do with me. Maybe what I see as a bad situation and evil intentions on their part began in their innocent decision to buy a winery in the area. Brad did say they weren't staying permanently in the cottages and that they were only there while remodeling was being done on the winery house."

"'Tis is a possibility."

"But . . ."

"What does yer gut tell ye, lass?"

"That's the problem. I don't know anymore."

Gran smiled encouragingly. "Don't fret, lass, and don't overthink. Ye know what happens when ye do." She patted Shay's arm. "The honeysuckle and message from Bridget could mean many things and apply to many situations." A gleam twinkled from Gran's eyes. "Maybe the message is the misunderstanding between ye and Liam. Could be she's telling you that Liam is not as bad as you think he is, and that his bad-boy behavior, as the young'uns say nowadays, has no real bad intent?"

"I think, Gran, that you need to come to terms with the idea that the fairies might be wrong about this one." Shay forced a nonchalant tone to her voice, but Gran's snort signaled the old woman had seen through the façade. Sighing, Shay crossed her arms and slouched back in her chair. "Have you ever been wrong, Gran?"

"Aye, many times—"

"See, then you might be—"

Gran held up a gnarled finger. "But I've never been wrong about the fairies"—she tapped the side of her nose—"or love."

"I give up. Let's agree to disagree, shall we?" At Gran's harrumph, Shay shrugged. "Right now, I don't have time to figure out the cryptic message from Bridget. I need to get back on track with Cora's murder and the reason for the buried shoes."

"Have ye figured out how to get a handwriting sample from Madam Malvina?"

"No, but you're right. I was getting too lost in my thoughts, in the nuance of everything. I need to get back to facts, and the handwriting in the book of poisons is vital to figuring all of this out." She pointed to a pencil and a pad of paper sitting in front of Gran. "Can I borrow that?"

Gran pushed it across to her.

"Thanks. My mind's been such a jumble with Brad's sudden appearance. A list will help me keep my thoughts straight, right?" She looked hopefully at Gran.

"It can't hurt, lass."

"Okay, of course, most of this is a guess, but . . ." Shay wrote *Cora—dead on hilltop—obvious ceremony—no tracks—killer covered up footprints, stole blue bottle, buried shoes. Poisoned with belladonna—*

There was a fact niggling at the back of her mind. A fact Dean had told her. Something about the poison. She rubbed her temples. *Think, Shay, think. Ah-ha! According to the coroner's report, the poison had been building up in her system over time. The final dose took her over the edge, apparently, and was the fatal blow. So either the killer didn't know she'd been preparing for a Samhain night ceremony to connect with the fairy world and gave her a dose he or she guessed wouldn't kill her, or the killer knew, because he or she had been slowly poisoning her and hoped the final dose given would be fatal, and it would look like a conjuring gone wrong and not a murder.* She scribbled on the notepad and then reread her words.

"Don't forget her readings with ye and me, and that when she didn't get the answers she was seeking, she sought out Madam Malvina."

Shay created a heading titled *Madam Malvina* and wrote *readings—book of poisons?—connection to blue bottle?—connection to Brad and Angela?* Shay was about to note Liam's questionable connection with Madam Malvina, but under Gran's watchful gaze, she stored that question away in her mind to deal with later. "I have more questions than answers about Madam Malvina's connection to the case. But everything always circles back to her, doesn't it?"

Gran took the pencil from her hand, folded the paper, and placed it in Shay's hand. "Then ye better start figurin' out who that handwriting belongs to."

"We're pretty sure it's hers, aren't we? At least, that's what Tassi said as soon as she saw it."

"Then get the proof and give it to the Gardaí."

"You mean the police?"

"Yes, lass, and do it soon. Ye can't keep putting ye and Tassi in the Madam's and Doyle's line of sight, and I fear that's all ye've been doing with asking yer questions."

Shay sat back, her heart pounding in her ears with the forcefulness of Gran's tone. Then her stomach twisted when she recalled she still hadn't given Dean the shoes they found. "I gotta go!" She jumped up and fled down the stairs.

Chapter 23

"If you tap your toes any longer, you'll wear a hole right through the floor." Jen wiped off a recently vacated table and centered the crystal vase containing freshly cut flowers from Shay's greenhouse.

Shay winced with her sister's reprimand, stopped her toe tapping, and massaged the back of her neck. Today had been one of the tea shop's best since Madam Malvina's theft of Shay's customers, and despite her aching feet, Shay knew she should feel happier. But that recent, all-too-familiar sense of dread diminished any sense of joy.

After her conversation with Gran, Shay had dashed off to the police station to give the shoes to Dean, with the hope that he also might fill her in on any leads they were following. As luck would have it, he was out on a call. Knowing she was already withholding evidence about the poison book, she relented and left the shoes with the deputy on the desk, who took one look at the backpack she had stored the shoes in and insisted she leave that too. He explained, with a touch of rebuke to his voice, that since she had contaminated them by not only touching them but using the wrong storage method, any potential evidence they found on the shoes would have to be checked against the interior of the pack, to help them determine the source and check them against her DNA or other interfering material. She had blushed and apologized and left feeling rather amateurish because she knew better. This wasn't her first case.

Through the entire afternoon tea service, Shay had waited for Dean to come through the door to ask about the shoes and worried about how to get Madam Malvina's handwriting, and in both matters, she had come up with nothing. Nothing good anyway.

Jen dropped the rag in a pail of water and walked over to Shay, wrapping her arm around Shay's shoulder. "You look exhausted. Why don't you go home after Tassi gets here?"

Shay glanced at the clock on the wall behind the sales counter. 3:55. Tassi should be walking through the door soon, but then Shay would need to make up an excuse to get her alone so they could discuss plans.

The front door opened, and Mayor Sutton walked in, his face etched with new wrinkles. His bloodshot eyes were rimmed with purple smudges; clearly, he hadn't slept in days.

"Mayor, come on in and have a seat. Can I get you something? I have a blend that would be perfect for you. On the house."

He waved away Shay's offer of a seat or tea. "I can't stay." He pinned her with a hopeful gaze. "Have you—" His gaze flicked to Jen. "Can I speak with you outside for a moment, Shay?"

Shay smiled apologetically at Jen and shrugged as if she had no clue why the mayor wanted to speak with her alone and followed him out the door.

He gazed kitty-corner across the street at the refurbished, brick façade of a new business promising the perfect spa day. The elderly couple who had previously run a mom-and-pop souvenir shop had recently retired and moved to Arizona. Shay had not known the couple all that well and had yet to meet the young businesswoman who'd purchased the building next door to Cuppa-Jo.

Mayor Sutton jerked his chin at the Rejuvenation Spa and Wine Bar. "Cora would have been a regular, I believe."

Shay nodded. Anything that screamed wealth or at least the pretension of it attracted Cora like flies to honey. "I'm sure she would have enjoyed the pampering, and I'm sure she'd deserve every bit of it." While Shay hadn't quite liked the woman, Mayor Sutton had never done her wrong, and if she could offer a kind word about his deceased wife, she would.

"Yes, I'm sure you're right. Have you . . . ah . . . gotten any further with the book?" His voice dropped on the last word as a group of shoppers passed them.

"No, not yet." She held up a hand when the mayor's face filled with disappointment. "But I promise I will get to the bottom of it. It's just that things have to be done correctly so we can take hard evidence to the police and she can be arrested on the spot. Otherwise, this will all explode in our faces. Please trust me. I'll let you know as soon as I do, okay?" She glanced through the window into her shop and noticed Jen studiously gazing at them. "I think it's best that you don't come by the tea shop just to talk with me. People might start getting suspicious. If you need me or something urgent comes up, text me." Shay checked that he had her number and watched him walk away, his head hung low and his feet shuffling along the herringbone-brick sidewalk.

Shay pushed the front door open and met Jen's questioning gaze.

"You and the mayor seemed chatty."

An unwelcome heat spread over Shay's cheeks. Quick, Shay, quick, think of something! "He's making the rounds of the surrounding businesses, asking if any would be willing to donate products or services for the upcoming charity Christmas bazaar." Shay's insides recoiled at the lie. She needed to come clean with Jen, but the pile of lies she'd already told her might as well be Mount Everest by now, and there was no way Jen was going to understand, let alone forgive her, for leaving her in the dark.

"And I couldn't be part of the conversation?"

This is why you don't lie, Shay. She opened her mouth to try to give a reasonable explanation when the front door slammed open, sending the bells jingling.

Liam loomed over Shay, and his face was tight with anger. "Gran and I had a little chat just a bit ago, *a chara*, and I'd like to have a wee bit of your time, if you please."

He didn't seem pleased at all. Gran must have told him about her silly nighttime adventure.

"Good afternoon, Liam," Shay said brightly. While she didn't necessarily enjoy his hulking presence and the sermon she knew he had in store for her, his arrival had saved her from digging herself deeper into a hole with Jen.

She glanced sheepishly at Jen, who added a crossed set of arms to her still-raised, mother-scolding eyebrows. Shay was tempted to tell her that if she kept her face like that, it would freeze that way, but from her sister's added toe tapping, Shay figured she'd better leave well enough alone.

"Do you mind if Liam borrows me for a bit? I promise not to be long." She walked through the shop toward the back room. Needing more privacy for the sermon that was sure to come, she headed up the greenhouse steps. "Oh," she called out, "please send Tassi up when she arrives. I promised her I'd show her another step in harvesting the herbs we use in our tea blends." That, at least, wasn't a lie. She had promised Tassi to do exactly that.

"Yes, ma'am!"

Shay internally cringed. Jen's voice held such a note of sarcasm that Shay could almost see her sister salute those words.

Liam slid her a glance, but Shay ignored him, headed up the staircase, and settled on the bench. "If you've come to preach at me, I advise you to hold your breath. I've already been scolded by Gran and Tassi, and even Spirit looks at me as if I were—in the words of Gran—daft."

Liam cocked his head. "I have no clue what yer talking about."

"But you're vibrating with anger. I figured you were mad about my nighttime . . ." She snapped her mouth shut. No sense in letting him in on her little secret. But it was too late. She could almost see his cop sense quiver to life.

"Your nighttime what?" He sat next to her and turned to face her.

"Never mind. If it was your business, I'd tell you. But I don't possibly see how it is." She folded her hands in her lap and tried to look as innocent as possible. "Now, tell me what has you so upset?"

"Conor. Do ye think it's possible to disown a cousin?"

Shay choked on a laugh. "Sorry, didn't mean to laugh. What has he done now that has you wanting to disown him?"

"He's . . . he's . . ." Liam jumped to his feet and paced. "He's crowing about town that he and you shared a kiss."

Shay's face burned hot, and she placed the back of her hands against her cheeks. Good grief. Just when she thought things couldn't get worse. Perhaps Bridget had installed a secret hole in the floor that would, upon request, open up and suck Shay into its depths.

"I'm sorry, but what?" Shay croaked out.

"He 'claims' it's for the benefit of Madam Malvina, that it will bolster the fact that it was you and him kissing instead of me and"—his gaze warmed as he studied her face—"you. I told him no one in town would believe you'd kissed him, what with that ugly mug of his."

Shay bit back a grin. "You and he look exactly the same."

Liam waved away her words. "What do we do with this new set of events my idiotic cousin has created? What will the town think?"

"Let them think what they will. Them thinking I'm going around kissing one of the Madigan cousins is far better than when they all thought I was practicing witchcraft." Shay shuddered at the memory of those horrible weeks. No, people thinking she was kissing an attractive man was far better than those awful rumors from last year, rumors spread by Tassi's father.

Speaking of Tassi, Shay checked her phone. It was ten past four. Where was that girl? Worry tugged at the back of her mind, but she ignored it. Tassi had often reminded her that she could take care of herself. A class must have gone late.

"So," Liam's voice broke into her thoughts, "what do you want to do about the Conor problem?"

"I think we let it do its thing. It'll be the talk of the town for a day or two, and then people will move on with their lives. Besides, he might be right." Shay chuckled at Liam's grunt of derision. "With that rumor going around, Madam Malvina will no doubt believe you when you tell her it wasn't you and I kissing under her awning. Your cover is not blown."

Liam sighed and sat back down beside her. "You're right."

Shay nudged his shoulder with hers. "Can I have that in writing?"

Liam grinned. "No." He leaned back against the raised bed at their backs. "What's next with Madam Malvina?"

"We still need to get a sample of her handwriting, and I was hoping to talk with Tassi this afternoon about ways to get it."

Light footsteps echoed up the staircase. "Shay," Tassi said as she ascended the last step, "I'm so sorry I'm late. The professor got rather long-winded toward the end of class, and Orion wanted me to wait for him. He walked me to work." A blush stained her cheeks. She smiled at Liam. "Oh, hi. Didn't know you were up here." She dropped her backpack on the floor with a thud and reached for a pair of gardening gloves from the potting table. "Jen said you had a harvesting lesson for me?"

The amulet warmed against her skin. Shay jerked. It had rarely acted as her conscience before, but she was glad it had gotten her attention, whether that was its intention or not. "Yes"—definite change of afternoon plans needed—"it'll be a mini-lesson, but something to get us started." Shay paused and glanced at Liam, who gave her a supportive smile. "I was hoping you had come up with a way to get Madam Malvina's handwriting."

Tassi lit up. "I was actually thinking about that during class and not what Professor 'Yada-Yada' was yammering on about."

Liam snorted and grinned. "All my teachers during school sounded the same too, lass."

Tassi shrugged. "Not sure how I'll perform on the test tomorrow." She pinned Shay with a gaze. "Please, don't tell Aunt Jo. I know she's already worried sick about me. Probably thinks I'm about to flunk out. I certainly can't tell her the real reason, can I? If she knew I was on the hunt for a killer, she'd lock me in the house."

Shay grimaced. If only Tassi had known she was the subject of such a conversation hours earlier. "It's a good thing that you have an aunt who cares about you." Shay gathered her own set of gardening gloves and handed Tassi a pair of garden shears and placed a set in her leather apron pocket. "Now, what was your idea?"

"Well, Orion's birthday is coming up, and I thought I could ask if she wanted to go in on a gift for him. That way she could sign the card and wouldn't be suspicious about it."

"That's brilliant, Tassi." Shay's smiled slipped. "Wait. When is his birthday?"

"Next week."

"We really need that sample sooner."

Tassi pulled a flyer from her backpack and handed it to Shay. "No problem there. I want to take him to the Grungefest concert this weekend. It's got all the awesome cover bands of the grunge movement from the nineties. It'll be his early birthday gift."

Shay shared the flyer with Liam, and from the nostalgic look on his face, Shay figured he'd been a grunge-rock listening teenager. "Today's Thursday, right?"

Tassi nodded. "Last time I checked."

"When do you plan on giving him the card and tickets?" Shay asked.

"Tomorrow. Is that soon enough?"

"That works." Shay nearly did a celebratory dance. "Now, Liam, if you don't mind leaving, I have horticultural secrets only Tassi can hear." She shooed him away, and after he left, Shay began showing Tassi more about the art of harvesting herbs.

Chapter 24

Twenty-four hours had never gone by more slowly. Business activity had diminished to a crawl; Bray Harbor residents looking for weekend entertainment this time of year generally left in search of excitement elsewhere. As for the influx of tourists with Bray Harbor as their destination, the annual Thanksgiving and Christmas festivities were still nearly a month away. Even Jen had taken the day off for one of Maddie's dance recitals, so Shay had only her own nerves to occupy her mind.

Shay had lost count of how many times she'd wiped down already cleaned tables or rearranged the shelves or popped quickly upstairs to double-check her perfectly pruned and healthy greenhouse plants. Now the only thing left to do was watch the over-the-counter clock's second hand tick each annoying moment away.

At four o'clock, like clockwork, Tassi ran through the door. The sudden movement didn't allow the overhead doorbells to tinkle merrily but sent out one solid, off-tune clattering chord. "Got it." She waved the card and slapped it on the sales counter.

"How'd you manage to get the card. Didn't you give it to Orion?"

"I did." Tassi grinned. "But I convinced him he'd just

lose it and the tickets before the big event tomorrow and that I should take it for safekeeping."

"You are a genius." Shay squeezed Tassi's shoulder and then scanned the birthday card in her hand. She smiled when she read the cheesy birthday message on the front and then flipped the card open and laughed at the punch line. "I take it you picked out the card?"

"Of course. I'm not even sure Madam Malvina knows what a fuzzy navel is. I mean, fun could clamber all over her face, and she'd probably swat it away."

"How do you know what a fuzzy navel is?"

"Really? I am in college, remember?"

"You're right." Shay sighed and thought of her own rebellious-youth stage. "Does Orion know a fuzzy navel is an alcoholic drink?"

Tassi shook her head as if she was truly disappointed in her boyfriend's lack of knowledge concerning mixed drinks. "No. He thought it actually was a card about belly button lint. I really do worry about that boy sometimes, but with a mother like Madam Malvina . . ." Tassi shrugged. "Anyway, do you think the sample is large enough to be an accurate representation of her handwriting?"

Shay studied the scribbled note Madam Malvina wrote to Orion. Nothing overly sentimental, which didn't surprise Shay in the least. "I think we have enough. Now I have to call in a favor."

Tassi eyed the empty tea shop. "Need me to hang around?"

Shay chuckled. "I'll need you for a bit, just in case anyone does show up while I go find Liam, okay?"

"Sure thing." Tassi settled herself at the nearest table, pulled her phone from her pocket, and started scrolling social media.

"Don't rot your brain with that stuff," Shay warned as she carefully placed the birthday card in her purse, recalling her lecture on contamination of evidence, and slung her bag over her shoulder.

"Yes, Mom."

Shay shook her head and left the tea shop, glad that Tassi, while a great kid, was not her responsibility. Shay wasn't sure she could survive a teenage daughter.

A moment later, Shay pushed through the front door of Madigan's Pub. Liam was behind the bar, and when he saw her, his face lit up in a grin. Shay told her rapidly firing heart palpitations to settle down as she reciprocated with an awkward smile and gave him a finger wave.

Liam gestured with his head to meet him upstairs, and as she climbed the wide staircase, she reminded her heart and her head that Liam thought of her as a friend, at best, and to not get her hopes up for anything other than that. The kiss they had shared was work for him. He'd used it as a means to help him procure a confession from a suspected killer, that's all.

The office was empty and, after she took a seat, she began drumming her fingers on her lap. Time ticked by slowly, and just as she was about to go find Liam, he walked through the door and sat in the chair behind the large walnut desk.

"What brings you here, *a chara*?"

Shay placed the birthday card on the desk. "I need to call in a favor. I'm sure you know someone from your police days who can help us identify the handwriting and compare it to"—she pulled the book of poisons from her purse and opened up to the first page with handwritten notes—"the writing in this book."

Liam's eyes narrowed as he studied the pieces of handwriting side by side. "To my untrained eye, they look remarkably similar." Liam pulled his phone from his back pocket and took pictures of the handwriting.

"That's what I thought, but before I go to Dean with this, I want definitive proof that she is behind all this."

Liam leaned back in the chair and studied her. "What's yer next move? Yer not thinking about confronting Madam Malvina, are ye?"

"No, no!" At his incredulous look, she sighed. "Yes, I was considering it." She scowled. "Don't look at me that way. I'm serious. Besides, I'd be interested to see how she reacts when confronted with the book. Maybe she'll give herself away without us even trying."

"She's got a better poker face than ye give her credit for. Look how she hoodwinked ye into thinking you two were friends."

Shay shifted in her chair. "Your point is true but painful. She broke fairly well, though, when I confronted her at the carnival. At the mention of the police, she confessed knowing about the blue bottle and to giving Cora a spell to follow."

"I don't suppose I can convince ye to not confront Madam Malvina?"

"You suppose right." Shay stashed the book and the birthday card back in her purse. "I won't do it in a lonely, secluded spot, though, if that's what you're worried about."

Liam shook his head. "This case just doesn't sit right in my gut. There's something I can't place my finger on, and it has me on edge." He came around the desk and enfolded her hand in his. "I can't stop you from speaking to Madam Malvina, but please promise to not do something stupid."

"When's the last time I did that?"

Liam's left eyebrow nearly touched his hairline. "I can pull up my list at a moment's notice."

Shay pulled from his grasp. "You . . . you . . ."

Liam smiled lazily. "Yes? I'm waiting for all my positive attributes that are so many ye are clearly having trouble listing them all."

Shay growled and left the room, her ears ringing with Liam's laughter. Men. Who needed them anyway?

After checking in on Tassi and making the executive decision to close an hour earlier than normal, Shay warned Tassi to be careful and not do anything she'd regret at the upcoming music festival, which earned her an exaggerated sigh and eye roll.

Shay locked up and walked her bike down to the boardwalk to the café. After ordering a ham-and-cheese melt with a side of fries, she scooted into a window booth and watched the passersby. She rummaged around in her purse for paper and pen and, as she waited for her food, jotted down notes. When she was done, she glared at the number of questions, which far outnumbered the facts.

Why did the killer do everything to cover his/her tracks, including literally erasing all footsteps, even Cora's, but then bury the shoes?

There were no signs of a struggle, so did Cora understand the enormity of her undertaking and was she so set on communicating with the fairies that she was willing to flirt with death, or did Cora think the ceremony was purely theatrical and see no danger in the performance or ritual?

If the poison book and handwriting is Madam Malvina's, which could point to her as the killer, what was the motive? What did she have on Cora or over Cora that Cora had to die? Did she kill on the orders of Doyle?

If Madam Malvina isn't the killer, was she simply a patsy for Doyle, the person whom all the evidence points to? What did Doyle have on her that she'd be willing to take the fall for murder?

And what in the world do the twinberry honeysuckle and Bridget's cryptic message mean?

Shay stared at her written questions and rubbed her

throbbing temples. A flash of white outside the window grabbed her attention. She smiled at Spirit, sitting on his haunches, facing the window, his tongue loping in and out of his mouth. Shay waved at him, and he yipped in response. When she turned back to her list, Spirit barked louder, and when she looked back at him, he cocked his head as if wondering what was taking her so long.

She chuckled and shook her head. "I'm coming," she mouthed out the glass window.

After shoving her note in her purse, she asked for her order to be changed to "to go" and exited the café with a paper bag stuffed with a piping-hot sandwich and fries.

Her stomach rumbled, and she contemplated making Spirit learn some patience, but after he all but walked her to her bike and used his nose to push her leg toward the pedal, she sighed and stashed the bag in the bike's basket.

She frowned at the white German shepherd. "You'll owe me another sandwich if I can't eat it while it's hot."

Spirit yipped and trotted off down the sidewalk in the direction of Madam Malvina's shop. Shay followed him and came to a halt a few businesses down from the tea shop. Shielded by a large inflatable tube man flailing and gyrating in celebration of a BOGO fudge sale, Shay sat on a bench with her back to the harbor. Spirit sat at her feet, blocking her from standing, much less walking.

"Okay, Spirit, okay. I get it. I'll sit and wait and watch." Shay dug out her sandwich, took a bite, and closed her eyes in culinary appreciation.

Spirit whined.

Shay peeked open one eye and laughed at the large, age-indeterminate dog giving her puppy-dog eyes. "You are much to old for these shenanigans, I think."

Doggie drool leaked from the corners of his mouth, and his tail thumped the sidewalk.

Shay sighed and pinched off a bit of ham and tossed it

in the air. Spirit caught it and lay down at her feet. "There, good boy. Now the rest is mine."

Minutes went by, and there was no movement into or out of Madam Malvina's shop. Shay polished off the rest of her sandwich and was on the last of the fries when the door opened and Angela and Brad exited the shop. They looked angry, and when Brad leaned down to whisper in Angela's ear, she jerked away and speed-walked to escape him.

"Interesting," Shay whispered to Spirit, who had come to attention and sat, ears perked, watching the couple intently.

When Spirit moved out of Shay's way, she took that as a sign to follow Brad and Angela. Keeping a distance between them, Shay walked her bike along the boardwalk, Spirit flanking her. With the colder temperatures coming off the ocean, most of the businesses that would ordinarily be clogging up the boardwalk were closed, leaving the normally busy space eerily empty. Shay shivered and created more distance between her and the couple. With no place to hide or duck behind, she was a sitting duck if they happened to turn around.

But as they were walking toward the cottages, she could always make the excuse that she was headed home. Practicing her speech if she did get caught, she nearly missed them as they turned off down one of the side streets leading back into the heart of Bray Harbor. If it hadn't been for Spirit, who guided her off the boardwalk, she'd have lost them.

Slivers of unease prickled at the back of her neck, and she glanced over her shoulder. This part of Bray Harbor, while not inhospitable, was home to shops with a reputation for either selling extremely cheap touristy items at astronomical prices or selling questionably legal items for cheap. Most locals avoided them, but the owners of these shops were able to make up the loss with unsuspecting tourists who had little knowledge or common sense and a lot of money.

Spirit paused in the shadow of an alley opening, and Shay took that as a sign to follow. After parking her bike in the alley, she peeked around the corner in time to see Brad and Angela go into the less-than-reputable homeopathic boutique Nature's Offerings, which promoted health and wellness. Shay snorted. If she could believe the rumors about town, the health and wellness the owners promoted was often chemically induced; they only used the welcoming storefront and legitimate tinctures, lotions, and potions to keep the Health Department and city council from asking too many questions.

"Now, what are those two up to?" Shay glanced down at Spirit, who cocked his head and whined.

Chapter 25

Shay crept along the opposite sidewalk and kept her gaze fixed on the front door of Nature's Offerings. She was thankful that twilight had fully descended, and she took advantage of the added cover the waning daylight offered. However, if Brad and Angela walked out of the store and so much as glanced across the street, she'd have a hard time escaping their notice.

Spirit nudged her hip with his nose, and she bumped into the brick wall of the store she was walking next to.

"What's gotten into you, boy?"

Spirit nudged her again, and when she moved to walk around him, he sat in front of her.

"For goodness' sake." Shay looked about to see if anyone noticed the hulking white dog herding her as if she were a sheep. She looked into the large storefront window of the building Spirit pushed her against and grinned and patted Spirit's head. "Well, done, boy. Stay here. I'll be right back."

She pushed the door open and smiled. Much like her own shop, bells tinkled out her arrival. She scanned the small storefront filled with hats of all sorts. Racks and shelves marked SHAWLS and CAPES and PONCHOS took up an entire corner. In another corner was leftover summer tourist paraphernalia, meant to tantalize all who entered with flashy overhead CLEARANCE SALE signage. Red tags dangled off most of the merchandise, with some racks marked down seventy percent.

As tempting as it was, Shay had run out of storage room and struggled to shove what little she did have in the sparse space her cottage offered, but any diehard autumn tourist not afraid to risk what locals thought to be days too cold for the beach would discover a gold mine at these prices. She paused and glanced at the tag on a cute two-piece swimsuit. She would have to tell Jen and Maddie about this store for next summer. She dropped the swim-suit tag and moved away from the temptation.

"Good evening."

Shay turned and smiled at the young lady behind the sales counter. Except for having the current trend of the split left eyebrow, she reminded Shay of Tassi, minus her charcoal liner. "Hello."

"My name's Brooke. Can I help you find anything? We have a sale on beach supplies, if you're interested in stock-ing up for next summer." Brooke gestured to the summer-sale corner.

"Yes, I was just checking it out, but I'm looking for a wide-brimmed hat and a shawl today." She needed some-thing to shield her bright red hair from Brad and Angela, and with the setting sun, the temperature had dipped fur-ther than she had anticipated.

"Of course. As you can see, our hats are spread out around the store, but the shawls are all in the corner by the front window. We got a special shipment just the other day from our supplier in Ireland." Brooke led Shay over to the display and handed Shay a dark green wool shawl. "The company's based in County Kildare, and all their garments are knitted from pure merino wool. This color looks magnificent with your red hair and makes your dark-brown topaz eyes sparkle absolutely golden."

"You're some saleswoman, aren't you?" Shay chuckled when she found herself reaching for her wallet. She gulped at the price tag. "Perhaps another time." And another pay-check. Shay's accounts were still reeling from months of little business. "Do you have anything a little less expen-sive?" Shay felt her cheeks warm and appreciated that Brooke didn't make her feel awkward about asking for something less costly.

"Sure thing. We still have high-quality shawls for some-thing a little easier on the wallet." She directed her atten-tion to another rack and walked away, leaving Shay to contemplate. She snuck a glance out the window and across to Nature's Offerings and caught sight of Brad and Angela still wandering the store. Not wanting to waste an oppor-tunity, Shay grabbed the cheapest garment, a blue-and-green-checkered wool shawl, and a dark-brown, wide-brimmed hat, paid for them, thanked Brooke for her help, and promised to be back to take a closer look at the expensive wool products.

After tucking her hair up under the hat, Shay stepped out of the shop and wrapped herself tightly in the shawl. It was enough to keep her warm and, with the help of the hat, should shield her from the notice of Brad and Angela. She walked farther down the sidewalk and settled on a bench.

"Look, Spirit, we have a bird's-eye view of our quarry."

Spirit rested his chin on her lap and looked up at her.

"I knew you'd like the hat." She chuckled and scratched his ear.

Nature's Offerings' door opened, and out stepped Brad and Angela, a brown paper bag swinging from Angela's fin-gers. Shay zeroed in on the package as the couple started walking away from Shay, back toward the boardwalk. Shay sighed in relief. She hadn't needed to buy the hat and shawl, after all.

She glanced back and saw Brooke folding up the sidewalk sandwich-board sign. If she hadn't gone into her store, though, she never would have discovered the best place in town to buy authentic Irish woolen garments, not to mention the summer sale of the century. There were no accidents in life, her adoptive mother would always say. Everything happened for a reason, and stumbling into Brooke's shop must have been one too. Perhaps she should give the girl her card and offer to do a free reading.

With Brad and Angela heading off in the opposite direction, her disguise wasn't needed, but just as she stood to go back in before Brooke locked up for the night, Angela turned her head to say something to Brad and broke out into a wide-mouthed grin.

"Brad, darling, look back over there at that beautiful dog." Angela's voice sailed across the street and pierced Shay's ears.

Oh no! *This can't be happening.* Shay sat back down. What was the use of buying the hat and shawl when her hulking, white dog attracted attention wherever he went?

Shay dipped her head enough to hide her face and still manage to see them. "Now what, Spirit?" she muttered under her breath. Brad had met Spirit a few nights earlier when she and Liam had pretended to be a couple. Hopefully, Brad was stupid enough to mistake one big white dog for any other big white dog.

Footsteps clicked closer and echoed on the cobblestone road that most of the historic sections of Bray Harbor still boasted. "Come on, honey, I'm going to ask her if we can pet it," Angela called over her shoulder to Brad, who huffed and pulled his phone out of his back pocket and started scrolling.

Bouts of nausea ebbed and surged in Shay's stomach. As Angela's footsteps came closer, Shay tucked her chin down and pretended to scroll on her own phone. Next to her, Spirit growled low in his throat. "Spirit, stop!" Shay murmured.

"Say, miss, can I pet your dog? He's—"

Spirit's low growl escalated to a teeth-baring snarl, and he rose from his lying position at Shay's feet to his full, wolf-sized height and took one step toward Angela.

Goose bumps littered Shay's skin, and she feared that Spirit had finally snapped, that his overprotectiveness of her had superseded what was necessary. Shay was about to reveal her true identity when Angela turned on her heel and hurriedly walked across the street back to Brad. Shay couldn't hear what she told him, but from the frequent glances at her and Spirit, she guessed he was getting quite the story.

Brad shook his head, patted Angela's hand, and nearly dragged her down the sidewalk, away from the homeopathic store and Shay.

Shay rested her forehead on Spirit's. "You weren't really going to hurt her, were you, boy? You were just trying to get rid of her for me, weren't you?"

Spirit licked her cheek.

"What would I do without you?"

Spirit whimpered and nudged her off the bench and in the direction of the homeopathic store.

"Stay here and keep watch. I'll see if I can find out what those two purchased, either aboveboard or under the table, if the rumors about this place are true." She pulled her shawl tighter around her shoulders and crossed the road, hoping she wouldn't find another dead end, like all the leads in the case had so far led her to.

*   *   *

Unlike the kind young woman at the hat store, the store clerk—tall, with dreads hanging past his shoulders—barely glanced at Shay, much less offered a greeting, leaving Shay to wander the store, reading labels and sniffing testers. One made her sneeze, and the clerk glared at her from behind the sales counter. "Sorry," she whispered and continued around the store, pretending to be interested in the cheap imitations and knockoffs of herbal products.

The lavender lotions were clearly chemically engineered, and a few of the labels that claimed to be purely natural products had the words "artificially colored" or "artificially flavored" in tiny print on the back label. Keeping her snorts of contempt to herself, she picked up a clear glass bottle containing white round pills that claimed to calm anxiety. The ingredient label was dubious at best, and while she grew many of the herbs listed, none of the ingredients did what the claim promised and, in fact, when in combination with each other, could have negative effects. Figuring the clerk wouldn't know or care about the less-than-honest advertising and health promises, Shay made a mental note to alert the powers that be about the unethical products. After all, she did have and "in" with both the chief of police and the mayor now.

After several minutes, the clerk, clearly annoyed with her presence, approached her. "Can I help you find anything specific?"

Shay glanced at his name tag. "Actually, Sean, there is. I was supposed to meet some friends here who were going to help me purchase some products. I'm afraid I was running behind, and my phone died, so I can't text them. I don't suppose you could tell me if they've been here already. Brad and Angela. The cutest couple you've ever seen." Shay's throat burned as the words left her mouth.

"You just missed them."

"Shoot." She thrust her hip out and gave her gums a finale chomp for effect. "I'm such a dunce when it comes to all this"—she gestured to all the products—"and Brad and Angela were going to prove me wrong. I don't suppose you could tell me what they bought. I'd hate to buy the wrong thing, especially as they were going to help me make my first purchase." Shay pulled her wallet out of her purse.

Sean, who had been paying more attention to his phone than to Shay, focused on her wallet. "Sure thing, miss." He sauntered behind the sales counter and tapped a few buttons on the iPad screen in front of him. "Looks like they purchased dandelion tea tinctures, our specialty lavender scrub, and a few bath salts."

"That's all?" Shay drew out her debit card and tapped the corner on the sales counter.

"That's it. Would you like to order the same?" He still refused to meet her gaze, and while he had been scrolling social media before, his current evasion tactics hinted at deception instead of inattention.

The amulet warmed against her skin. Its heat forecasted what she already assumed. Sean was lying. About what, she didn't know. She needed to get a look behind the sales counter. Brad and Angela had purchased something other than dandelion tea and bath salts.

Think, Shay, think. She needed a distraction, and she knew just the person. She leaned on the counter and beamed a smile at Sean. "When do you close?"

"In about an hour."

"Good. I have another friend who is an absolute expert in all this hooey—" She smiled sheepishly. "Sorry. No offense meant."

"None taken." And from his tone, Shay guessed that Sean wouldn't care if the shop disappeared one day, taking all its fake products with it.

"I'll be back soon." She left the store, called for Spirit, and ran as fast as she could to Crystal Beach Cottages.

She arrived breathless at Gran and Liam's front door, and before she could knock, Gran answered, her feet already encased in white sneakers and her coat firmly fastened. "Well, where are we going?"

"How do you do this?" Shay gestured to the woman's outfit. "It's like you were ready and waiting for me."

"Who's to say I wasn't?" Gran's faded blue eyes sparkled with a hint of impishness, as she cupped Shay's cheek. "The moment ye let go, you'll finally see." Gran patted her cheek twice and then descended the porch steps. "What are ye waiting for?"

Shay gaped at Gran. "See what?" She followed Gran down the steps. "What am I letting go of?"

"Ye'll see."

Spirit whined at Shay's feet.

"I know, boy, I'm confused too."

Gran chuckled and continued walking down the boardwalk. "Come on, ye two. I've got me evening telly shows to watch, and I can't do that until this night's errand's done."

Shay caught up with Gran in three big steps and fell in stride with her. "And how do you know the night's errand?"

"Ye can't get as old as I am and not have gained a sharp sense of intuition. Besides, the fairies told me." Gran gave her an exaggerated wink.

"Gran." Shay sighed and laughed. "You don't know what we're doing, do you?"

"Not one bit." She chuckled. "I sensed ye needed me, but beyond that, ye'll have to fill me in, lass."

Shay brought Gran up to speed on the night's events and grinned. "How do you feel about being a distraction, Gran? How's your acting?"

"Fair to middlin', and if this Sean is as dense as I sense he is, I have a fair shake of pulling off the perfect farce."

Chapter 26

Ten minutes later, Shay pushed through the front door of Nature's Offerings, Gran following behind. "I'm back." Shay smiled at Sean, who offered a flat stare in return.

Thankfully, the store was empty of customers as Gran and Shay leisurely wandered the aisles, finally taking up a position in the back corner, near the sales counter. They lowered their voices and perused the shelves. Shay randomly removed bottles and packages, pretended to read the labels, all while attempting to give the impression that they were interested in the various products. After a few minutes, Shay nudged Gran's arm, signaling she was ready to set their plan in motion.

Gran set her large purse on the sales counter and ambled toward the front of the shop. "I think I saw that product we were discussing earlier, deary, over here on the front shelf." Gran took a few more steps, let out a slight shriek, and crumpled to the floor.

"Gran!" Shay cried out and sprinted over to Gran's prone body. "Can you hear me?"

Sean joined her and knelt beside Gran, who was lying in a heap on the floor. "Ma'am, are you okay?" There was a look of such genuine concern on his face that Shay felt guilty for their ruse.

Gran groaned and clutched at her chest. "My pills, lass. In my purse. Hurry."

Shay hurried to Gran's purse, positioned perfectly to give the illusion she was riffling through it, when all the while she was searching the shelves behind the sales counter. Sweat beaded on her forehead when Sean got to his feet. If he came closer, he'd see she wasn't searching Gran's purse.

Gran grasped his hand and pulled him back down. "Don't leave me, young man."

"But I should call the ambul—"

"My friend is getting my pills. I'll be okay. 'Tis this old heart of mine, ye see. Some say I'm older than the hills, and while I feel as young as the day I was born, my heart says otherwise. Why just the other day, the fairies told me—"

"Fairies?"

Shay smiled at the incredulous tone in Sean's voice and the story Gran started telling him about her life among the fairies. Shay blew out a breath in relief. That tall tale should buy her some more time at least. As quickly as she could without making too much noise, she searched the shelves under the counter and came across a ledger, pulled it out, opened it to the last page, revealing names and figures and dates, and snapped a picture.

"Gran, where's your bottle of pills? I can't find it." She fingered through the ledger, took a few more pictures, and replaced the book in the exact spot she'd found it.

"Fool girl," Gran said, "it's in a blue zipper bag. It has fairies on it."

Shay chuckled to herself when she unearthed the blue bag decorated with dancing fairies. "Found it."

"Quick, lass, quick. I can see the light."

Shay rolled her eyes, ran back to Gran, plastered a look

of concern on her face, and handed her a small white pill. What she was actually handing the old woman, she didn't know, but as Gran swallowed it with no concern, Shay figured it wouldn't do her any harm.

"There, there, I'll be as right as rain in a moment." She clutched Sean's arm. "Would ye mind helping me to my feet, lad?"

Sean looked at her uncertainly, but did as she asked. "Are you sure you don't want me to call you an ambulance? You know, just to be sure?" he said, not releasing her elbow until she was steady on her feet.

"Lad, if I called the ambulance every time I fell or had an attack, they'd start charging me extra on account of me being a nuisance." She waved away his concern. "Now, where's me handbag?"

Shay retrieved it for her and smiled at Sean. "Thank you for your help with Gran. I've never had to find her pills before, so I'm glad you were there to keep her occupied and her mind off the situation while I hunted for them."

Sean grinned, revealing a warmth he'd hidden well earlier. "I'm just glad she's okay." He leaned toward Shay and lowered his voice. "She's just as stubborn as my grandmother."

Shay nodded knowingly and thanked him again, looped her arm through Gran's, and assisted the frail-appearing woman out the door. They kept the charade up until they were well around the corner and back on the boardwalk.

When the coast was clear, Shay stopped and hugged Gran. "You were magnificent."

Gran patted Shay's back and slipped from the embrace. "Well, lass, I do what I can. Did a little bit of acting back in the old country, ye know."

"Really?"

"Most folk said they'd never seen a better Juliet."

Despite the darkness, the antique streetlamps bordering

the boardwalk illuminated the night enough for Shay to see the blush on Gran's face. "Did it have anything to do with who was playing Romeo?"

Gran snorted. "None of that nonsense, lass. Let's see what evidence ye gathered."

Twenty minutes later, Gran and Shay settled around Gran's kitchen table, a teapot and two steaming cups of chamomile tea in front of them. Shay tapped the photos icon on her phone screen and enlarged the first picture she had taken. Before she could get a closer look, the front door opened.

"Gran, sorry I'm late. Conor and I were—" Liam stepped into the kitchen and halted. "Shay, what a nice surprise."

"Liam, take a seat." Gran patted the chair next to her. "Shay and I had a grand adventure tonight."

Liam looked at Shay for an explanation, and after he sat down, they filled him in on her evening.

"Nature's Offerings, you say?" Liam massaged the back of his neck. "Word about town is that it's the place to go if you want something a little stronger than herbal teas and tinctures."

Shay pushed her phone toward him. "I think we have a little more proof than just rumor. Look." She pointed at Brad and Angela's name scrawled in one column, followed by the date and amount and product. "Why on earth would they need this amount of Ambien and whatever these three are."

Liam squinted at the screen. "Whoa. These are powerful drugs, opioids." His gaze met hers, and the rock she'd carried in the pit of her stomach all evening plunged.

"You're kidding—it was opioids?"

"Yeah. I think this must have been what they were drugging you with back in New Mexico. Ambien alone would have caused the memory loss you mentioned, not being able to remember what was going on, and the other three?" He shook his head. "They would have caused the confusion and brain fog, and also contributed to memory loss. Brad and possibly Angela were consistently drugging you, probably through your coffee to hide the bitter taste of the crushed-up pills. I'm sorry."

The reality of the situation, the fact that Brad, the man she had once been crazy in love with, could do such a thing to her—violate her memory, her thoughts, her ability to function—stabbed her in the heart. Gray dots sparkled at the edge of Shay's vision, but Liam's warm touch and gentle voice brought her back to reality.

"Shay?" Liam squeezed her hand. "He can't hurt you anymore. You're not ignorant of his actions, and you know his secret. That makes you more powerful than him. You are no longer his victim."

Shay blinked to clear her vision, and she concentrated on Liam's face. He had moved to her side and knelt before her. "You're right."

"Can I get that in writing?"

"Not a chance." She laughed and did it ever feel good. Even with having an answer to all her nagging questions about how her foolproof instincts could have let her down so much, all she felt, in the moment, was a deep sense of relief. If what Liam proposed was true, then just knowing how Brad had managed to steal her business, her life, her reputation made it all easier to bear.

Liam's grin slipped. "Question is, why are they purchasing such a large amount now?"

Shay gasped. "Madam Malvina."

A muscle in Liam's jaw ticked. "Probably, but are they purchased on her behalf, for some nefarious business of her own, or do they plan on doing the same thing to her as they did to you?"

The amulet warmed Shay's skin, and she shivered.

Gran studied her over the rim of her teacup. "Don't fear it. Use it. Ye have the gift."

Shay eased her grip on the teacup handle. Gran was right. She had to stop fearing the greatest gift—besides life—that Bridget had left her and begin to embrace it. Maybe that was why she only ever received cryptic visions or visions that were clear but made no sense.

She glanced down at Liam, who studied her with quiet understanding.

"I can leave if ye want me to." He got to his feet.

Shay reached her his arm. "No, that's okay. You can stay." She wanted—needed—him to stay, but she couldn't say the words. Instead, she forced a laugh. "The more the merrier, as they say."

He looked questioningly at her.

"Here, lass." Gran placed a candle in front of Shay and placed a warm hand on her shoulder. "I believe in ye, but ye need to believe in yerself."

Shay couldn't speak around the lump in her throat, so she gently squeezed Gran's hand and pulled the leather-encased bottle from under her shirt. She held it over the candle's flame and waited for the tiny bubbles to dance inside the glass. As soon as they appeared, Shay held the bottle against her forehead, closed her eyes, and inhaled deeply to center herself.

Gray fog and silence swirled in her mind's eye.

She gritted her teeth in frustration, and the gray fog darkened until she stared into a black abyss. She could hear nothing except for the sound of her teeth grinding. Some gift she had.

A warm touch calmed her negative thoughts. She knew it was Liam's hand on her forearm, and the heat of his hand melted away her frustration, and she was centered again. The darkness lifted, and the gray fog descended to swirl at her feet as she stood in the middle of an abandoned room. Shay couldn't tell what room, but it appeared familiar. Someone was sobbing with such pain and heart-wrenching gasps that tears sprang up in Shay's eyes.

With quiet steps, Shay moved through her vision, the fog circling her feet and crawling up the walls of the room. Her heart pounded as she approached a wooden door. The sobs escalated, occasionally broken by guttural groans of deep pain. Shay stopped and placed her hand on the doorframe, supporting herself as her wobbling knees threatened to give out on her.

She took a deep breath, grasped the door handle, turned it slowly, pushed the door open, and stepped into another realm, it seemed. She squinted and shifted in her chair. It wasn't another room, but a meadow, and she found herself in the middle of the deadly fairy ring. Gone was Cora's body. It had been replaced with a wreath of deadly nightshade. Shay peered intently at the colorful ring and crouched down beside it. No, it wasn't nightshade. It was twinberry honeysuckle. She reached out to touch one of the black berries, but a cry, the same sobs from the mysterious room behind her, made her twist around to see . . . danger.

But it wasn't a person in trouble or pain. It was Doyle. Her early visions of the balding man had increased to the full form of him, and his wicked grin pierced Shay's soul. "Be careful of what you seek. You might not like what you find."

Anger replaced fear, and Shay jumped to her feet, crossed over the boundary of the fairy circle, and ran right through Doyle's body, his form diluting and becoming one with the fog at her feet.

"Shay?" A far-off voice echoed through her mind, and she turned in circles, trying to find the source. She clutched her chest, and her lungs struggled to fill.

"Shay, you're safe." A warm hand encased hers, and the soft Irish lilt of a familiar voice called to her. "Shay, open your eyes."

Shay obeyed the voice and gazed into Liam's electric-blue eyes. The concern in them brought her to attention, and she eased her hand from his. "I . . . I . . ." Shay gulped and dropped her gaze.

"Ye saw, didn't you? A full vision?" Gran asked, her voice laced with equal parts concern and excitement.

Shay nodded her head. Exhaustion seeped into her bones. She was weightless yet heavy with the enormity of what had just occurred.

"What did ye see?" Gran prodded.

Shay clutched her hands in her lap and squeezed until her knuckles whitened. "I was in a room. It felt familiar, but I didn't recognize it. Someone was crying. It sounded like a child, but I can't be sure. Whoever it was, they were in such deep agony that I started crying."

"We saw the tears running down yer cheeks," Liam said gently.

Shay swiped at her cheeks. "It felt so real. It was uncanny really." She shook herself. "Anyway, there was a door, and when I opened it, it led me to the fairy ring where we found Cora's body, but instead of finding her, there was a wreath of what I thought was deadly nightshade but turned out to be twinberry honeysuckle."

"That couldn't have made ye cry out, though." Gran studied Shay.

"I cried out?"

"Aye. Liam here wanted to pull ye from yer trance, but I stopped him."

Of course, he did. Shay's heart skipped a beat. He always wanted to protect her, even, so it seemed, from imaginary evils.

"Doyle was there," Shay whispered as if just saying his name would conjure his appearance. "And it wasn't a snapshot of him this time. It was his whole body, and he spoke to me."

Gran leaned toward Shay and rested her wrinkled hand over Shay's. "What did he say?"

Shay swallowed. "That I should be careful what I look for because I might not like what I find."

"Was there anything about Brad or Angela and the drugs they purchased?" Liam asked.

"No. Not even a hint of them."

"Maybe it's a sign that they aren't involved," Liam said.

"I don't know if we should rule them out yet," Shay said. "Their activities alone are suspicious enough to keep them on our radar. It's the repetition of the innocuous plant and the verbal warning that gets me."

"This is not the first time you've gotten the message that things might not be what they seem," said Liam.

Shay rested her head against the back of the kitchen chair and stared at the ceiling. "I have the sense that we've been looking at this case wrong from the beginning and that Doyle, who we thought was on the sidelines, acting as the puppeteer to his stooges, is actually at the heart of this case. And if Conor was right about seeing Doyle with Madam Malvina, she's caught up in all this as well."

Chapter 27

Saturday dawned earlier than Shay anticipated, and she stumbled to her kitchen. The previous night's vision had left her drained in a way she had never experienced. Visions of fairy rings and nightshade and Doyle's warning had plagued her dreams, and this morning she knew, in both mind and body, that she'd be useless in the shop.

Spirit whined at Shay and pawed at the kitchen door.

"I'm coming, boy." She shuffled over to the door, opened it, and, after closing it, leaned back against it. The clock above her kitchen stove told her she'd gotten at least six hours of sleep, but her misfiring brain and sluggish feet indicated she'd spent most of that time tossing and turning.

She trudged to the fridge, opened it, and groaned. Not a thing to eat unless a singular block of moldy cheese was her new breakfast of choice.

The cupboards revealed nothing either, except a nearly empty jar of peanut butter and the heel of a loaf of bread. She'd have to make a quick grocery run before going to the shop. Sleep or no sleep, a woman still had to eat.

After starting her morning coffee, she hurriedly got dressed, throwing on a pair of black leggings and an emerald-green, oversized sweater. She looped gold hoops through her ears, piled her hair into a messy bun, squinted into the bathroom mirror, and patted her fingertip over the bags under her eyes. Knowing she had nothing to deflate them, not even a cucumber, which she added to her mental shopping list, she poured her coffee into a to-go cup, snatched her temporary bag from its hook, since the police still had her backpack, and let Spirit in.

"Wanna go to the store?"

Spirit did his doggy dance at her feet and yipped.

"I'm buying human food. Not dog food." She laughed at his twitching ears. "Never mind. Come along then. And if you're a good boy, I'll get you a treat."

Spirit's tongue rolled out of his mouth, and he darted out the door as soon as Shay opened it.

"Wait for me." Shay hopped on her bike and hurried to catch up with him. "Now, the store's not going anywhere, so can we slow down," she said as she pulled up beside him.

In a few moments, she parked her bike in front of the local mom-and-pop grocery store and told Spirit to stay put and be a good boy. She didn't have time to check off everything on her list, but she grabbed essentials like milk, eggs, bread, and an assortment of fruits and vegetables. Not that she wanted them, but she had almost reached a year of keeping her New Year's resolution from eleven months ago to eat more of them. She wasn't about to let a hiccup in her life cause her to lose the only resolution she'd ever made and kept. And she desperately needed a win.

Shay reached for the last item on her must-have list, her morning coffee, when a grocery cart slammed into hers. Her to-go cup went flying, and one of the back wheels rammed into her big toe. She hissed in pain.

"Excuse me—" Shay snapped her mouth shut when she

saw Madam Malvina behind the offending cart. From the glint in Madam Malvina's eyes, the head-on collision was not accidental.

"Mom . . ." Orion shuffled his feet and had the decency to blush. "You should apologize," he whispered.

"I will do no such thing to a hussy like her."

Shay gasped and backed up a few steps. "I'm sorry, but what did you just say?"

"You heard me." A piece of Madam Malvina's black hair slipped out from under her black turban-styled head wrap. She blew it out of her eyes, but it fell right back.

Shay thought it would almost be comical, were it not for the malicious glint in Madam Malvina's eyes and the glimmering diamond eyes of the skull pendant hanging from under her turban in the center of her forehead. Shay wasn't sure which set of eyes she should focus on—those of the empty skull or Madam Malvina's, which burned with venom. She opted for the skull just above the woman's blazing eyes.

"I know we've had our differences in the past, but I don't understand what I did for you say something like that to me."

"You think I'm stupid enough to fall for Liam's lie that it was Conor kissing you under my store's awning?" Madam Malvina snorted. "After all the mooning you've done over that worthless man. Who, by the way, I've kicked to the curb. Told him so this morning when he came around to proclaim his innocence." She nudged Orion with her shoulder. "Isn't that right?"

Orion studied the tips of his sneakers and remained silent.

Mooning? Shay bit her tongue. She had to play her hand well. One misdeal and Madam Malvina would know they were up to more than performing a fake kiss in front of her business. "You're right."

Madam Malvina, who had opened her mouth to voice another tirade, gaped at her.

"It was all my fault. And I'm sorry."

Madam Malvina tilted her head and studied Shay, as if she were studying her prey. "And exactly how is it your fault?"

Shay forced a brave bravado. "I was provoking Liam." Blend truth with fiction so everything seems like truth. "He's been flaunting his endless stream of women in front of me all year, and I wanted him to have a taste of his own medicine, so I told him I had kissed Conor and that I bet that his cousin could kiss better than he could." Shay's face burned hot, and she hoped Madam Malvina mistook it for shame instead of the disappointment she had in herself for lying so easily to the person she once considered a friend.

Madam Malvina's lips slowly pulled back in a grin. "A bet Liam seemed to take pleasure in taking." She waved her hand dismissively. "If I were you, I'd stay a million miles away from the Madigan cousins. They're nothing but trouble."

Shay pretended to agree. "I'm sorry that my stupid bet caused you any pain. Liam didn't kiss me because he likes me. He was proving the exact opposite." Her heart pinched at the truth of those words. Liam had had many chances to make their accidental kiss into something, but he hadn't, and time was proving her assumptions that he only saw her as a good friend a reality.

"Well, who needs men anyway? They only end up hurting you in the end. Besides, I have my Orion, don't I?" She moved to give Orion's cheeks a pinch, which he ducked with a quickness Shay hadn't expected.

The cover of *A Layman's Guide to Poison* flitted into Shay's mind. Now was as good a time as any to see how Madam Malvina reacted to the mention of it. Liam had not heard back from his contacts about the handwriting, but if Shay could get a read on whether Madam Malvina knew of its existence, that would point them in the right direction.

"Well, I'd better go," said Shay. "Sorry again for the trouble I caused. If only I had listened to everyone who told me gambling would only cause trouble, right?" Shay chuckled and started to turn her cart around. She stopped. "Actually, I do have a question for you. I had a customer come in the other day asking if I had a certain book. I had never heard of it, but I promised to ask around." Shay adopted a nonchalant stance, resting her forearms on the cart's front bar. "He was asking about a book entitled *A Layman's Guide to Poison*. Have you heard of it?"

Madam Malvina pursed her lips. "I've heard of it, of course. You can't be an expert in herbs and potions like I am and not have heard of it." Her pointed look communicated quite clearly that she did not consider Shay an expert in anything. "I don't have the book, nor have I read it. What did this man want it for?"

"Mother, we should go. We'll be late opening up the tea shop." Orion tapped his foot and checked his smartwatch. "You have a client right away, remember?"

"They can wait." She pinned Shay with a pointed gaze. "Well?"

Shay's amulet scorched her skin, and she coughed to cover up her gasp of pain.

"Um . . . he said it was for research. That he was writing a book and wanted to be accurate in his descriptions."

Madam Malvina grunted. "And I'm the queen of the fairies. People who request books like that are usually in the business of learning the business, if you know what I mean." She adjusted her black shawl and stuck her chin out. "Now, if you don't mind, I'm behind schedule. Come, Orion."

Orion followed her down the aisle like a dejected puppy.

After making sure no one was looking, Shay clutched the burning amulet. If Madam Malvina wasn't lying, Shay would be very surprised. Content with the knowledge that Madam Malvina at least knew of the book's existence, Shay rolled her cart to the checkout aisle and paid for her purchases.

An hour later, Shay unlocked the front door to Crystals & CuriosiTEAS and pushed it open. The bells tinkled a welcoming hello, and she breathed in the familiar scents of her tea shop. For the first time in weeks, she felt settled instead of uneasy, and she wasn't sure why. It was not as if she had solved Cora's murder or figured out the role Brad and Angela played in all this or could prove that Madam Malvina was involved in Cora's death. Nor had she and Liam come to a mutual understanding. No, besides her business being back on its feet, everything was still up in the air, and with that thought, she shivered.

The past few years, she had been reluctant to celebrate any steps forward because it always meant the universe had other plans. This upbeat energy coursing through her at the moment might mean only one thing. It was a short reprieve before her life was about to topple back down to the ground, and everyone around her was about to become collateral damage in the deluge of problems that still were left unresolved.

She inhaled the comforting scent again to ground herself and headed up the stairs to her greenhouse. After sitting on the bench, she closed her eyes and quieted her thoughts. A sense of peace washed through her, and she smiled. Even though Bridget's voice was silent, Shay felt the presence of her mother and leaned into it. There was a different aura than normal. There was a sense of pride in the air.

"Are you proud of me, Mother?" Shay whispered to the empty room. "My vision last night was clearer than ever."

A vision of Liam flitted through her mind, and she smiled. "Perhaps Gran is right. Maybe Liam and I are made for each other." Shay remembered how it was his comforting touch that had cleared her vision. She shook her head. The magic was hers, not his, but his effect on her was undeniable.

For the next thirty minutes, she reflected and tried to soak in all the positivity from what her mother had created in the greenhouse. Something told her that she would need an abundant stash of it going forward when the deluge began.

The jingling of bells pulled Shay from her trance, and she stood and stretched. "Well, here we go." She descended the steps, marched through the back room, and stuttered to a stop at seeing Mayor Sutton standing in the middle of her tea shop, a look of utter despair on his face.

"Mayor?" Shay, afraid she'd scare him away, took a few tentative steps toward him. "What's wrong?"

Wordlessly, he held out a letter to her. From the looks of the paper, it had been folded and unfolded several times, and the edges were crinkled as if being crumbled over and over again in a fist.

She carefully unfolded it, read it, and met Cliff Sutton's mournful gaze. "She wrote this for your anniversary message?"

He nodded.

"It is clear she had a special surprise for you, something that would change both of your lives." There was no mention of the blue bottle or what Cora had envisioned she could do with it, but there was no denying that Cora wanted to surprise her husband with the ultimate anniversary gift. And from her scrawled words—"someone special is helping me to give you the most incredible gift, and I cannot wait to share it with you"—Cora had clearly enlisted the help of someone. Someone who probably turned out to be her killer. The hair at the back of her neck rose, and Shay shivered.

"But the ending—" His voice cracked, and he cleared his throat. "What does it mean?"

Shay squinted at the cursive writing, which by its messier scrawl indicated Cora had been rushed for time. Was she rushed for time because she was meeting the person she thought was going to help her break through the boundary of this world into the world of the fairies?

She read the last lines out loud, "My dearest Cliff, the adventure I'm embarking on is not a simple one, and although I have no fear, I am not sure of the outcome either. I am willing to risk it all for the chance I have been gifted because I know it will bring us both such happiness. If something does occur and I cannot make it back to you, know that I am safe, and please remember how much I love you."

Mayor Sutton collapsed in the nearest chair, hid his face in his hands, and wept.

Shay pulled a chair next to him and took a seat. She knew there was nothing she could say to comfort him, and anger burned inside her. Cora had obviously trusted the person and went willingly into a ceremony that she thought, at the worst, would trap her in the land of the fairies. Shay only wished Cora was safely with the fairies. No, someone had misused Cora's trust, and now her husband sat next to Shay, weeping.

Shay patted his shoulder. "I'm so sorry. I promised you I would help find out who did this, and I'm working on it. It's been slow going, but I have a strange feeling that we're getting closer."

Mayor Sutton looked at her through tear-blurred eyes. "Thank you. Sorry I lost control of my emotions. It's been rough."

"Don't apologize. Would you like some tea to help take the edge off?"

He smiled sadly. "No, thank you. As much as Cora tried, she could never make a tea drinker out of me." After hauling himself to his feet, he held his hand out to Shay. "Thank you. Please let me know the minute you have something solid, okay?"

Shay promised and opened the door for him and watched as he walked down the sidewalk, his head down and his shoulders slumped.

"Poor man," she muttered, flipped the sign to OPEN, and double-checked that all was ready for the first tea service of the morning.

The bells tinkled, and Shay turned, a welcoming smile on her face, which quickly slipped into a frown at the look on Liam's face. "What's wrong?"

"I got the report back on the handwriting."

Chapter 28

"You said it could take a few days. You only took the pictures yesterday. That's a fast turnaround." Shay adjusted the placement of an already-centered flower arrangement at the nearest table to settle her nerves. She sensed the news Liam was about to give was the opposite of what they'd assumed.

"Well, when you save a man's life, the favor is returned pretty quickly." He waved away her intrigued look. "That's a story for another day, *a chara*." He tapped his phone screen, quickly scrolled, and was about to hand it to her when the door opened, and customers walked in.

Shay sighed. "This will have to wait. With Jen out and Tassi taking Orion to the Grungefest later, I'm all alone."

After a warm greeting, Shay got the four customers squared away at their tables and jotted down their orders.

"Want some help?" Liam fell into step with her as she headed to the back room.

"Really?" She narrowed her gaze at him. "Don't offer anything you're not actually prepared to do."

"I have experience, and from the looks of it"—he jerked his chin at the filling tea shop—"you need all the help you can get right now."

Shay grinned. "You're a lifesaver, and with that charming smile of yours, I'm sure you'll make all the ladies swoon."

"You think I'm charming?"

"No. But most of my customers are older and have poor vision, so they probably can't see clearly anyway." She chuckled at his shocked inhale. "Go." She gave him a slight shove toward the tables and entered the back room to gather all the baked goods and different teas.

Two hours later, Shay and Liam waved to the last of the white-haired ladies as she swaggered out the door. Shay turned to Liam and chuckled. "I don't think I've seen Mrs. Hampton sashay her rear end like that since her hip replacement last year."

"What can I say? I have that effect on the ladies."

If Liam hadn't been important to her success through the morning's service, she'd have swatted him. But after one look at the tip jar, which had filled up over the course of the morning, she let his comment slide and rewarded him with only a glare. "You might as well take that—you earned it. I've never seen anyone shimmy away, shielding his back end from so many ladies with twitchy pinchers outside an all-male dance show."

"*A chara*. I'm shocked. I never took ye as the type."

"I'm not, but I've seen the *Magic Mike* movie." She rolled her eyes and brushed her hands across the front of her apron. "I think we have some time before the next big rush for us to discuss your contact's report on the handwriting."

"Right." Liam pulled out his phone, tapped the screen, and handed it to her.

Shay scanned the text thread between Liam and his contact. "This seems to say that the handwriting is inconclusive."

"Handwriting analysis is still a tricky science and usually isn't allowed in a court of law, unless, of course, the court agrees that the person is indeed an expert in his or her field, and it's usually accompanied by other pieces of evidence to make the case stick."

"He says here that the handwriting is a match for Madam Malvina's, but that there are enough inconsistencies that he can't claim that it's one hundred percent hers."

"What now?"

"I think we continue down this path. If Conor is correct and he saw Doyle and Madam Malvina together, he is most certainly connected to this case. Cora's death has to boil down to Doyle and/or Madam Malvina. Either way, keeping tabs on Madam Malvina might lead us to Doyle. Who knows, they might slip up and get careless about who sees them together."

The door opened, and a fresh batch of customers entered. When they all smiled at Liam and tittered amongst themselves, he groaned.

It appeared the word-of-mouth communication train in Bray Harbor was as reliable as usual, and his fan club was growing by the minute. Shay laughed and nudged his arm. "Word must have spread that one of the Madigan boys was serving tea." She shooed him forward and cut him off when he opened his mouth to speak. "I know, I know. I owe you big-time. We'll talk about your price after we're done."

For the rest of the day, Liam and Shay worked side by side and in perfect harmony. Shay closed the door after the last customer, flipped the lock, turned the sign to CLOSED, and leaned her back against the door.

"What a whirlwind." She sighed and massaged the back of her neck.

Liam chuckled and fanned out several pieces of paper. "You're telling me."

"What are those?"

"Phone numbers."

"You're kidding me."

"Wish I was." He tossed them in the garbage can next to the sales counter. "Need help cleaning up?"

"No, you go. There are a few things I want to do before leaving for the night." She stepped around him, but he moved in front of her.

"We work well together, don't we, *a chara*?" He stepped closer, his gaze concentrating on her face.

Shay's mouth went dry, and her heart pounded against her ribs. "So it seems."

"I . . . uh . . . I've been thinking, and—"

At a knock on the window, they both jumped. Shay slammed her hand over her erratically pounding chest and glared at Conor, who had stuck his face to the window and was mouthing, "Let me in."

Shay wrenched it open so quickly that Conor stumbled in. "You scared the bejeezus out of us. You could have knocked like a normal person."

Conor looked back at the door and then at her in confusion. "I did." He studied her and Liam, and a grin spread across his lips. "Ah, I see."

"What do you mean, *I see*?" Shay crossed her arms over her chest.

Liam scowled at Conor. "He sees nothing, that's what he sees."

Conor shook his head. "What I see now is not as important as what I just saw. Madam Malvina and Doyle. Quickly." When Liam and Shay stood motionless, he gestured to the door. "Come on."

"Okay, okay," said Shay, as she grabbed her bag and followed him and Liam out, locking the door behind them and following Conor in the direction of Madam Malvina's tea shop.

"When did you see them?" Shay panted as she power-walked to keep up with the Madigan boys' longer strides.

"Just under ten minutes ago," Conor said over this shoulder.

Shivers skittered up Shay's spine. They could be too late. She picked up her pace and soon left Liam and Conor behind her, slowing down only as she neared the shop. They finally caught up to her, both huffing and puffing. "Boy, yer a hard lass to catch." Liam panted.

Conor grinned. "But I thought all the ladies ran *to* ye, cousin, not away."

"Shush." Shay held her hand up. "What's our game plan? We can't just go waltzing in there. She's definitely not a fan of yours right now, Liam."

"Don't I know that. My ears are still ringing from this morning's phone call." He pulled at his left earlobe. "She claimed you told her it was all your fault, and that I should steer clear of women like you."

"Like me?" Shay snorted. "And she told me I should stay away from you and you"—she pointed to Conor—"and that she didn't need a man anyway."

A sudden gust of wind swirled from the beach, and Shay shivered. "This is ridiculous. We need to find a way in without being noticed."

Liam pulled out his phone and tapped in a number. "Got it."

"Who are you calling?" Shay asked, her teeth chattering when another gust of northerly winds wrapped frigid tendrils around her.

"Madam Malvina," Liam mouthed, holding the phone to his ear.

"What for?" Shay shared a confused look with Conor, who simply shrugged his shoulders.

Liam help up a finger. "Hello, Malvina, darling."

Shay's shoulders arched at the sweet lilt to his voice, and her hand shot to her mouth to stem back her sudden bout of nausea.

"Now, now, darling, I know yer upset with me. I completely understand why yer angry with me. I know . . . Shay distracted me for only a moment." He rolled his eyes at Shay and twirled his index finger at his temple. "Yes, yes, I will stay as far away as possible from her from now on. I was hoping to come and see ye tonight."

Shay glared at him.

"Yer doing a reading?" Liam grinned at Shay and Conor and gave a thumbs-up. "It sounds like yer outside, though. Are ye sure the breeze isn't too cold for ye? I'd hate for ye to catch a chill." Liam chuckled. "Of course, the fire pit. I'd forgotten about our favorite spot to sit a while."

Shay opened her mouth to speak. It was only Conor's hand on her arm and the slight shake of his head that kept her from crying out her disbelief at what she was hearing. How close had Liam and Malvina actually become?

"Yes, dear, we can plan on another night. Good night, my love." Liam hung up and turned a blinding grin on Shay, a grin that slipped quickly into a frown. "Now what?"

"You . . . you . . ."

"Toad?"

"How'd you know what I was going to call you?"

"I've heard it before and recently too, if my memory serves me right." Liam lightly squeezed her shoulder and gazed into her eyes. "There's only one woman for me, and I assure you and swear by the fairies that Madam Malvina is not her."

From the look in his eyes, Shay suspected a deeper meaning to his words, but with Conor watching them intently and the unrelenting brisk ocean breeze, Shay didn't want to delve into that at the moment. Besides, with everything up in the air, she wasn't sure she had the physical or mental strength to deal with a conversation that would irrevocably change her life for better or worse.

Conor cleared his throat. "Come on, you two. We can sneak down the alley toward the back of her shop. Her patio is enclosed with a wood fence, so we can freely listen to whatever they're talking about, if they are actually out there."

Shay shivered and wrapped her new shawl more tightly about her shoulders. "They'd both have to be idiots to think being outside tonight is a great idea."

"Her firepit area is actually quite nice and . . ." Liam swallowed at Shay's glare. "Right, after you." He gestured for Conor to go into the alley first and then followed Shay.

The alley acted like a wind tunnel, and Shay clung onto her shawl to keep it from flying away. Dumb, dumb, dumb! A storm must be brewing, and instead of being tucked up in her nice, warm cottage, she was hiding behind a wooden fence, her ear pressed against a crack in the wooden slats.

For a moment, she was afraid that Madam Malvina and the man Conor thought was Doyle had gone back inside. If that was the case, her investigation would take a hit, and she'd be none the wiser on who was behind Cora's death.

"I told you, Doyle, people might start getting suspicious that you keep turning up here like you do." Madam Malvina's voice cut through the fence. "Someone's bound to notice. This town is full of gossip mongers."

Shay's sense of relief was cut short when a man's harsh laugh pierced her eardrums. From the look on Conor's face, Shay assumed the man's laugh was Doyle's.

"Come now, Malvina. You claiming there are gossiping biddies in this town is as good as pointing the finger at yourself. I know you."

"*Knew* me." Madam Malvina's tone hardened. "You knew me, once, Doyle, a long time ago. You do not *know* me or what I've endured to get where I am today."

"You mean this little shop. What do you call it, again? Celestial Treasures and Teas?" He scoffed. "I could buy this out from under you in a heartbeat, and then where would you be? Would you run back to Monterey with your tail tucked between your legs? We both know you can't go back there, don't we? Customers generally don't like being lied to by a charlatan."

Madam Malvina sucked in a breath and coughed. "How dare you?"

"How dare I what? State the truth? We both know your powers are nothing but smoke and mirrors, and we both know you're as blond as they come under that black dye."

Shay shared a startled look with Liam and Conor. Madam Malvina a natural blond? Shay tried to picture it and shook her head. The woman would certainly be less terrifying if she'd stuck with her natural hair color.

"What good would it do for you to buy me out, ruin my business?"

Doyle chuckled, and Shay's skin crawled at his cheerless tone. "I rarely do anything for the good of anybody or anything. I simply do because I can."

Shay wished she could see the expressions on Madam Malvina and Doyle's faces, but the crack she was trying to spy through wasn't at the right angle, no matter how she twisted her neck and tilted her head.

"Look, I did what you asked. After you realized I had made a connection with Shay, I did your bidding. I pretended to be her friend. I spied on her and even encouraged Orion to befriend Shay's strange little friend Tassi."

Shay's ears went hot at Madam Malvina's words, and her heart thumped erratically against her rib cage. While Madam Malvina's words about her stung, her rage boiled over at the thought of Tassi being lied to. People could mess with Shay all they wanted, but the moment they hurt those she cared about . . . Shay's fingernails bit into her palms, and she flinched.

Liam pried apart her left fist, gently held her hand in his, smiled, and softly shook his head.

"And if that's not enough," Madam Malvina snapped, "I was the one—at your command, by the way—who encouraged Brad and Angela to buy the winery here."

"Tsk, tsk, my dear Malvina, I believe you do protest your innocence too much. Remember, I see everything you do. I have eyes all over, including in this piddly seaside village. If customers catch on that you're spiking their tea with opioids to make them dupes in your I'm-a-real-seer act, what made you run from Monterey will seem like a picnic."

Shay squeezed Liam's hand. The connection between the opioids and Brad and Angela and Madam Malvina finally connected. Madam Malvina must be blackmailing Brad and Angela with what she knew about them. *Perhaps even what they did to me back in Santa Fe.* Could that blackmail be forcing them to buy contraband opioids for her?

"And if I don't keep playing your little game?" Madam Malvina's voice sounded tired and defeated.

For a moment, the only sounds were the cracklings of logs burning in the fire pit from within the fenced-off area and the wind howling down the alley.

"I'm sure," said Doyle, cooly, "that the Bray Harbor Police Department will be very interested in your little shop of horrors."

"What about Orion?" Madam Malvina hissed. "Surely you wouldn't want to hurt him or do anything to make his life any harder than what it already is, would you?"

"And why should I care about a weirdo like him?"

"Because he's your son."

Shay sucked in a breath so hard, she nearly coughed. Her eyes stung with tears as she struggled to regulate her breathing. Orion was Doyle's son? That meant that if that were indeed true, and Doyle was Shay's father as well, Orion was Shay's half brother.

Liam gripped Shay's hand and pulled her in to his side.

"And like I've told you a dozen times before now," Doyle added, his tone as cool as ice, "I might have planted that seed, but that makeup-wearing, weird kid is no son of mine, you hear?"

Chapter 29

Shay couldn't stay to hear anymore. With her heartbeat pounding in her ears, she sprinted down the alley, veered left, and continued at full speed until she reached the front row of the shops running along the boardwalk. Once there and well away from Madam Malvina and Doyle's soul-crushing words, she leaned over and planted her hands on her knees, panting. No matter how hard she tried, she couldn't catch her breath. She feared she'd never be able to breathe freely again, a sensation she hadn't felt since hearing the devastating news of her adoptive parents' death all those years ago.

The wind whipped at her hair, and the waves crashed on the beach with an intensity to rival her churning emotions. Poor Tassi. Poor Orion. And for the first time in a long time, she felt pity for Madam Malvina.

Her amulet burned against her skin, and Shay winced. She had considered Doyle a foe, but had never felt such evil emanating from a being like this before. Whatever ran through his veins, it certainly wasn't the same life-giving blood that ran through the rest of humanity.

Gran had been right about the whole situation. There was an undercurrent of hatred and evil that threatened to overtake them all if Shay couldn't figure out Cora's murder.

Never before had she felt such a necessity of solving a case, and never before had the feeling of impending doom suffocated her at the thought of failing.

A warm hand rested on her back, and soft words caressed her cheek. "Breathe, *a chara,* breathe."

Shay tried to obey Liam's gentle, singsong voice, but her lungs wouldn't cooperate. An overwhelming sense of dread consumed her, and unwanted images of herself as a teenager, hearing the tragic news about her parents, flickered through her mind. Her aunt had finally found a paper bag for her to use, which had worked like a charm, but as there was no paper bag in sight, Shay feared she'd never escape this overpowering sense of foreboding.

"Shay, yer going to be okay. Look at me," Liam said quietly.

She couldn't ignore the calm command and gazed into his eyes. While there was concern there, she didn't see panic.

"Good. Now, do me a favor, lass. Purse yer lips like yer about to whistle."

Shay did as he instructed.

"Good. Now, regulate your breathing through them. No, keep them pursed. There you go. Good lass."

Somewhere in Shay's mind, she felt the need to scold him for talking to her as if she were a child or scared puppy, but the technique was working, so she was too grateful to remind him she was a grown woman.

After several moments of breathing through her pursed lips and listening to Liam's soothing voice, Shay could finally breathe easy again. She straightened to her full height and sighed. Exhaustion replaced panic, and she rested her forehead against Liam's chest. "Thank you," she whispered, not knowing if he heard her or if the wind had stolen her words and sent them off unheard into the night air.

"Yer welcome." There was a gravelly tone to his voice that she hadn't heard before.

She lifted her head and studied him. "What's wrong?"

"Nothing. I'm just glad yer okay."

Shay looked skeptically at him, but let the subject drop. Madam Malvina's declaration that Orion was Doyle's son echoed painfully through her head. "Do you think that Orion is actually my . . . my half brother?"

"I think we dig deeper and wait until we have definitive proof before jumping to any conclusions."

If that were true, and if Doyle was in fact her father, what did this news change for her? She had wanted connection to family, but Orion, a teenager, with whom she had nothing in common . . . ? Beyond having a friendship with Tassi, they were as different as night and day, and after what Madam Malvina said about forcing Orion to build a relationship with Tassi, she wasn't sure they had even that in common anymore.

Fresh anger bubbled up inside her. Half brother or not, she wouldn't let Orion deceive her friend any longer. Stinging pain in her palms forced her from her fuming thoughts. She opened her fists to find half-moon shapes embedded in her palms. A whispered voice brushed her cheeks. *Remember the raven and Gran's words. Listen, watch, and learn, as not everything ill began with evil intentions.*

What do you mean, Bridget? What am I missing!

Shay focused on her breathing. Perhaps Orion had no choice but to do his mother's bidding, but had, in the course of his relationship with Tassi, come to have real feelings for her. He certainly looked at her with an intensity that felt real.

Shay shook off those gloomy thoughts and looked over Liam's shoulder. "Where's Conor?"

"He stayed behind to continue eavesdropping." He wrapped his arm around her shoulder. "Let's get ye home."

Five minutes later, Liam and Shay reached her front porch and an awaiting Spirit, who looked very much like her adoptive mother did when teenage Shay tried to slip in the door a few minutes past curfew.

She patted Spirit's head. "I'm sorry. I know you were worried. How about I give you an extra treat to make up for my lateness?"

Spirit yipped, cocked his head, and perked his ears.

She chuckled as she unlocked the door, dropped her bag on the floor, and tossed two doggie treats in the air for Spirit to catch. Then she sank into the sofa and put her feet up on her trunk coffee table. "I'm done."

"I'll make you some tea," said Liam, as he laid a throw from the back of the sofa over her.

Shay curled up into a ball and nestled under the blanket. There was something comforting in listening to Liam working in her kitchen: the sound of the water pouring into the kettle, the opening and shutting of the cupboard as he gathered mugs, the clicking and clanking of the porcelain, the softly hissed swear words, indicating not all was going as he wanted it to. Shay smiled and closed her eyes, keeping track of his motions in her mind's eye as she listened to his movements. Somewhere there was a soft clicking of the door, but Shay was too tired to open her eyes to check. Darkness soon took over.

"Shay?"

Shay, startled, opened her eyes, and peered up at Liam. "What? What happened?"

He chuckled, set her mug on the coffee table next to the sofa, and sat beside her. "Nothing happened. I have yer tea."

After struggling to get into a sitting position, Shay grabbed the teacup and curled her cold hands around it. The warmth of the cup seeped into her bones, and she took a bracing sip. "This is good. But it's not one of my brews."

There was an impish gleam in Liam's eyes. "Aye, you'd be correct. This is an old family recipe. Ye needed something to put some color back in yer cheeks and fire back in yer spirit."

Shay narrowed her gaze at him. "What'd you spike my tea with?"

"Ye like it?"

Shay took another sip. "I do. What is it, and what's in here? I taste a familiar herb."

"It's a hot toddy with Liam's special ingredient. And, no, I will not tell you what it is so you can knock it off with your puppy-dog eyes."

Shay blinked. "I wasn't giving you puppy-dog eyes." When he started to object, she held her hand up. "Besides, I don't keep whiskey in the cottage. Can't stand the stuff."

"First off, it's not whiskey. I use brandy, and I left you but for a moment to grab the ingredients from my cottage."

So that was the sound of the closing door. Shay took another sip, closed her eyes, and relished in the liquid heat and radiating warmth it provided. "Thank you. Someday you'll have to share your recipe."

"Then ye'll be waiting until the end of time for that."

"Fine. I'll just get it from Gran, then."

"She's the one who swore me to secrecy."

"Yes, but as I'm usually not a thorn in her side, unlike you and Conor, she might be more willing to share it with me." She gave him a cheeky grin.

"Why—"

The front door burst open, and Conor nearly fell through.

Liam jumped to his feet. "Haven't you heard of knocking?"

Conor closed the door with his foot. "Thought I had a standing invitation." At Shay's raised eyebrow, he blushed and massaged his neck. "Sorry. Want me to go back out and try again?"

"It's a little too late for that, don't ye think?" Liam bristled and sat back down next to Shay.

"It's alright, Conor," said Shay. "Have a seat. What did Madam Malvina and Doyle have to say after I . . . well . . . ran?"

"I don't blame you for running. If I'd been in your shoes, I would have." Conor settled back in the wing-backed chair beside the fireplace. "Nothing much, actually. Madam Malvina got real quiet after Doyle said what he did about his son, and after a few minutes with nothing but the hissing sound of water being dumped on the fire, they went back into her shop. I hung about to see if I could follow Doyle back to wherever he's staying, but he must have evaded me."

Shay fought her way out of the blanket, grabbed her bag, sat back down, and rummaged through it. After smoothing the folded paper with the questions she'd written down at the café earlier that week, she passed it to Liam. He scanned the paper and then handed it to Conor.

Conor took a quick scan and shook his head. "I don't know if I can answer all the questions on your list, but I think we're close to answering two of them." He held the paper up and read aloud. "Did she kill on the orders of Doyle? And if Madam Malvina isn't the killer, was she simply a patsy for Doyle, the person whom all the evidence points to? What did Doyle have on her that she'd be willing to take the fall for murder?"

"It looks like Doyle knew all of Madam Malvina's dirty business secrets," said Shay. "So, if she was drugging her clients to make them more susceptible to her readings, that would not only end her business but send her to prison." Shay shook her head in disgust. "Which means, if it's true, that the hold he had over her was huge. With everything at stake, I can only guess that when he said jump, she had no choice but to ask how high."

"Do you think it's possible that she drugged Cora to make the poor woman more open to her suggestions?" Liam asked.

"That's a possibility that I haven't ruled out. It's clear from the note she left for her husband that Cora trusted the person 'helping' her with the ceremony. With this new evidence, however, it might be that Cora was under a spell of sorts that was caused by the opioids."

"Could be that the opioids sped up the effects of the belladonna in her system," Conor added. "Maybe the person responsible for her death didn't mean to kill her. If the killer wasn't Madam Malvina, he or she wouldn't know about the drugs in her system from the readings, right?"

"Don't forget that, according to the pathologist, the belladonna had been built up in her system over time," Shay said.

"What if there are two people involved? The poisoner, who had evil intentions toward Cora, and the killer, who ironically enough, had no knowledge of the poisoning via belladonna or the opioids." Liam sat up straight, and his gaze flipped between Shay and Conor.

A vision of twinberry honeysuckle flitted through Shay's mind, and she swore she heard again Bridget's whispered warning that not all that ends badly began with bad intentions.

Shay jumped to her feet. "What does it all mean?" she muttered to herself as she paced the room, ignoring Liam and Conor's quizzical gazes. "What in the world do the twinberry honeysuckle and Bridget's cryptic message mean?" Shay mumbled and continued pacing, her lips moving silently as she processed her thoughts. The twinberry honeysuckle, although not as deadly as belladonna, was still considered a toxic plant and could cause harm if too much was ingested. Her amulet warmed against her skin. The cryptic message from Bridget echoed through her mind.

Not all that ends ill began with evil intentions. But there were still intentions behind it. Someone started a process and, even though he or she had no evil in mind, had set fate in motion and now could not prevent it all turning horribly wrong.

The fairy ring, the ceremonial theatrics of it all, the missing bottle, the remaining pouch, the Samhain eve timeline, the buried shoes, all pointed to an inexperienced killer. A killer who paid far more attention to the little details in setting up the scene than he or she did to cleaning it up afterward. Doyle would not have wasted his time with all the pomp and circumstance. If he'd wanted Cora's bottle—which he wouldn't in the first place, because he knew who held the true power—he'd have killed Cora outright and cleaned up after himself.

"I think you're right, Liam." Shay stopped pacing. "I think there are two people involved, but they are not working in tandem. They didn't know about the other's actions, and poor Cora got caught in the middle of all this madness."

Liam and Conor gaped at her.

"Don't you see? The twinberry honeysuckle is still a dangerous plant, if used improperly, and can cause harm under the right circumstances. I think the person ultimately responsible for Cora's death meant to steal the bottle or trick Cora into giving it to them. Intention for harm was there, but I do not believe intention to kill was. After Cora died, I think this individual panicked, grabbed the bottle, and left the pouch behind, which wasn't too big of a deal. They probably thought it would point nicely back to me, as it came from my shop."

"What about the shoes?" Liam asked.

"That's why I think the killer panicked. He or she saw what had happened and was left with a dead woman's pair of shoes. An unmistakable pair. Not many people around here can afford Prada anything. Panicked people never make good decisions, and I think they buried the shoes, thinking the police would concentrate their efforts on the fairy ring crime scene instead of a random boulder on the outskirts. It would have worked too, if Tassi hadn't had the same dream as I did, and . . . apparently Gran."

"Doyle wouldn't screw up like that," Conor said.

"That's what I think too, which again points to one person as the most logical killer."

"Madam Malvina," Liam and Conor cried instantaneously.

Chapter 30

Sunday dawned with low-hanging storm clouds and roaring winds smashing raindrops across the cottage's windows. When Shay's alarm blared its morning wakeup call, she groaned and buried her head under her covers. She was about to hit the snooze button when a knock on her door ended that fairy-tale dream.

"Coming," she muttered as she slipped into her slippers and tied her robe. Something about the rainy, cloudy weather chilled her to her bones, and she shivered as she walked toward the front door.

Another loud knock sounded before she could unlock and open it.

"I said I was coming," she said as she flung it open. "Dean?" Shay stepped aside. "Come in out of that weather."

"Thanks." He stepped in and looked down at the water pouring off him onto her welcome mat. "Sorry about that."

"It'll dry." She grinned. "Whereas you might never be dry again by the look of you."

"Tell me about it."

"Want some coffee?" She scanned him head to toe. "And maybe a towel?"

"As tempting as that sounds, I'll pass. I can't stay long. I thought you'd like news about the shoes."

"Are you offering to tell me something and not have me finagle the information out of you, like normal?"

"Don't get used to it. There's nothing definitive yet, as the lab's not done processing everything, and that could take weeks. But we did find something—a piece of gum stuck to the bottom of one of her sandals."

Shay frowned. How had she missed that? "She could have picked that up anywhere. There were hundreds of people milling around during the Halloween festival, and who knows how many kids simply spit theirs out."

"Maybe, but the lab thinks it was picked up much later in the evening, closer to the crime scene, because of the amount of California sagebrush and other vegetation found only on the bluff in question that was captured in the gum wad. We're still waiting on definitive results, but I'd bet my next paycheck that's correct."

"I know that California sagebrush grows back quickly after fires and that while it's not actually sage, it has the smell of it, but what does that have to do with proving where she picked it up?"

"Think, Shay. You never see it in people's gardens, right?"

"Right."

"Never thought I'd hear those words from you."

Shay grinned. "Well, are you going to fill me in or not?"

"California sagebrush doesn't take too kindly to neighbors and will actually inhibit the growth of nearby plants. It's rare to find it in town, but there is an abundance of this plant along the coast and especially on the bluffs, like the one where Cora was killed."

"And you think this is where Cora stepped on the wad of gum?"

"Again, I'm still waiting for conclusive evidence, but

that's what my cop gut is telling me. I do know it's not Cora's," Dean said. "I already checked with the mayor, and he claims Cora never chewed gum as she thought it made her seem uncouth."

"Which means the gum could be the killer's?"

"Perhaps. I'm keeping an open mind. It could have been a random hiker's too. But it would have had to have been fairly fresh to stick to Cora's shoe." He sighed. "I can't help but feel like I'm grasping at straws. Nothing about this case adds up or makes sense."

"If it is the killer's, you have his or her DNA."

"Which only counts if we have the killer's DNA already on file. If not, it's a waiting game that could lead to nothing."

The look of dejection on Dean's face caused Shay a pang of guilt for not coming clean about the book of poisons. After he'd given her more information than he normally did, she'd knowingly kept a piece of evidence from him. Granted, he'd have told her it was only supposition and not worth anything until there was proof behind it, but she should have at least let him know about it.

"Hang on. I'll be right back." She hurried to her bedroom, unearthed the book from its hiding place in her sock drawer, and clutched it to her chest as she walked back toward Dean. "Please don't be angry with me."

"Shay, what have you done?" Dean held his hand out for the book and flipped through the pages.

She shuffled her weight from one foot to the other. "I . . . ah . . . Mayor Sutton gave this to me because Cora had it, and he wanted to know more about it. And there were handwritten recipes and notes in the margins, and I wanted to confirm that the handwriting belonged to the person I thought—Madam Malvina—before giving the book to you. I didn't want to waste your time, and you're always going on and on about needing proof and—"

"Darn it, Shay! I should have at least known about it, don't you think? Keeping this from me, from the police, has possibly set back this investigation by weeks." Dean's face reddened. "Do you honestly think I just sit in my office with my feet on my desk, waiting for you to trot on in with whatever you've managed to dig up? I have a job to do, and that's to protect the people of this community, and if I don't have all the facts—whether you think they are pertinent or not—I can't do my job. Do you understand?" He didn't wait for her answer and instead shook his head. "And here I thought I'd extend a little courtesy your way, allowing you access to facts I normally wouldn't, and this is how you repay me?"

"Dean, I'm sorry, but I honestly—"

"I could arrest you for impeding an investigation, you know." Dean pinned her with a fierce gaze.

"Jen would put you in the doghouse and never let you back out if you did that."

"Yeah, well, I'm already in the doghouse, so there's not much for me to lose, now is there?" Dean's shoulders stooped.

"Wait, what? What happened?"

"Never mind." He puffed out his cheeks and exhaled. "Look, I'm sorry for scolding you. I took my stress out on you, and that's not fair. With the mayor breathing down my neck and me getting nowhere with this case, I—" He studied the tips of his black boots. "I snapped, and I'm sorry."

"No, you're right. I should have shared the book with you when the mayor first brought it to me. I was worried about unnecessarily stirring things up if I was wrong, though." She gestured to the cover of the book clutched in his hands. "You should know too that Liam had one of his contacts compare the handwriting, but the results were inconclusive. The sample from the birthday card we know was written by Madam Malvina, because Tassi watched her write it, wasn't a conclusive match to the handwritten notes in the poison book. There's just enough of a discrepancy between them to give the expert pause."

"And when were you going to pass along this tidbit of information?"

Shay's cheeks burned. "After I had confronted Madam Malvina about it."

"And did you?"

"I confronted her about the book, asking if she'd heard of it. I didn't ask her about the handwriting in it."

"And?"

"I got the sense she was lying when she said she'd never heard of it, and the amulet warmed as well, so I'm leaning toward her at least knowing about its existence. Which is something to go on, at least."

"I'll be the judge of that." He tucked the book under his arm. "Let me be clear about one thing, Shay. I think you and I could actually work well together, and while I can't officially use your help or anything like that, I'd like to know that when I need you, I can trust you. Please don't keep any more evidence from me, okay?"

"I promise." Looking at his creased brow, she crossed herself. "Cross my heart. I never will again."

"Let's just hope that in the future there aren't any more murders in town; then I won't have to worry about what you're digging up behind my back." Dean's radio squawked, and he sighed. "Well, I'd better get going. Stay out of trouble, and let me know the moment you figure out anything or hear anything or even suspect anything." He tucked the book inside his jacket, opened the door, and dashed out into the rain.

Shay closed the door, berating herself. Her action had risked alienating her brother-in-law, who, over the course of the past two years, had always tried to keep her on the sidelines of an investigation. Then, after finally relenting—for whatever reason, and completely out of character—he had started to share facts with her, and how did she repay him? She'd held back a major clue.

Sure, she hadn't done it for any nefarious reasons. She just didn't want to again hear the words "I need proof," which were generally followed up with the proverbial pat on the head and him asking her to run along and let him get back to work. But the fact was that, even though she had fully intended to share what she found out with him as soon as she had that all-elusive proof, her lack of two-way communication with him had now strained their relationship.

That's what happens when you keep secrets, though, isn't it? You end up hurting a lot of people, including yourself, in the end. Maybe it was because she was born in secret, raised in secret, and then endured secrets from the man who had sworn to love her until death did them part that she continued to perpetuate the cycle, even though she hated it.

No. She would break the cycle. And she'd start with Jen. The time for secrets between them was over.

An hour later, she hopped from the taxi she'd taken to her shop, due to the downpour, and sprinted to her front door. The awning did little to protect her from the deluge, as a wind had picked up, causing the rain to fall sideways. By the time she got the door unlocked and entered the tea shop, she was dripping wet.

She scowled at the squishing sound that echoed up with each step she took in her sopping-wet booties. Good thing her jacket had protected her wool sweater from the rain, and while her black leggings would dry quickly, she feared she'd have squishy socks all day. Shuddering at that idea, she made a mental note to keep an extra set of clothes at the shop.

She ignored the squishing between her toes and readied the tea shop for customers brave enough to venture out in the weather. She glanced up at the wall clock. Jen would be in soon, and in order to refocus her scattered thoughts, Shay climbed the steps to her greenhouse and sat, as usual, until she heard the doorbells jingle out her sister's arrival.

"Shay?" Jen's voice sailed up the steps, along with the scent of coffee.

Shay blew out a breath. "I'm up here!"

All too soon, Jen stood in front of her, coffee cups in hand. The words Shay had been rehearsing quickly evaporated from her mind.

"You look as if you've seen a ghost," said Jen, handing her a take-out cup. "Here, and I don't think we need to rush this morning. I doubt we'll have any customers until this storm passes."

Shay fiddled with the lid of the cup and wished the conversation was already over, that Jen had already forgiven her, and that they were back to normal. But it wasn't over, and the only way it would be was if she started it.

"Shay, you're starting to scare me. Are you not feeling well? Did you get bad news?" Jen rested her hand on Shay's forearm. "Did Liam break your heart . . . again? If that's the case, I'll hunt him down and—"

"It's not Liam." Well, it was not *not* Liam, but that was a conversation for another day. Today was all about Shay and the untruths she'd allowed to come between her and her sister. "It's me."

"I'm not sure I understand," said Jen, staring blankly at her.

Shay didn't blame Jen, as she hardly understood herself. "I have to apologize to you."

"For what?"

"I . . . I've been keeping secrets from you."

Jen slid her hand from Shay's arm. "We're under no obligation to tell each other everything, so don't feel like you—"

"No, these are secrets I kept from you because I didn't trust you enough, and that's not a wall I want between us."

"I don't understand." Jen's shoulders slumped. "You don't trust me?"

"No. Yes. No, I do." Shay grabbed for Jen's hand. "No, see? This is why I need to come clean because I do trust you. I was afraid for you. Does that make sense?"

Jen's quizzical gaze indicated it did not make one bit of sense.

Shay squeezed her sister's hand. "I've come to realize, over the past few weeks, especially with all the secrets and lies surrounding Cora's death, that I don't want secrets or half-truths to rule my life anymore. There is one secret that I have to keep from the world, but you are not that world. You're my sister."

"What are you saying?" Jen pulled her hand away. "Have I ever done anything that would make you think you can't trust me? I mean, even when you found out who Bridget was in your life, I accepted you as my blood relative and—"

"I know, and I don't know where the feeling of wanting to live in secrecy comes from. I was thinking that perhaps it was because that's all I've ever known since I discovered that my life in Santa Fe and then my entire childhood were lies." She massaged her temples. "But the why doesn't matter now. No more secrets."

Jen's face was ashen, and Shay reached inside her sweater, pulled out the leather pouch encasing the blue bottle, and placed it on the bench between them. "What do you know about this?"

Jen narrowed her eyes at Shay, as if expecting a trick

question. "It's an heirloom from Bridget, your birth mother, and you sometimes use it to enhance your readings."

"That's not all." Shay inhaled and exhaled to steady her nerves. "There's a priceless blue diamond in the bottle. It's the major part of the Early family legacy and the object that gives great power to the possessor, and . . . and there's a man who is after it—Doyle, to be exact."

"Doyle? Isn't that the man you think could be your birth father? A rare blue diamond? This is crazy."

"Tell me about it, but yes, and Doyle wants nothing more than to take the blue bottle from me, by force if necessary."

Jen gasped and placed her hand over her heart. "Shay, I—"

"That's not all. He's tried before, and I'll be under his shadow until, well . . ." Shay swallowed against the lump in her throat. She'd never really processed the future with Doyle always on the fringes of her life. He wouldn't stop until he had the blue diamond. She straightened her shoulders. She would not let Doyle rule her life with fear.

Tears welled up in Jen's eyes. "Oh, Shay, I don't know what to say."

"That's not all." Shay smiled sadly. "I . . . ah . . . I have to tell you now about all this because the blue bottle is at the center of Cora's murder, and Doyle is in town and may or may not be involved in and/or connected to all of it."

Red splotches expanded on Jen's cheeks. "So, he could harm you . . . kill you even . . . at any moment, then?"

Shay's heartbeat pounded in her ears. "Yes, which also puts everyone I know in danger too, and why I never told you about the diamond and its powers before. Dean told me not to because if you didn't know, you'd be easier to protect, but now I'm afraid for everyone I care about because Doyle is so—"

"Wait! Dean knows about this priceless diamond, and you didn't tell me this because . . . ?"

"Because I thought . . . we thought . . . if you didn't know, then you'd be safer and"—Shay dropped her gaze and whispered—"I didn't want you mothering me and living your life in fear for mine."

Chapter 31

The silence was unbearable, and Shay finally looked up from the floor and met Jen's tear-filled eyes. "Oh, don't cry. Please don't. If you start crying, I'll start crying, and you know how puffy and red my face gets. Neither of us will be fit to be seen when customers arrive."

Thunder rolled in the distance, and the rain beat harder against the greenhouse windows.

"Not much chance of anyone coming out in this," Jen mumbled and swiped hard at her damp cheeks.

"Go ahead and yell at me. I deserve it. I've kept this secret from you for two years, and the lies and half-truths I've told in the past few weeks are too many to count."

When Jen remained silent, Shay squirmed in her chair. "Please, say something. Anything. Tell me what a horrible sister I've been, because that's the truth."

"No." Jen got to her feet and paced. "That's not true. You're an excellent sister, and one I missed horribly while you were away. Our lives moved so quickly in different directions that I lost my purpose in your life. It should have been to support you"—a harsh laugh ripped from her chest—"but as I didn't know about your struggles with Brad until you landed on my doorstep, I did a horrible job of that."

"You didn't know because I didn't tell you. I was embarrassed by how easily he duped me, and that's—"

"You didn't tell me because you didn't think you could, and that is entirely my fault. I should have maintained contact, checked in on you after you left Bray Harbor." Jen paused her pacing and studied Shay's face. "I always knew there was something different, something special about you. I never knew the reason until you told me, but our parents were always so protective of you, and after they died, I stepped into that role. Part of me feels guilty that I didn't protect you from Brad, and I'm making up for lost time, I guess." Jen sat back down and cradled Shay's hands in hers. "You've had so much thrown at you that I want to protect you from all I can. So, you are right, I do mother-smother you, and I'm sorry." A large tear slid down her cheek. "I hate the fact that there's someone out there who wants to harm you, Shay, and I hate the fact that I'm powerless against it. If I could protect you, I would."

"But you can't, so—"

Jen smiled. "Quit interrupting me, little sister. Because I can't protect you, I won't even try. I will walk through this with you side by side. How does that sound?" She held out her pinky finger. "How about we enact the sacred pinky swear of our childhood, huh? I promise to try not to mother you, and you promise to not keep secrets that could break our trust."

Shay held out her pinky finger, which she could barely make out due to her tear-blurred vision. "This is unbreakable, you know."

"I know." Jen pulled Shay into a hug. "Thank you for telling me. I don't like it, and I hate this guy with every bone in my body, by the way."

"Join the club." Shay eased out of Jen's hug. "And thank

you for not going ballistic on me, even though I deserved the scolding."

"Well," said Jen, "I probably would have gone berserk if I didn't have a secret I've been keeping from you." She took a few deep breaths. "Ever since Dean got promoted to sheriff, our marriage has been on the rocks. We both thought the promotion would be a good move, as he'd have a more stable schedule, but it seems like it's killing our marriage, and I don't know why." Jen hid her face in her hands and sobbed.

Shay shifted closer to her on the bench and embraced her in a side hug. "I figured something was up when Dean alluded to the fact that he was in the doghouse this morning." At Jen's thunderous look, which rivaled what was happening outside now, Shay wished she could take her words back. There was no sense in pitting them against each other. "He wasn't throwing you under the bus, Jen; he was more scolding me because I withheld evidence from him. He seems really stressed."

"That's the problem. There is so much responsibility on his shoulders with this new position, and it's not getting better. And now with Cora's murder, the mayor is really breathing down Dean's neck for answers, and Dean takes his frustrations out on me and the kids."

Shay gasped. "He's not—"

"No, nothing like that. Dean would never do that. He just comes home grumpy and sullen. I can't remember the last time we had quality time together or the last time he went to one of Maddie's recitals or played baseball with Hunter in the backyard. We've become more roommates who tolerate each other than the loving couple we once were, and I'm scared that this is the end."

Shay held her sister as she wept. "Why didn't you tell me?"

Jen sniffled. "Because I knew how stressed you already

were, and I didn't want to add to it. It's my job to take care of you, not the other way around."

"Looks like we both underestimated how much we could support each other." Shay grabbed Jen by the shoulders and forced her sister to look at her. "When this is all done, you and Dean go off to some tropical island together. Dean has to have vacation days built up, as I've never known him to take time off. Tassi and I can cover the shop, and I will watch Maddie and Hunter. You and Dean need to reconnect, and you can't do it here or with kids around."

"You're right."

"You know, a lot of people have been telling me that lately." She recalled Dean's words, and a smile formed on her lips. "I really need to get this 'you're right' thing in writing for later when everyone thinks I am wrong again."

A weak smile came to Jen's lips, and she hugged Shay. "Thank you for trusting me enough to tell me your secret. Now"—she held Shay at arm's length—"fill me in on the Cora case. We have time, and I think you owe me at least that much, don't you?"

"Yeah, sorry about all the cloak-and-dagger meetings behind your back while you dealt with the business. I really don't know what I'd do without you."

"Knowing you, you'd figure out some genius plan, like what you did with the bubbling witch's brew."

Shay's face grew warm with her sister's compliment. "Thank you." She dug out the sheet with her scrawled questions, smoothed out the crinkled paper, and filled Jen in on the case. "So, I'm left with these questions"—she tapped her finger on the paper—"and Liam, Conor, and I agree that there are two people involved: the poisoner, who for some reason was poisoning Cora with belladonna over a period of time, and the killer, who unintentionally dealt the final blow."

"And you think this all because of a cryptic message from Bridget?" Jen asked.

"Yes. There has to be meaning behind it."

"And the blue bottle is at the heart of this crime?"

"I believe so; otherwise, there's no sense in stealing it. Someone wanted the bottle, and believing Cora had the real thing, he or she devised a plan to get it from her."

"But they could have easily stolen it from her, ripped it from her neck, or cut the leather thong while she was alive. There would be no reason to kill her to get the bottle. I'm sure that if someone pulled a knife on her and ordered her to give it over, she would have. Cora might have been a difficult woman, but she was no idiot."

The cryptic messages from both Bridget and Doyle and the vivid vision of the crying individual echoed through her mind. Her amulet warmed, and she flinched, not from the heat of the bottle but from the pain-filled sobbing of the person she'd failed to identify. The more she thought, the more she knew it was the crying of a child. But this didn't make sense because there was no child in this case.

Bridget's whispered words rang through Shay's mind. *Remember, not all that ends ill began with evil intentions.*

Doyle's face popped up in Shay's vision. *Be careful what you look for because you might find the answer you don't want.*

Sweat beaded on her forehead. Shay jumped to her feet. "Oh my gosh, Cora wasn't supposed to die. No one wanted to kill her. There are two, possibly three people involved."

Jen gaped at her. "Did you just solve the case?"

"Maybe." Shay snapped her fingers as she thought. "I have to go check something."

Jen gestured to the back window of the greenhouse, which was weeping with rain. "In this?"

"I don't have a choice." Shay grabbed her jacket and hurried toward the spiral staircase. "If I'm right, another life is on the line."

"Shay, do you want me to call Dean?"

Shay paused, her hand on the railing. She had promised Dean to share what she knew, but there was no time to wait. With worry swirling in her stomach and the amulet burning at her skin, she knew there was no time to lose. A vision of the bluff where Cora's body was found flashed in her mind. "Tell him to meet me at the bluff. And tell him to hurry. I'm afraid it's a matter of life and death. Can I take your car?"

Wordlessly, Jen dug in her purse and tossed her the keys. "Be careful."

With Jen's words of caution still ringing in her ears, Shay dashed through the tea shop, out into the pouring rain, and raced down the street to her sister's SUV. Her heart pounded so loudly in her ears that it drowned out the sounds of the lashing winds and torrential rain. To make matters worse, despite her so-called rainproof jacket and the quick sprint to the SUV, Shay still got soaked from head to toe.

She swiped at the beads of rainwater running off her hood into her eyes, but it didn't make a difference. She still could barely see through the windshield because the wipers couldn't keep up with the deluge. As she did a quick shoulder check and pulled away from the curb, she decided that, if her gut and the amulet were correct, by the time she was done with the incident she anticipated she was about to encounter, she'd be just as sopping wet as she would be coming out of a refreshing shower, but this encounter wouldn't feel as luxurious as that. She stepped on the gas pedal.

Shay drove up the winding road that led to the bluff and parked as close as she could to the wooded area that separated the ocean and bluff from the roadway. The rain had not stopped, and Shay searched about for an umbrella. After finding one shoved under the front driver's seat, she took a few bracing breaths, opened the door and her umbrella, and slogged forward through the puddles and tiny rivulets of water cutting through the sandy soil. Rain pinged at the umbrella, and the whipping wind threatened to tear it from her hands.

When she finally reached the wooded area, she was now faced with the uphill trudge while dealing with the dense foliage and trees in a rainstorm. She collapsed the umbrella and clawed her way up as fast as she dared, slipping and tripping through the undergrowth, keeping the victorious image of her reaching the top, before it was too late, firmly planted in her mind. When her phone rang, she ignored the twigs tearing at her hair and struggled to dig her ringing phone from her jacket pocket. "Hello?"

"Shay, thank goodness you picked up. I must have just missed you." Tassi's voice cracked with emotion.

"What's wrong?" The amulet went from burning to scorching, and Shay hissed in pain.

"I found something . . . something that doesn't look good."

Shay finally saw the end of the woods and could make out the flat land of the bluff. "Tassi, just come out with it."

"I found other samples of Madam Malvina's handwriting . . ." A sob tore from Tassi's throat.

"That's actually a good thing. That gives the handwriting experts more to work with, and maybe it will be a definitive match to Madam Mal—"

"No . . . they're not Madam Malvina's."

Shay gritted her teeth as she pulled herself over the top

of the bluff. "Tassi, please," she groaned. "If they're not Madam Malvina's, whose are they?"

There was an eerie silence from Tassi as Shay struggled to get to her feet and move through the last of the underbrush onto the wide-open bluff. A figure paced at the edge of the cliff, and there was no mistaking the recognizable form.

"Orion!" Shay yelled over the screaming wind and pounding rain at the exact moment Tassi whispered his name into the phone.

Chapter 32

"Tassi, call Dean. Tell him I'm on the cliff by my house, bring backup and to hurry." Shay gripped her phone in her hand and launched into a sprint, hoping to get to Orion before he made the ultimate fatal decision.

It appeared that Orion hadn't heard her over the sound of the storm and continued to pace along the cliff's edge. The amulet seared Shay's skin, and she swore it branded her. Not wanting to startle him, she pulled up a few feet from him. Her breath came heavy and labored as she fought to fill her lungs. It was clear he still hadn't noticed her, and she took a moment to gather her racing thoughts. If she came across as panicked, he would be too, and that would only end in disaster when she visualized how high they were above the rocks and crashing waves below.

After a few moments and after finally controlling her breathing, she drew in a deep breath. "Orion?" she called, loudly enough to be heard over the storm.

He spun around and gaped at her. His wild, red-rimmed eyes bugged out when he set them on her. His skin, normally pale, glowed translucent in the gray murky light. "Shay?" he whispered, the wind catching his words and whipping them back out to sea.

Shay took one step forward, but stopped the moment he took a step back, bringing him closer to the ledge. She held her hands out. "I won't hurt you, Orion. I just want to talk. Is that okay?"

Orion shook his head and looked back over his shoulder. A shudder wracked his body, and Shay feared the force of it alone would send the boy over onto the rocks below. He whipped his head around and locked gazes with her. "What are you doing here?"

"I'm here to help you."

A harsh laughed ripped from his chest. "You're a little too late for that."

The pain in Orion's eyes mirrored the pain of the crying child from her vision, and everything clicked into place. "No, it's never too late to do the right thing."

"You have a spell that can bring Cora back from the dead?"

Shay flinched at his cutting sarcasm. "No, but you have the power to bring justice to her."

"Justice?" He nearly spat the word. "If there was any justice in the world, Cora would be alive, and I wouldn't be on this ledge—" His voice cracked, and tears sprung into his eyes.

"You have the choice to back away from it, Orion."

"That's where you're wrong. I am out of choices." Orion took another step closer to the edge.

Rain lashed at Shay's face, as she peered past him to the cliff top and feared the unrelenting rain had made the rocks at the edge slippery and unstable. "I know, Orion. I know you didn't mean to kill Cora."

"How do you know that?"

"Because I—"

"You are the real thing, aren't you? You saw, didn't you? Mother has always yammered on and on about what a fraud you were and that your scheming ways would put her out of business, but it turns out that she's the fraud, isn't she?"

"I'm not here to talk about your mother. I'm here to talk about you." Shay held her hands out. "Please, Orion, come away from the ledge."

"No. I can talk from here."

Shay took a steadying breath. "Tell me what happened between you and Cora. Now I know you never meant to harm her."

"I only wanted the blue bottle, but I didn't want her to know I was the one to take it. It all seemed so easy at first. I knew she'd been coming in to see my mother. I eavesdropped on their conversations to know enough about what Cora wanted." Orion shivered and wrapped his arms around his chest. "I . . . ah . . . bought the book of poisons online—"

"So your mother really didn't know about the book?" Shay thought back to her run-in with Madam Malvina at the grocery store and sucked in a breath. The amulet's warming hadn't had anything to do with Madam Malvina's supposed lies but was about Orion, who had stood next to his mother. Shay had misinterpreted the amulet's warming. She'd been so set against Madam Malvina that she hadn't even considered the other possibility, that Orion was involved in Cora's death. Shay just hoped that she wasn't too late in trying to rectify it all and could bring Orion safely back from the edge.

"Not that I know. I didn't get the book from her or her shop, if that's what you're asking." His voice was filled with frustration.

Shay held her hands up. "Sorry, I didn't mean anything by that. I was just curious. Please continue." Shay wanted to check the time on her phone, but knew that would send the wrong message. In her mind, it seemed that she'd been on the ledge in the wind and rain for hours, but it could only have been minutes. If only Dean would hurry. *Keep him talking, Shay. You have to buy time!* "So, what happened?"

Orion glanced back over his shoulder. "I . . . uh . . . knew Cora had come to believe everything my mother was telling her and was open to suggestion, so I did some research. It wouldn't take much to convince Cora, but I knew she wouldn't instinctively trust me. So I copied my mother's handwriting, and after I had mastered it enough to trick Cora, I texted her from my mother's phone and wrote something about Orion having a book he was going to drop off, and if Cora was willing, Orion could walk her through a special ceremony. She fell for it. Then I deleted the text thread from my mother's phone, so she wouldn't see the conversation."

"But the text thread would have shown up on Cora's phone."

"I had her delete it before the ceremony. I told her that what we were doing was highly irregular, and as she was the mayor's wife, she should probably get rid of all the evidence." He dragged his wet hair from his eyes. "I knew I had to give her something to bring about the visions she was looking for. I was unsure how to do this until I came across a vial of belladonna in my mother's shop."

Shay gasped. "Your mother had a vial of it?"

"It was locked away, but I'd learned at a very early age to get into those hiding places. Don't you see, I was desperate to get the blue bottle, and when I found the belladonna, I knew I had my answer. I researched how to use it and took a nonlethal dose to the fairy ring. I figured that after she fell into her trance, I could steal the blue bottle from her, and she'd wake up none the wiser in the middle of the fairy ring and believe she'd communed with the fairies."

"And the missing bottle?"

"I was hoping she'd assume the fairies took it or she'd lost it in their world or something. I hadn't thought that far, to be honest."

"And then she died."

Orion gulped and clasped his hands to his throat. "I . . . I panicked. I had researched so carefully. I had done the math so many times, I saw it in my dreams. I was confident that all I was doing was giving her a pretty sweet hallucination, allowing her to see what she wanted to see, and taking the bottle. I needed it more than she did, after all."

Shay heard the echoes of the crying child from her visions and shuddered at the pain echoing in those heart-wrenching sounds. Even though Shay sensed she knew the answer, she asked, "Why did you need it more than she did?"

"My father." His tears mingled with the rain dripping down his face. "I knew he hated me, never wanted any part of my life, thought of me a freak, a waste of time. When I overheard him and my mother talking about the blue bottle and how badly he wanted it, I thought that perhaps if I could get it and give it to him, he . . . he might finally love me . . . want me for his son." His voice broke, and sobs wracked his body.

Tears burned at the back of Shay's eyes, and she swallowed hard past the lump in her throat. She too wanted the love of a father, and with the high possibility it was Doyle, it was a love she would never get. While she would never stoop to the actions Orion had, she understood that the pain he had felt was too much for the lost young man.

"What happened after that, Orion, after you realized she was dead?"

"I . . . ah . . . knew I had to cover my tracks, and in doing so, I erased hers. I realized my mistake after I had done it and knew immediately I had signed my own death warrant. I tried to get rid of all the evidence that I could. I left the pouch thinking it would lead back to you." He shook his head. "Sorry about that, by the way. You've never shown me anything but kindness, and I was willing to throw you under the bus in a second."

"Don't worry about it." Shay quickly calculated the time she thought had passed. It felt like an eternity since she'd reached the bluff. She had to keep him talking. Distract him. "What about the shoes? Why didn't you throw them over the bluff and into the ocean?"

"I figured they'd make it ashore somehow, and not many people wear Prada around here, and the moment they were found, they would be identified as Cora's. I panicked and buried them in the only ground I could find loose enough for me to use my pocketknife."

Sirens cut through the wind and rain.

Orion sniffled, wiped his nose, and narrowed his eyes at Shay. "I thought you said you were here to help me. You called the police, didn't you?" He took a step closer to the edge, and lose stones fell over the side. Orion swallowed hard and watched them plummet to the sharp rocks below.

"Orion, don't."

"Give me one good reason not to."

"Tassi."

Orion stared at her. "Do you really think Tassi will want anything to do with me after she knows what I've done?"

"I don't know what she'll do, but I do know that you jumping to your death will ruin her life forever and will impact her future. I know you care about her too much to inflict that pain on her. You love her."

A sob broke from his chest. "Yes, yes, I do."

"Then walk away from the ledge, Orion. Take four big steps toward me, and I'll wait with you." Shay held her hand out toward him. "Please. For Tassi."

Orion gazed down over the edge.

"Orion, please . . ." Shay pleaded through tears.

He turned toward Shay and raised his leg to take a step toward her. At that moment, gale force winds ripped through the clearing, catching Orion off guard. He teetered, and the foot he had planted on the slippery rocks on the ledge lost its grip. Arms flailing, Orion began sliding over the edge.

Shay screamed and launched herself at him. She lay on the ground, dug her toes into the sodden earth, and grabbed his jacket sleeve. "I've got you."

But she didn't have him. Orion was heavier than he looked, and Shay's grip on his sleeve slipped. "Orion, grab onto the rock near your right hand. There, now, try pulling yourself up, okay?"

"I can't. It's not worth it. I'm not worth it."

"Yes, you are. I will not let you die on my watch. Now do as I say," Shay growled through gritted teeth.

Orion grunted as he began pulling himself up. His grip slipped, and he slid further off the ledge, pulling Shay toward him.

"Help, someone, please help!" she called. Then, through the wind, she faintly heard voices calling her name. Yes, Dean was here, but from the sound of the voices accompanying his, they were still too far off to help. If she didn't do something, and fast, Orion and possibly she too, would slide over the edge to the rocks below.

Shay swore under her breath and struggled for a foothold, digging her toes into the saturated soil.

"Just let me go, Shay."

"No." Shay's toes slipped between two rocks, finally

finding an anchor for her body. "Latch onto my arms, Orion, and use me to pull yourself up."

"But I'll pull you down with me."

"No, you won't. Just do as I say." Shay held her breath and wedged her toes even harder into the crevice. Her right hand latched onto another nearby rock, and she used that to push against.

Slowly, so slowly Shay thought time had stopped, Orion pulled himself up over the ledge, using her forearms, then her upper arms, and finally her back as leverage to crawl away from danger. Once safe, Orion collapsed onto his back next to Shay and gulped in air.

Shay, with her right cheek firmly dug into the mud and her body too exhausted to move, studied the boy next to her out of her left eye. "Orion?"

He twisted his neck and looked at her. "Yeah."

"Don't ever do anything foolish like this again, do you hear me?"

"Yes, ma'am."

"And don't call me ma'am. Makes me feel old."

"Shay?" Orion reached out his hand and grasped hers. "Thank you." He turned his face back to the sky, closed his eyes, and didn't bother protecting his face from the pelting rain.

Chapter 33

"Shay!" Dean's voice didn't sound far off, and Shay knew her brother-in-law and his posse would reach her and Orion within seconds. Comfortable in that thought, her heightened level of adrenaline began to fade, and exhaustion seeped into her bones. Drenched from the onslaught of rain, she shivered. Her teeth chattered uncontrollably, and even though the mud was cold against her cheek, she didn't have the energy to lift her head. This is where she'd remain. Cold and tired and next to her probable half brother, a young man who, in desperation for his father's love and approval, had almost taken his own life.

"Shay!"

It wasn't Dean's voice this time. The Irish lilt to it could only mean one person. And when his strong arms wrapped around her and pulled her to her feet and into his chest, she broke down and wept. The sound of Orion's voice filled her ears, but with the wind whipping around them and Liam's heart thudding in his chest, she could make no sense of the words.

Dean's voice cut through Shay's sobs, and she withdrew from Liam's arms in time to see him leading Orion away, the boy's arms behind his back. When Shay started to follow, Liam grasped her hand and pulled her back to him. "Let Dean do his job."

"But—" Shay pulled from Liam's grip. "I need to talk to him, to explain, to—"

"Dean knows what he's doing. Orion confessed to everything."

"I need to speak to him. Dean needs to know—"

"And ye can when everything calms down and ye've taken care of yerself." Liam held his hand out and waited until Shay entwined her fingers through his. "Come. I'll take ye home."

Too tired to argue, Shay walked with Liam past Jen's SUV in the small public parking lot behind the cottages, through her back gate. She robotically climbed the stairs to her back door, where she made her way through the kitchen to her living room, curled up on the sofa, and promptly fell asleep, only to awaken at Liam's light touch in what felt like mere seconds later.

"*A chara?*"

Shay squinted at the face before her. "Did you break every speed limit known to man to get to the bluff?"

A muscle in Liam's jaw ticked. "Getting to the bluff after Dean's phone call? Aye." He cupped Shay's jaw. "And I was still too late."

The warmth from his hand heated Shay from the inside, and goose bumps erupted on her arms. "But you came. And that's all that matters."

"Not if ye'd gone over the edge." He closed his eyes and visibly shuddered.

When he opened his eyes again, they radiated an emotion Shay hadn't seen in them before, and a warm blush crept across her cheeks. "But I didn't," she whispered, "and that's all that matters." She faintly smiled and jerked her head toward the kitchen. "Care for a cup of tea?"

"Ye can have yer tea. I'm going to have something a little stronger." Liam chuckled. "If ye don't mind, I'll pop over to my cottage. That is, if you feel okay about being left alone for a moment?"

"Of course, I'm okay, now." She pushed herself up into a sitting position. "But take my umbrella by the door."

Liam scowled at the rain streaming down the cottage windows. "Yeah, it doesn't look like there's much chance of me getting there and back without one." His warm gaze met hers. "Thanks, I'll be back." As if on impulse, he pressed a kiss to her forehead and ran out the back door, slamming it behind him.

Shay stared at the doorway he had disappeared through for several moments before shaking herself into action. When Liam came back, she didn't want to look like a drowned rat. She sniffed her clothes and crinkled her nose. Surely, she had time for a quick shower too.

Ten minutes later and swathed in dry leggings and an oversized sweater, she headed to the kitchen, gathered the tea supplies, and put the kettle on to boil. A knock sounded on her door, and Liam, in his bright yellow rain gear, opened it and stepped onto her welcome mat and shook out the umbrella under the protection of the back-step awning.

"If someone said it was raining cats and dogs, I'd believe them." He slid out of his wet rain gear, piled them neatly beside the door, and walked toward her, a warmth in his eyes, a smile on his face, fresh black slacks encasing his legs, and an off-white cable-knit fisherman's sweater showing off his muscular physique.

Shay's face grew warm, and she inwardly fought her instinct to draw him toward her. She had to learn to let him go, to forget him, and, worst and hardest of all, think of him only as a friend. She wasn't sure her heart could take that, but it was obvious that's all he wanted from her. He'd made that clear time and time again this past year. She spun around toward the stove, masking her flushing skin, and set about rearranging everything she had already organized.

She sensed him before she felt his hands on her shoulders. "Shay?"

Something in his voice had fire and ice running through her veins. She didn't turn around. Instead, she steadied her thoughts and hands at the task before her and poured the boiling water into the teapot. "There," she said aloud, more to herself than Liam, "in five minutes we'll have some tea."

He gently turned her around and gazed into her eyes. Electricity snapped between them, and the amulet warmed against her skin. It wasn't a scorching or painful heat, but a comforting one. Between the heat from his touch and the comforting sensation of the warm amulet, Shay thought she'd melt to the floor in a puddle, much like the rainwater dripping off his rubber boots.

The new look he'd given her earlier was steady in his eyes. "Care to sit a while? I have a confession to make, *a chara*."

Shay followed him wordlessly to her living room and sank beside him on the sofa. Before she could open her mouth to say anything that would break the magnetic pull between them, he sank his fingers into his hair, pulled, and shook his head.

"Shay, I'm a feckin' eejit."

Shay snorted a laugh at the very Irish and polite way to call someone an idiot. "And this is news to you?" She grinned.

He didn't reciprocate her smile, but continued gazing at her with an intensity that had her squirming. "No, I am.

All jokes aside. For the first time in my life, I've been faced with my own stupidity and brainlessness. Shay"—his hands found hers and clasped them—"today on the bluff, seeing ye near the cliff's edge, yer body flat on the ground . . . I . . ." He closed his eyes and drew in a deep breath. "I'm tired of running from my past, from the ghosts that lurk there, and I think in running from what I didn't understand, I tried to find comfort in many things. Women being one of them." He caressed his thumb over the back of her right hand. "From the day I met ye two years ago, I ran even farther, hid even deeper because I didn't understand the pull ye had on me. I didn't want to open my heart to trust anyone ever again. That was the hardest thing I ever had to do."

Shay blinked, trying to compute the words she was hearing. "Liam, I don't understand—"

"What I'm trying to say is that to escape the pull ye had on me, I ran from ye. I didn't understand it, so I feared it, feared ye." He shifted closer to her, his thigh pressing against hers. "Problem was, no woman filled me or gave me what I needed, and those relationships crashed and burned because . . . well . . ." He cupped her cheek. "Because they weren't you, *mo anam cara*. I love you. Yer the other half to me heart and soul. My fairy princess."

Shay was afraid her heart would beat a rhythm right out of her chest, and tears burned at the back of her eyes. She blinked and squeezed them to stop them, but they fell down her cheeks anyway. "Oh, Liam, I don't know what to say. I've wanted to hear these words from you for so long now that I can't believe you're actually saying them." All the women he'd paraded in front of her filed through her mind. She shook her head. "What's to say that tomorrow you won't find another one or get bored with me or realize you only thought you loved me, that the danger on the bluff—"

Liam kissed her and cupped the back of her neck, urging her closer.

Shay lost track of time and lost herself in Liam's kiss and arms. All too soon, he broke the kiss and rested his forehead against hers. His warm breath fanned her face.

Pounding on the front door reverberated through the cottage, and Shay jumped off Liam's lap.

"Shayleigh Myers, you open this door this instant."

Shay pressed her hand to her burning cheek and then finger-combed through her hair, which was messy thanks to Liam's exploratory fingers. "Jen sounds upset."

"If you don't open this door, Shay, I will have Dean bring the police battering ram, and I will break down this door."

"Spirit's really worried about you." Tassi's voice was accompanied by a well-timed howl by the German shepherd.

"Aye, I agree with yer sister, but we don't need a battering ram. I know where ye hide the key, lass." Gran's voice sifted through the keyhole, and Shay envisioned the eighty-something-year-old bending over and trying to get a peek through the small opening.

Under his breath, Liam muttered something in Gaelic Shay didn't understand and hauled himself to his feet. He grabbed Shay one more time, pressed a hard kiss to her lips, and murmured against her ear. "We are not done with this conversation, *mo grá.*"

Shay grinned. "We weren't doing much talking."

"Exactly, and I'd like to continue that, but—"

The sound of a key being inserted into the door had them jumping apart as if they were teenagers caught in a naughty act by their parents.

Shay stomped to the door and yanked it open, revealing Jen, Gran, and Tassi all looking as guilty as housebreakers should be. "Why, hello, you three. What brings you by on this fair day?"

Tassi nearly knocked Shay over in a huge bear hug. "Thank you. Thank you for saving Orion's life," she whispered and clung to Shay for a few more seconds before Gran peeled her off.

Jen scowled at her. "Fine day? First the never-ending rain that has me thinking we should all build arks, then your mad dash into one of the worst storms in Bray Harbor's history, and then the phone call from Dean that . . . that"—Jen's voice broke, and she crushed Shay in a hug. "I know I pinky swore to not mother you, but, darn it, Shay, you could have died!"

Spirit, who'd been circling her legs, yipped at her, as if saying "I agree" to Jen's comment.

Shay's cheeks burned, and she knew her face must resemble a mottled red apple. She pulled from Jen's embrace and locked gazes with her. "I'm sorry. You're right, but I didn't have time, and the thought of Orion doing the unthinkable . . ." She shivered and sank down into a chair. "Forgive me?"

"Of course, I forgive you. Your kindness and protective spirit are what make you the best person I know. I wouldn't want you any other way." Jen sat in the chair beside her at the kitchen table. "Dean said he'll be by as soon as he can to get your statement. He wanted to make sure Orion was settled properly and then grab a dry uniform."

Tassi sat cross-legged on the chair across the table from Shay, and despite her red-rimmed eyes and puffy face, she smiled at her friend. "You are the bravest person I know. I don't know how to thank you." She sank her fingers in Spirit's fur when he laid his giant head on her lap.

"You just did," Shay said.

"I'm just worried about Orion. What happens now?"

"Whatever happens, just know I'll be by your side the entire time, okay? You're not alone in this." Shay flashed her a supportive smile.

Gran, who had been silently watching, sat in the chair across from Jen, tilted her head, and studied Shay, then looked up at Liam. Gran had obviously not missed his arm snaking around Shay's shoulders when they had barged in. She grinned, and her eyes twinkled. "Aye, I told ye the fairies are never wrong."

"Gran," cried both Shay and Liam.

"'Tis the fairies, and now that ye've found each other, nothing will break ye apart." Tears welled up in Gran's eyes and trickled down her craggy cheeks. "Here I thought I'd have to lock ye two in a closet until ye both came to yer senses, ye daft young'uns."

Jen's gaze zeroed in on Liam's hand on Shay's shoulder. She rose to her feet, gesturing to the living room. "Mind if I have a moment of your time?"

Liam slid a glance at Shay, shrugged his shoulders, and then turned his blinding smile back on Jen. "Sure thing. Lead the way."

Liam followed Jen out of the kitchen, through the living room, and down the short hall leading to Shay's bedroom.

Shay looked helplessly at Gran. "What's that all about?"

"I'm sure Jen will give Liam a piece of her mind and warn him that if he hurts ye, she'll kill him."

"I told her to quit mothering me, and she's already broken her promise."

"Well, if he hurts you, and Jen does nothing about it, I'll fill in for her. I have a few tricks up my sleeve," Tassi said.

"'Tis not mothering she's doing," Gran said. "As ye have no direct kin around, she's taking on the role of protector. And ye needn't worry; if he breaks yer heart, even though he is my kin and me grandson, I'll do the job if she doesn't."

Shay chuckled and then swallowed the laugh threatening to choke her. Gran looked as serious as ever, and there was a hard glint in her eyes Shay had never seen. "You're not joking, are you?"

Gran smiled, and Shay shivered, making a mental note to never, ever get on Gran's bad side.

Chapter 34

Hours later and tucked up in the corner of the couch, Shay, feeling somewhat refreshed after the nap Gran had forced her to take, sipped her tea. Over the rim of her cup she studied the group of people in her living room, all seemingly lost in their own thoughts.

Gran sat, her eyes glazed over with a blanket draped across her knees in a chair beside the fireplace. Spirit lay at her feet, his head resting on her white tennis shoes. Jen was in the chair opposite Gran on the other side of the fireplace with Dean at her feet, while her hand mindlessly rubbed his neck as she stared into the dying embers of the fire. Beside Shay, Liam lounged on the couch, his head back, eyes closed and his warm body pressed against hers. Tassi, who was the only one absent, had gone home after Shay encouraged her to come clean with her aunt Joanne.

When Shay had first awoken, the events of the previous hours had seemed like a dream, and she wondered if the Sunday that had started with her almost alienating her brother-in-law was still the same Sunday that had revealed a killer, almost gotten her killed, and instigated a confession of love from Liam.

She contentedly smiled, resting her head against Liam's shoulder. While she didn't know what the future held for them, she knew it was worth the risk. Her blood warmed at her closeness to him, and if her living room hadn't been packed with people, she would have snuggled right into his chest and—

Dean cleared his throat breaking the silence of the room. "So, Shay," the tips of his ears reddening, "it looks like I owe you one . . . again."

"I was just following my instincts," she said, slowly lifting her head from Liam's shoulder. "Which told me to get to the bluff as quickly as possible."

"Then you knew it was Orion when you ran out of the tea shop?" Jen asked.

"Let's just say I had a very strong inky feeling." She uneasily smiled. "I figured if I was wrong, I'd simply get wet and find an empty bluff. If I was right, though"—Shay shivered at the memory of finding Orion ready to jump— "I had to try to stop a young man from doing something he could never take back. To be honest though, it was Tassi's phone call that told me my sense of urgency to get there, wasn't wrong." She furrowed her brow and sat upright. "Dean, I've been thinking and did Orion say anything to you beyond confessing to Cora's murder?"

"He corroborated what you told me he had said. He wanted the love of his father so much that he was willing to trick Cora out of the blue bottle. He had no idea it wasn't the real thing. He still doesn't. Your secret, at least, is safe from those who didn't already know about it."

Jen squeezed his shoulder. "No thanks to you and Shay's assumptions that I can't keep a secret or handle the responsibility of it."

Dean patted her hand and gazed up at her. "I really am sorry. I was only trying to protect you."

Jen smiled. "I know, you both were and I forgive you." She pressed a kiss to his temple.

Shay hoped this was a sign that the couple were well on their way to being lovebirds again. "Then he really didn't know that someone else was poisoning her?"

Dean shook his head. "No, he had no clue. I've done some digging and got a search warrant for Madam Malvina's tea shop. The vial he claimed he'd found wasn't there anymore, and we couldn't find any evidence of illegal drugs or deadly herbs in the shop, but I highly suspect Madam Malvina had been drugging Cora to make her more open to Malvina's suggestions. "Right now," Dean shrugged helplessly, "there is nothing pointing to Madam Malvina directly, even though I highly suspect she is the reason Cora died. All the evidence we have so far points to Orion as Cora's killer."

"Like what?" asked Shay.

"It's his forged handwriting in the book of poisons, it's his confession of giving her a dose of belladonna on the bluff, and it's his covering up the crime scene and burying the shoes—by the way, DNA proved it was his gum on the sole—and along with his confession and fingerprints on the blue bottle we found hidden in his room of their cottage. It doesn't look good for him."

"She must have cleaned out the tea shop not even thinking of cleaning out her cottage of evidence that might be there, which ended up pointing to her own son."

"Unless her intention was for the evidence to point to Orion?" Jen said.

"Who knows, and we might never find out. All we know for sure is that she's a slippery one." Shay frowned. "Which means with no proof, you can't make an arrest, right?"

"No, but I guarantee you Madam Malvina is on our list, and we'll be keeping a closer eye on her. Oh, and also the so-called homeopathic store," Dean roguishly grinned.

"Let's just say that the owner, employees, and a certain Brad and Angela, who are now suspected drug runners, are on our radar too."

"I always knew Madam Malvina was a fraud." Gran tsked. "I wouldn't give it too long before she's packing her bags and moving to the next town where she can set herself up again."

To Shay the idea of Brad and Angela having a long-time association with Madam Malvina made her skin crawl. Brad and Angela were slimy, that was for sure, but Shay didn't think they'd openly conspire to bring about someone's death. However, being naive to what was going on right under her nose back in New Mexico proved to Shay that there was a lot she had to learn about her ex-husband and his new wife.

It all made her question if she was actually the one who had initially introduced them when Angela came to work as her assistant, or if they were already old *friends* and their meeting and what followed was staged as part of a 'long con'? She shook her head. There was time to think about that later. She needed to focus on what was important now.

"What will happen to Orion, though?" asked Shay. "I know he was the last one with Cora and it was his dose that caused her death, but the motive wasn't there. The jury will take that into consideration, right? I know he has to pay the price for taking someone's life, but if he's really my half brother, I want to do anything in my power to make sure he's got a good team of lawyers."

"There is one more thing."

Shay's skin prickled at Dean's tone. "What now? I really don't know if I can take any more surprises or bad news."

"I don't know what kind of news this is, but it's quite

clear from Orion's confession that he is Doyle's one and only child."

Shay's breath caught in her throat. "What? How'd he know? What did he tell you?"

Dean massaged the back of his neck and blew out a breath. "What started out as a police interview changed quickly into a counseling session. The life that kid has led makes me want to weep, and, just ask Jen, I don't feel compelled to do that often."

Jen pressed her hand onto Dean's shoulder and gave him a comforting smile.

"He claimed that, on multiple occasions, he overheard Doyle railing to his mother about his one and only child, a ridiculous makeup-wearing kid, and why on earth he only had a weird, useless son to carry on his lineage."

"But Orion could be mistaken."

"There's always that possibility, but after all I heard from Orion, I'm willing to bet my retirement funds that Doyle is not your father. However"—Dean shifted on the floor—"we could, with Orion's permission, of course, run a DNA test to see if you are siblings. That might really put your mind at ease."

While Shay didn't hear Bridget's voice, a sense of relief flooded through her, and she felt her late mother's presence wrap around her like a soft blanket. The amulet stayed cool against her skin, and Shay took it as a sign that Doyle, the man who wanted to steal the amulet from her, was not tied to her through blood. Her real father, the one who had tried to strangle her mother to get the bottle all those years ago, would have killed Shay by now for it. In her gut, she knew Doyle wasn't that man. Unless, of course, with his advancing years, he had learned not to just take what he wanted, but to enjoy the chase and toy with his prey first . . .

She blew out a raspy breath to shake it off. "No, I have to trust my gut. I don't think that's necessary. I've never felt so relieved in my life, so I'll take that as a good omen. Besides, I'd hate to have Orion go through any more emotional trauma as we waited for the results," Shay said. "Still, I want to do all I can for him. You understand, don't you?" Tears welled up in her eyes. "Especially, if his mother is letting him take the fall for something she did."

Dean nodded. "The mayor even feels bad for him and doesn't want to press charges, but my hands are tied right now. His actions caused a death and the DA is involved. I can't guarantee anything, but I will do what I can to make sure his appointed attorney is a good one."

"Thank you," whispered Shay as she sat back and glanced questioningly at an unusually quiet Liam whose tender smile filled her heart when she gently rested her head on his shoulder again.

Even though she'd napped, she was exhausted, and hashing over the details again with Dean had left her feeling wilted and haunted by all the unknowns that still existed. Right now though, she didn't want to think about any of that and wished the whole world could disappear because this was exactly where she wanted to be—snuggled up beside Liam, who cradled her close as his fingers gently trailed up and down her forearm.

Jen stood and motioned for Dean to join her. "I think it's time we head home now, and let Shay get some rest."

Dean moaned as he got to his feet. "These bones don't get any younger, and I swear this weather is making it worse." He eyed Liam, who wasn't making any attempt to leave. "A word, Madigan."

Liam rolled his eyes, uncurled his arm from around Shay, stood, and faced Dean. "I know, I know, if I hurt Shay . . . I've heard it twice already, three times if you count Spirit's bared teeth when Shay broke the news to him earlier."

Dean pointed to the front door and ushered Liam out under the protection of the awning.

After the front door closed behind them, Shay sighed. "Now he's mothering me too."

"Nah, he's probably making a bet on when you wise up and kick him to the curb." Jen grinned and nudged Shay's shoulder.

The door banged open, and Shay, Gran, and Jen jumped. Liam stormed through and paced in the small entrance. "Gran, I told ye he was a rat!"

Gran sighed and rested her hand over her heart. "Take care, Liam, of speaking of yer cousin like that. He's a good lad, he is."

Shay looked from Gran to Liam and back again. "What's going on?"

The two in question stared at each other, leaving Shay as much in the dark as ever. She was about to ask her question again when Dean walked through, a sheepish look on his face. "Sorry to be the buzzkill around here. I had a message to give Liam from Conor, and from the looks of things, your new boyfriend doesn't like it."

Liam held up a slip of paper and shook it. "Just when I thought I could trust him, that he wouldn't run off and break Gran's heart again, he vanishes with nothing more than a flippant note."

Shay plucked the note from Liam's shaking fist. She read it out loud, "Liam and Gran, gotta go. Have a drink at the pub for me. After Doyle. *Slán go fóill.*" Shay looked at a red-faced Liam. "What's that last bit?"

"Bye for now." Liam's jaw ticked. "That, that . . ."

"He's a lost lad, Liam, and until a few hours ago, ye were too, until . . ." Gran pointed to Shay. "Would ye care to dig up yer old wild ways and sins?" At the shake of his head, Gran grinned triumphantly. "That's too bad, as I've quite a long list."

"But going after Doyle is as near a death sentence for him as possible. He's being reckless and stupid and—"

"He's doing what he thinks he has to do. Conor is a smart lad. He'll figure it out and surely be waltzing through our doors once again." Gran patted Liam's cheek. "I'll be off now, as ye two"—she wagged her finger between Shay and Liam—"have a wee bit of catching up to do."

Liam coughed, and Shay's face heated. She pressed her fingers to her hot cheeks to hide the mottled scarlet stains she knew were no doubt exploding across her face. With knowing looks among them, Gran, Jen, and Dean walked out of the cottage, leaving Shay and Liam completely alone. A crackling buzz filled the air as Liam closed the door and slowly turned toward her. Her chest swirled with butterflies when he locked his gaze with hers.

"Well, *mo grá*," he hoarsely whispered. "I do believe we have some unfinished business. Now, where were we?" He moved toward her and swept her into his arms. "I love ye so, so much," he murmured, placing feather-soft kisses across her cheek.

Breathless, Shay pulled back and stared into his eyes. She finally understood what she'd seen in them earlier, and a shy smile dangled at the corners of her mouth. She drew in an unsteady breath, stood on tiptoes, closed her eyes, and softly pressed her lips to his.

Her universe, for the first time in weeks, had finally stopped spinning, and while she knew the continuing questions she had surrounding her real father and Orion's upcoming trial—not to mention still having her ex-husband and ex-best friend as next-door neighbors—would all prove challenging, to say the least, she knew she'd get through it as long as she remembered the messages of the raven.

Right now, though, this minute, she didn't feel alone. She felt . . . free at last and something else—what was it . . . powerful? It didn't matter, except perhaps Gran was right after all. Maybe she and Liam were in fact royalty of the High Seelie Court, and with their alliance finally made, together they would be . . . powerful. No, unstoppable.

"I love you too," she murmured and hungrily sought out Liam's lips with hers.